Praise for

Praise for *The Tongue Collector*

"Loved this book! I couldn't put it down. The main characters, Detective Noah and his partner, Holly, have great chemistry. The book pays careful attention to police procedures and forensics which is refreshing. You think by the title this book would be gory, but it's written very well. It's a great suspense thriller that will keep you on the edge of your seat. Can't wait for the next book to come out."

— Mike, Reader Review

"Cowboy detective Noah McGraw & his partner Holly Roark are back. In this book, they are challenged to catch a narcissistic, psychopathic serial killer who works in the criminal justice system. The killer knows how to keep a crime scene clean so there are very few clues. However, he makes some mistakes & detective, Noah McGraw is smarter than the killer. The book is fast paced with an interesting story line that keeps the reader guessing. When it all starts to fall together, I could not put it down. Add a little romance & the result is a nice read."

— Allison, Reader Review

Praise for *You'll Never See Me Again*

"I absolutely loved this book, I couldn't put it down. The details and thought put into this book by Dr. Magarian are absolutely amazing. I felt as if I was in the book myself."

— Brooke, Amazon reviewer

"Loved the book. It kept my attention, kept me guessing and kept me reading. I didn't want to put it down. Highly recommend it."

— Nancy Loyd, Amazon reviewer

Praise for *The Watchman*

"*The Watchman* came to life for me, because it is so well written and instills a sense of caution as you read. I am delighted to have had the pleasure of discovering Robert Magarian and his talent."

— Bea Kunz, reader review

Praise for *72 Hours*

"I was compelled to carry *72 Hours* around with me. It's a blend of trouble both personal and political, with an evil that will stop at nothing and a CDC that may—or may not—have found the only salvation. Here, also, is a family in pain. Suspenseful, timely, and breath-catching."

— Carolyn Wall, author of *Sweeping Up Glass*

Praise for *Follow Your Dream*

"In *Follow Your Dream*, Robert Magarian provides a template for turning a dream into reality, step-by-step. In 1987 Magarian created the first annual Norman Community Christmas Dinner, serving a free meal to individuals and family who would have been alone on Christmas Day. In the years hence, the event has grown to serve 1,600 people, with 200 volunteers. This is a remarkable story of what one person can do with a dream and how that dream can change many lives."

— Robert L. Ferrier, reader review

"How does God want you to relate to Him? The same way you would to the least of our brethren. And that is what author Robert Magarian has done as so succinctly shared in this inspiring story, showing that the efforts of one mobilized an entire community to care for each other. THIS IS A MUST READ!"

— Mike Tomasco, reader review

Also by Robert Magarian

FICTION

The Watchman

72 Hours

You'll Never See Me Again, A Crime to Remember

The Tongue Collector

ESSAYS

Follow Your Dream

A Journey into Faith

Pride goes before destruction,
A haughty spirit before a fall.

Proverbs 16:18

Dedication

In loving memory of our daughter,
Paula Marie Magarian,
(September 25, 1956 – July 9, 2020)
and
In loving memory of my brother,
Dr. Edward O. Magarian,
(October 3, 1935 – November 6, 2021)

Chapter 1

Fourteen Years Earlier

Twenty-one-year-old Michael Mordecai slips out of bed, rubs his eyes, and looks at the clock.

Eleven a.m.

He heads into the bathroom and showers.

After dressing, he goes down the stairs to the kitchen in this million-dollar home, which belongs to his parents, Weldon, and Gail Mordecai. He ambles over to the frig and reaches for the box of cereal on top, then opens the frig to retrieve the milk. He looks around, not really expecting to see anyone. His mother, a surgical nurse at St. John's Hospital, is at work. His father, oh, yes, his father, Weldon, the doctor, a neurosurgeon. He's at his office.

Michael goes to the free-standing table in the center of the kitchen, and grabs a bowl on the counter, pours in cereal, adds milk, sits on the bar stool and starts devouring his breakfast. Cell phone vibrates on the counter.

It's got to be mom. She's always on my ass about something. It must be the appointment with Dr. Horowitz.

He reaches for it. "I know what you're going to ask."

She wants to know if he's up and ready to go to the hospital research lab for his summer job interview, which she has arranged.

Crap. The interview isn't until one.

"Yes, I'm ready. I'll be there on time."

"You better. I went to a lot of trouble for you, son. Dad left his car for you."

Michael knows she doesn't believe him because he told her before she made the appointment that since he has this summer away from college, he wanted to take it easy. But his parents would have nothing of the sort.

Science always has been his interest from an early age, but he thinks about maybe skipping the cancer research interview at the hospital. Yet that's just a pipe dream. There's no way he cannot go. His dad would be all over him. After all, he's controlled Michael's life ever since he was old enough to know right from wrong and especially since his teen years. Consequently, they aren't on the best of terms, even though his dad took him hunting to bond. Didn't work. Not much better with his mother, either. He hates them both.

A few weeks ago, he heard his parents talking about him in the kitchen. They felt he was spoiled and lazy and they were at fault, giving him everything without making him work for it.

He sighed. *Maybe because I was the only child. Well, that's their fault. I didn't ask for them to be my parents. I inherited them.*

Ever since the first grade, they told him they wanted what was best for him and he had to do his part and excel in his studies. Michael did excel in school and in college. Now he's waiting for the fall semester to go to graduate school for the Ph.D. in genetics at Harvard. His parents had hoped he would go into medicine. Not for him. He doesn't like people and diagnosing patients' illnesses and handing out prescriptions is not very challenging, and not particularly helpful, especially if patients didn't comply. Then he'd have to let them have a piece of his mind. No, he's better off in the lab away from patients.

While eating, Michael fantasizes a scene where he sneaks into his parents' bedroom and stabs them in their throats in seconds with his favorite dagger while they slept. They'd never know what hit them. He became very skilled in handling knives, learned it from his maternal grandpa, Oscar. They whittled figures out of wood together.

There are several cars, boats, and wood figures in Michael's room that he had carved, which he admires. He and grandpa whittled for hours with several special knives, and even challenged each other at throwing them at targets nailed to the trees. They attended gun shows where Michael felt more attracted to knives. It thrilled Michael when he first spotted the sparkling daggers. He remembers the first time he held one in his hand. A dagger is for stabbing and is a weapon. Knives are primarily for cutting and slicing. What he could do with a dagger excited him. He ended up buying a Combat Commander Gladius Dagger.

Michael rises from the table, grabs his back pack, and heads out the front door for his appointment with Dr. Isaiah Horowitz, chief of the Oncology Department. He's running late. He races to the hospital in his dad's white caddy. St. John's is a six-story red brick building with large windows. The congestion around the hospital irritates Michael. His anger is compounded when he nearly runs into a woman stepping off the curb into the crosswalk, carrying a child. He screams at her. "Why don't you look where you're going, bitch!" She gives him the finger. He finds a doctor's parking space and pulls in. *Whomever the doc is, that's tough. Let them look for another place.*

He hops out and walks toward the entrance, waits for an ambulance to pass as he hurries to the sliding glass doors and enters the lobby. Patients are everywhere. Some are sitting on sofas and overstuffed chairs, while others are in the floral shop and at the coffee bar. There are two elevators in the back. He rushes to the one that opens, from which a bevy of people rushes out, nearly trampling him. As it empties, he enters, and it fills in seconds. He feels cramped as the doors close. He steps out on the sixth floor and looks to his left and to his right. The entire level houses research labs and offices as far as he can see. He turns to his left and finds the sign outside the lab with the doc's name. The door is open and the oncologist, Dr. Isaiah Horowitz, is seated at a desk against the wall in the corner of the lab, wearing a white coat and having the appearance of a little Einstein, bushy eyebrows and white hair, no mustache, and maybe around five foot two. The huge lab is well-lighted with many benches and tons of equipment scattered throughout the room and on top of the lab benches. One researcher is at the first bench watching a large flask twirling in a hot water bath to aid in the distillation of its liquid contents into another flask. As far as Michael could see, there were researchers working at what appears to be their own lab space.

Dr. Horowitz looks up and then at his watch, mentions Michael's tardiness, but Michael shrugs it off. Horowitz begins by chastising Michael and impresses on him that his researchers are never late for meetings and emphasizes that his people work long hours.

Yah, yah. I've heard all that bullshit before.

"Have a seat," the doc says, pointing to the chair next to his desk.

Michael sits. Horowitz looks down at a file on his desk with Michael's name on it, the one his mother submitted for him. He opens it and begins reviewing the pages. Horowitz looks at him and is about to begin the interview, but is interrupted with a phone call. "I will," he says. Thank you."

Then Horowitz shocks Michael with a question. "How can a measly four-year science major like yourself, without any graduate education or research experience, offer anything to my sophisticated cancer research lab?"

Michael is shocked and stammers under his breath. "You arrogant son-of-a-bitch."

He inhales and remains quiet for a few moments to regain his composure.

"I'm waiting, son," Horowitz says.

Michel believes the doc is pushing his buttons to see how devoted he is to research. "I'm a devoted learner and lab worker, sir, willing to do anything that could help your group in some way, if given direction. I did some research in my undergraduate training."

Horowitz just frowned at Michael for a few minutes under those bushy eyebrows, not saying a word.

Did I put it on too thick, Michael thinks? *What else could I say. Why doesn't the little shit say something?*

Horowitz stands and extends a hand. "I think we can find something for you in our tech group."

Michael jumps up surprised. Grabs Horowitz's hand. "Thank you, sir. You won't be disappointed."

"I hope not." He pauses. "And, by the way. Next time you come, don't park in the doctor's parking spot even though you are driving Dr. Mordecai's car. That was security on the phone earlier. You escaped a big fine this time because you came in your father's car."

Oh, shit. "I won't, sir. I promise."

"In case you're wondering how they knew it was you instead of your father, they saw you hop out."

Michael nodded, without saying a word.

After working in the lab for two weeks, Michael notices that many cancer patients coming into the hospital are middle-aged or older. That interests him and he wonders if age has something to do with cancer. This prompts him to spend time in the hospital library searching the scientific literature for articles on diseases affecting mostly the elderly. *If aging could be slowed or delayed, then maybe health issues could be prevented,* he thinks. During his time at the hospital, he searches the scientific literature for anything related to age and disease. He finds only a lot of statistics about diseases in the elderly but nothing about why they are affected the most. What about the mechanism of aging? Could it be studied in preventing diseases? He finds only articles where researchers in the U.S. are reporting substances that may promote longevity. Michael thinks they may be able to prevent disease like cancer. He searches for their results, realizing his hypothesis must be: *is old age more susceptible to disease*? He believes age has something to do with the immune system. Maybe he can proceed with his ideas for his doctoral degree at Harvard.

Chapter 2

Current day

Dr. Michael Mordecai, a thirty-five-year-old, blue-eyed, blond narcissist, has a slender body and stands under six feet tall, and was diagnosed with antisocial personality disorder (ASPD) when 15, which his parents revealed to no one.

They were warned that persons with Michael's condition tend to lie, break laws, act impulsively, show aggressive or aggravated behavior, consistently get into fights, or physically harm others, don't feel guilt or remorse for having harmed or mistreated others, and lack regard for their own safety or the safety of others. Michael consequently has no friends. At every turn in his life, his parents did what they could to help him, but he resisted them, thinking they were pressuring him to do well at everything.

Michael's handsome and single. He's never found a women that measures up to his standards—he believes women should be subservient, and not offer an opinion. Yet, he's been dating his dad's former nurse, Kendal Wilson, only because he thinks her professional training as a nurse may be helpful to him someday.

Michael's lives in his folk's home in Chastain Park with his mother, Gail. His father, a neurosurgeon for nearly forty years, died two years earlier of a heart attack. Gail had to retire early from St. John's Hospital due to advanced osteoarthritis, and is now confined to a wheelchair. Michael has an unmarried, middle-aged husky nurse's aide, Donna Harvey, come in six days a week to look after his mother, since he didn't want to spend any money placing her in an assisted living facility. Donna Harvey is reserved, talks very little about herself, but is kind and a good worker. He wonders why she drives a 15-seater white van?

Gail talks often about Kendal Wilson and asks Michael to bring her to their home more often. He knows mother is hoping they'll eventually marry, and she'll have some company.

The prodigal son, Michael, never worked a day in his life outside of college until he ended up at Biogen, one of the world's leading biomolecular companies, after he finished his Ph.D. at Harvard, and then a postdoc in genetics at Stanford.

Michel's education was supported by stipends and financial assistance from his father and mother. He and his mother now live off Michael's salary and Gail's retirement investments, since he squandered most of his inheritance. He loves expensive clothes and racing through Atlanta in his fancy red BMW. He answers to no one. There are times when Donna Harvey isn't at their home, and Michael loses patience with his mother when he's forced to help her.

At Biogen Labs, he works with Jessica (Jess) York, Ph.D. from MIT, another geneticist and confidant, and Dr. Corey Keller, MD, Ph.D. from Stanford is director of the Biogen lab, who Michael knew at Stanford. Keller is a tough supervisor.

Michael's stubbornness and dislike for Corey causes him to butt heads often with him. Michael thinks he deliberately sabotages his efforts to become a leader in the anti-aging field, which was once Keller's dream at Stanford, but his ego urged him to climb the ladder in administration and out of the lab.

Chapter 3

Cowboy Detective Noah McGraw, dressed in a starched white shirt, jeans, jean jacket and boots, and wearing a white Stetson, walks into the squad room of the Homicide Division of the Atlanta PD with his partner, Detective Sergeant Holly Roark, returning from the Pinelawn Cemetery where Laura Evans, the mother of serial killer, Jack Carter, who McGraw and Roark killed in a gun battle weeks ago, was buried this morning.

Noah McGraw is affectionately called the Marlboro Man around the station, mostly behind his back. In the Sixth Precinct the detectives work in a spacious area in the squad room called the bullpen or the pit. Drapes conceal what goes on inside the Capt.'s office, positioned across the room between two interview rooms along one wall, with a holding cell in the corner of the room.

McGraw removes his white Stetson and places it on the desk, reaches for his Braves cup and walks over to the coffee stand, fills it and returns to his desk. Holly is looking his way. He knows she senses something is bugging him. He's been quiet the whole time they rode back from the cemetery, wearing that serious look when something is on his mind.

"What's up with you, boss," Holly says as she sits at her desk facing him. Even though they're engaged to be married, she still calls him 'boss' as do the other detectives, when the team is in the bullpen.

"You haven't said a word since we left the cemetery. What's bugging you?"

"Nothing's bugging me."

"Oh, yeah. Who are you kidding? Come on, get it off your chest."

"It's personal," he says.

Again, she insists. "Come on. Get it off your chest. You know we no longer keep secrets from each other."

"It's not that. It's just that I don't know how you'd interpret what I'm feeling. It's no big deal."

"Yes, it is. You know me. I must know."

He takes a couple swigs of his coffee and frowns. "Okay. I guess you won't think it's crazy."

"Me," she says, slapping a hand to her chest and pushing herself back in her chair laughing. "No way."

"You're quite the actor," he says. "Okay. I guess I can tell you since we're alone. I think mom would be proud of me."

"In what way?" Roark asks, with a puzzled look.

"Let me finish."

Raising her hands above her head, she says, "Okay, okay."

"Something spiritual happened to me." He pauses as he looks at her, wondering if he should go on. "You know how I hated Laura Evans the way she treated Jack, causing him to hate people, which led him to killing some. Because of that I didn't think she deserved an elaborate funeral."

Holly nods. "Okay. But what happened to you?"

"Listening to the minister during the ceremony, this feeling came over me. A feeling I never witnessed before. It lifted this weight off my shoulders."

"That's good, isn't it?"

"I didn't know at the time what was happening. I was trying to understand what it meant."

"And did you?"

He feels himself nodding. "Forgiveness."

"Forgiveness?" she repeats.

"Yes. I hadn't realized my anger. Anger against Laura that was bottled up in me. During the minister's eulogy, something strange came over me and the anger lifted from my shoulders." He pauses. "I'm now willing to forgive her for the cruel things she did to Jack, which caused him to do bad things."

"Noah," she said with warmth in her voice "That's wonderful."

Just then, the two other members of their team, Detectives Ed Kramer and Juan Gomez enter the squad room. On the way to their desks, Gomez asks, "How'd everything go at the Evan's funeral, boss?"

You could hear a pin drop in the room.

Holly is waiting for Noah's answer. She knows he's debating what to say. "Did you hear Gomez, boss," she says.

"Yes, I heard him." He turns and says, "It went well, Gomez."

"Good to hear," Kramer says.

"Glad that's over," Gomez says. He turns and spots the Capt. "Here he comes," Gomez whispers.

Captain Dipple, Chief of Detectives, comes in from the Lion's Den, his office, named by the detective group, into the squad room and stops at McGraw's desk. For a few moments he scans his detectives without saying a word. The ex-hockey player from Minnesota, in his late forties, over six foot, has a muscular build, high forehead, dark hair and thick eyebrows. Friends tell him he has the smile and face of the actor Ernest Borgnine. He's heard a few weeks earlier that a detective said he has bulldog chops. He'd put his money on cowboy McGraw. Dipple has been on a diet and believes his chops have shrunk some.

He inhales a deep breath and says, "Cowboy. I heard from your FBI friend, Agent Drew, who described how well you analyzed the scene at Carter's lodge, and especially your knowing Jack wasn't killed in the house bomb while everyone else thought he was." He pauses again, frowning. "How did you do it?"

"Intuition, Chief. Got that feeling after analyzing the scene."

"Sergeant Roark? I'm aware of your contribution, too, in finishing off Jack Carter with McGraw. Great teamwork, you two."

The two detectives look at each other and smile. The Capt. isn't too loose with his compliments.

McGraw said, "Thank you, Capt." while Roark only nodded.

The Chief looked over at the other team members, again. "The Carter case now has been resolved," he says. "Good work, everyone." He turns and heads back to his office.

Roark turns to McGraw and says, "Noah, before I forget. Dusty will turn eleven next week."

"Are we celebrating with a party for my little buddy?"

"I'm planning on it."

"Can I help? I haven't seen Dusty in a while. Guess it's time for another novel plus something else."

"I can handle the party, but Dusty has been wondering why you haven't been to see us in weeks. He asks about you nearly every day. He still hasn't gotten over our leaving the Circle M and Texas Rodeo in December."

"I know. I've been thinking about that and may have a solution." He holds up his right hand. "I'm still wearing the leather bracelet he and Whitey made for me while you guys were with us." That was after he and Holly returned from the Ole Miss campus where the shootout with Max Kingston took place, and McGraw took a couple of rounds before they killed Kingston. Holly and Dusty stayed with McGraw for weeks while he recuperated from his gunshot wounds, then he and Holly returned to work.

"I'd like you to bring Anna Marie with you to his birthday party. Dusty really likes her."

"She'd love to come."

Chapter 4

That evening Noah McGraw leaves the station in the black Silverado SSV (Special Service Vehicle) that was awarded to him by Captain Dipple and the Police Chief after he returned to work from his time off to heal from his gunshot wounds received in Oxford, Mississippi. He entered a request a year before for an SSV but didn't expect it to be approved. He now thinks it's their way of rewarding him for his service and in solving the Max Kingston case.

The black monster really takes off, and he arrives at the Circle M before sunset, pulling into the driveway. The SSV has no police markings and the police lights are recessed inside as he requested. The APD mechanic had installed a computer and communication setup.

His sky-blue RAM 3500 pickup is not in its usual spot, which means his mother, Anna Marie, has taken it out shopping. This is not a bingo night. McGraw reaches for his cowboy hat, opens the car door, and walks up the flagstones to the two-story white frame antebellum that sits back two-hundred feet from the road. His German Shepherds, Prince, and Tucker, bark up a storm as he opens the door, jumping on him with their tails wagging. He knows what they want, and moves into the kitchen, reaches in the cabinet for a box of treats and slips them one. He notices the red light on the coffee pot and the odor from salmon mixed with veggies on the stove wafts his nostrils. This is the handiwork of his thoughtful mother, who has made one of his favorite dishes, but he's not hungry at the moment. Instead, he grabs his favorite coffee mug on the counter, fills it, adds cream to the brim and drinks some before carrying it outside with his canine buddies racing ahead of him, chasing cats, squirrels and rabbits that hang around the barn. The horizon is bright orange and the sky is blue. Whitey Berry, his ranch hand from Texas, is an old buddy that lives in the small house on the back of the property, oversees the ranch, the two horses, feeds the strays and sells the hay. They meet at the barn and talk briefly and McGraw does what he likes the best, talking to his horses, Mystery Lady, and TR (Texas Rodeo), and walking the property sipping his coffee and mulling over what's on his mind.

The ranch house, with its tall windows, enclosed wrap-around porch, is situated on two hundred acres of an old horse farm and a perennial garden with plants and flowers, a horse barn, abandoned chicken coop and acres of Timothy grass and alfalfa, sold as hay to the horse people. McGraw loves the smell of the roses that grow in his mother's garden when in season, the odor of hay, enjoys seeing animals roaming the property, and finds it relaxing when riding his horses and his father's Harley. All these things are part of his Texas upbringing.

Toughness and meekness were hard for this cowboy to balance in his early years. His mother told him he was a maverick, like the cows he couldn't brand. Anna Marie taught him to cook, because learning recipes would warm his heart. She instilled a respect for God in him from birth, and taught him, "Poverty and comfort separates us from our Lord." She read Scripture to him in the evenings hoping to cancel out some of his toughness. He found that the thirty-one chapters in Proverbs gave him wisdom, knowledge, and courage in his line of work today.

McGraw, the Eagle Scout, and valedictorian of his high school graduating class, chose to go into the Marines before college. After serving four years in the military police, he went to Harvard, graduated with a degree in psychology, and then on to the University of Maryland, earning a master's degree in Criminology and Law Enforcement. McGraw scored off the charts on the Civil Service exam while in the police academy, and during two years as an investigating officer for the Maryland Highway Patrol, he earned a reputation for being highly perceptive and analytical in his investigative skills.

McGraw joined the Atlanta PD in his thirties, went through the local police academy and spent two years in patrol, where he demonstrated street smarts and the ability to read people and to get them to talk. These skills propelled him into the Investigation Bureau of the Narcotics Division. The chief recognized McGraw's ability to multi-task and to lead an investigation, which opened the door to the Homicide Division. After two years in homicide, he was promoted to lieutenant and the department approved his request to go back to wearing starched white shirts with jeans, boots, and his Stetson. He liked being affectionately known as the Marlboro Man among the division, and was one of the finest investigators in Atlanta, if not in the entire east.

Chapter 5

The bright sun this early June morning blinds Michael Mordecai as he leaves his home, throws his backpack into the red BMW, hops in and races through the streets of Atlanta to Biogen, a prominent biotech company housed in a four-story glass-front building in which the ascending stairs are visible from the street. He maneuvers into the parking lot in the back, pulls into his parking spot next to Corey Keller's red Corvette convertible. He grabs his backpack, steps out, and ambles around the building to the front, where he meets up with one of his techs, a pretty, slender blond in her late twenties.

How are things, April?" he says as they head to the entrance. With a pretty smile, she says, "Fine, Dr. Mordecai. Another sunny one."

He nods. "The kind I like."

Glass doors open automatically into a spacious lobby. Cool air from the air conditioning system hits them in the face as they enter. A security desk is close to the entrance, the area behind it occupied with a decorative coffee shop in the middle and an open seating area with bespoke furniture placed throughout on oriental rugs. A bank of elevators is in the back, but Michael likes using the stairs to look out over the fast-moving traffic on the busy street below. He and April sign in at the security desk, and then he follows her, who also takes the stairs, two at a time. Instead of looking out at the traffic this time, he fixes his eyes on April's attractive rear end. Michael doesn't really have any feelings for women but he doesn't mind looking at them. He'd rather use them then love them.

They reach the well-lighted top floor with its narrow hall extending the length of the fourth floor. Michael grumbles at the white-haired man guiding a polishing machine over the vinyl tile floor when they nearly collide. He thinks of people like this guy as mere objects more than living creatures, which means he has no regret over how he manipulates and exploits them for his immediate enjoyment. And this custodian contributes very little to society, so Michael doesn't give him the time of day. He is adept at putting on charisma when he wants something; otherwise, he cares little for others.

April leads the way into the bioengineering lab supervised by Michael and Jessica York, and she walks over to where another technician, Simon, is working at one of the lab benches.

This Biogen lab is one of the best equipped Michael's ever seen, which reminds him somewhat of Dr. Horowitz's lab at St. John's Hospital. Biogen hasn't spared any expense to compete in the bioengineering world. There are several important molecular tools used in their work in genetic engineering, such as a Polymerase Chain Reaction (PCR) tool, which involves the process of replicating copies of the genes of interest; Restriction Enzymes (known as Molecular Scissors that cut out DNA at specific locations), and Super-Resolution Microscopy. The more advanced the microscope, the more things can be done, like examining biological tissue all the way down to its DNA caps on chromosomes, known as telomeres.

Dr. Jessica York, his geneticist colleague, is sitting at one of the high-powered microscopes examining mouse tissues when he walks up behind her, lowers his head inches from her silky brown, shoulder-length hair. He loves the smell of her shampoo. Jess turns around and scowls at him.

"Stop it, M&M. Can't you see I'm busy?"

She playfully labeled him with the moniker 'M&M' from the letters of his first and last name, and it stuck. She's a few inches taller than he, slimly built like a muscular gymnast in training, runs after work to keep in shape for her marathon, eats lots of veggies and fruits. Her smooth narrow face glows under the fluorescent lights. By any measure, she's what one would rate as a looker with inviting breasts and a well-built gluteus maximus, which shows below her short, white lab coat.

"Aw come on. You know you love it."

"That'll be the day," she says.

"I like the smell of your shampoo."

April and Simon look over at them, smiling.

He whispers, "Can't stop loving you, baby," as he moves over in his area.

"I heard that," Jess says.

He swings his backpack around, which flies on his desk, knocking over his keepsakes—wood carvings of human and animal figures he carved with grandpa Oscar. He pulls out his chair on wheels and sits, reaches for his carvings, and sets them up and out of the way. On the wall next to his desk hangs a dagger with the inscription, *Grandpa Oscar*. He lost his best friend years ago but thinks about him every day. He thinks about their visits to gun shows and his interest in knives.

Our favorite gun show was the annual Las Vegas Antique Gun and Knife show. Grandpa liked his Remington 870 Pump-Action Shotgun. I like knives of all kind. The first time I held a dagger in my hand, a sense of power came over me. I heard voices. "Kill, kill."

"What are you doing, M&M? Come here."

Michael is awakened from his reverie. He stands, inhales, reaches for his white lab coat on the hall tree in the corner, and slips into it and heads over to Jess.

"What are you examining, Jess?" he asks as he moves in next to her.

"It's about time you showed up," she says in a teasing tone. She was joking, of course, because he's never late, a discipline forced on him by Dr. Horowitz.

"I'm looking at some of the mice tissue telomeres. As expected, they've grown." She looks up at the wall clock. "Notice the time. We meet with Corey at nine."

He nods, heads back to his desk, and gathers up his research report, a copy of which he gave to the director earlier.

Biogen is one of the principal companies that has been researching anti-aging agents for over a decade, competing with several pharmaceutical companies. Anti-aging research is built on the idea that slowing the aging process can prevent multiple age-related diseases. Michael believes aging is related to telomere length. Telomeres are the protective end caps on chromosomes. Telomeres shorten with age and have been associated with increased incidence of diseases and poor survival. There is evidence of lifestyle factors affecting health and lifespan of an individual by affecting telomere length.

Clinical trials are currently underway across the country with drugs that have the potential of increasing the lifespan of humans, but do they increase telomere length? That's Michael's interest. The type-2 diabetic drug metformin has surfaced as a promising anti-aging agent. It has been tested in roundworms and in mice. The results in both are encouraging. The worms aged more slowly than the untreated ones, didn't develop wrinkles, and stayed healthier longer.

Michael has been studying the biology of aging since his Harvard days where he searched for drugs that act on pathways involved in cell growth. These drugs inhibit a protein in mammals known as *mTOR (mammalian target of rapamycin)*. He found that TOR exists in nonmammals; hence, just the name TOR is used. Michael found when he inhibited TOR, the lifespan in fruit flies to mice lengthens. At Biogen, he has developed an agent he's named RapTOR, an antagonist of TOR, which mimics the activity of rapamycin, an inhibitor of TOR, normally used as an immune-suppressing drug. He's excited and eager to get his agent into clinical trials to beat the other companies to market, but he knows he'll meet resistance from the director, Dr. Corey Keller, who always wants more and more testing. Michael has become adept in using devious measures to get what he wants from people, but knows Corey is sharp and not easily swayed. Michael will play along for now. only to get him to move on his agent.

During their walk down the hall to the conference room Michael says, "We'll see what Corey thinks about our study of RapTOR in the humanized mice."

Humanized mice carry human genes, cells, and tissue. At the end of their study, they found Michael's agent lengthens the average lifespan of mice by 50 percent, lengthening their telomeres.

"He should be really impressed with the telomere study," Jess says, as she leads the way into the room where Corey is sitting at the head of the shiny rectangular table surrounded by twelve red-leathered chairs. Behind him is a large green board and in one corner is an easel pad with 50 plain sheets of paper. Against the wall under the huge tinted glass window across from the entrance is a table covered with a white cloth, on it is a steaming carafe filled with coffee, cups, and a plate of fruit and a box of goodies.

"Help yourself to the coffee and goodies," Corey says, as he flips through what Michael knows is his report.

Both Jess and Michael nod and say "thanks," as they head for the coffee table. After filling their cups, Jess reaches for a couple of pieces of fruit while Michael goes for a jelly donut. They move to the chairs on each side of the table close to Corey. Jess on his right and Michael on his left, facing Jess.

"I've read over your research report on RapTOR Michael and find your results in the worms and humanized mice very, very interesting; especially the telomere results. You both have made significant strides toward unlocking the secret of longevity here at Biogen. Congratulations!"

Jess and Michael look at each other with a puzzled look on their faces. Michael thinks, *He's gonna want more. I can tell it in his voice.*

"I'm hearing a but, Corey, isn't that, right?" Michael says.

"Yes."

Michael squirms in his chair. *The bastard.* "Corey, listen. I think we need to move fast on our compound so Biogen can beat these other companies to market. RapTOR is ready for clinical trials and with your influence, we could move in a study right away."

Corey shakes his head. "No way. There is much more work to be done before we can move into clinical trials. FDA would never approve our request at this point in the investigation. They will require testing in larger animals."

"But you have influence," Michael says. "We could skip that step."

"You need to do a study of your compound on dogs and then I will think about the clinical trials."

"But—"

"No 'but' Michael," Corey says.

Michael jumps up, knocking his chair backwards on the floor, and storms out of the room with his report in hand.

Jess looks at Corey, who is shaking his head.

"Dr. York, you're the only one able to calm him down. See to it."

"I don't know if—"

"—You need to keep an eye on him," he says as he stands. "You know what to do. That's all for today." He grabs the papers in front of him, and rushes out the door.

Oh, my. Michael, you've overturned the apple cart.

Chapter 6

Michael pulls his red BMW into his driveway around five that evening, gets out and rushes up to the entrance of his home, still steaming over the meeting with Corey Keller. He could strangle the bastard.

He enters the marbled foyer. "You're home early, Dr. Mordecai," says Donna Harvey, who is in the kitchen to his left. "Anything wrong?" He usually comes home around seven.

"No, just finished early," he says as he moves through the family room with expensive leather furniture plush rugs and lots of lighting. He notices his mother sitting across the way in her favorite chair in the sunroom reading a novel and drinking her evening tea. He walks to his office at the end of the living room without saying a word, opens the door and throws his things on the badly worn overstuffed leather chair to his left that belonged to his grandfather, and is positioned in front of the floor-to-ceiling bookshelves containing a collection of the classics. His study is where he relaxes and does his best thinking.

There's a tap on the open door. "I brought you some hot tea, Dr. Mordecai. It seems you're in need of something," Donna Harvey says.

"Thank you. You're so observant and so kind," he says insincerely, but she'd never guess it the way he uses his pleasant tone. He does this with people to win them over because he never knows if he'll ever need them to do his bidding.

He moves across the ivory carpeted floor carrying the tea to the mahogany desk in front of a large window with its woodened blinds closed, pulls out the high-back leather chair and sets the hot tea cup on his desk near the phone.

I need something strong. Not this tea.

He goes to the apartment-size fridge in the corner by the door, on which are whiskey glasses and several bottles of Scotch. He pours a three-finger scotch, takes a couple swallows, and moves to his desk where he sets the glass, sits, closes his eyes, and inhales several deep breaths, then exhales. Minutes later, feeling better, he stares across the room at one of his favorite paintings hanging on the wall. One that his mother never approved of and wanted it out of her sight. He bought it rather cheap from an artist who had several paintings for sale at the gun show he and Grandpa Oscar attended. Probably no one wanted it is why he got it for almost nothing. The dark-haired man in the painting, possibly in his thirties, fair skin, is looking upwards with his mouth open in apparent agony from a dagger stuck in his throat, blood dripping out of the wound onto his white starched shirt.

That could be Corey, he thinks.

Michael finishes off his drink and for now ponders on how he can do his own clinical trials. He realizes there's no way he can perform a randomized double-blind-placebo-controlled study without lots of help. It's out of the question. Then what? How can he skirt the clinical studies established by the FDA? An idea flashes through his mind. What if he can find elderly patients to treat secretly without Biogen knowing about it?

He rises and goes for another three-finger scotch. Takes a few swallows.

I like that idea.

His girlfriend, Kendal Wilson, works at the Jefferson Nursing Home. Maybe he'd take her to dinner and convince her to help, but first he must begin that damn dog study. He pauses, just realizing that in his fit of anger he'd overlooked something important that he hadn't considered. That study would help him determine the Maximum Therapeutic Dose (MTD) of RapTOR, which will be more accurate in the dosage he'll used in his human trials.

Not all is lost. I hope Jess told the techs to bring up the dogs.

Now, feeling somewhat better, he walks over to the fridge for more scotch.

Chapter 7

The next morning, Michael enters the lab and asks Jess if she told the techs to bring up the dogs."

"They're in the animal room now," she says, as she rises from her desk and leads the way to the large animal room adjacent to the middle of the lab. The room was filled with cages of mice, but now is filled with five large dogs in large crates on the table in the center of the room. They barely bark when he and Jess walk in. Michael paces in front of the crates, pensively observing them as he peers in, one-by-one. You can hear a pin drop. The pitiful dogs struggle to stand from their arthritis when he taps on their crates. In the first crate is a black Doberman pincher. In the second is a brown Collie, in the third, a fawn, short-haired Boxer, in the fourth crate is a Dalmatian with a white coat marked with black-colored spots, and in the fifth crate is a black Lab. Their sad eyes in heads resting between their front paws, stare up at him. Even Michael's hard heart begins to soften.

Jess whispers to Michael. "I sure hope RapTOR can help these poor darlings."

"All but one," he whispers back. "The black Lab will be our control."

"Oh, the poor thing."

Michael doesn't respond. Instead, he is fixed on the condition of each animal.

"How old are these dogs?" he asks the techs. "They look like they're on their last leg."

Simon shrugs. "We followed your criteria, sir. They're around nine years old, weigh between 50 and 70 pounds and have a height close to 24 inches."

"Do you think your agent can help these poor things, Dr. Mordecai," April asks in tears.

"I'm counting on it." He pauses. "No more time to waste. Let's get started," he says. "One of you run down the protocol."

"Yes, sir," they said in unison.

April begins. Looking at each sheet of paper in her hands, she asks, "Which dog will be our control, Dr. Mordecai?"

"The black Lab in the fifth crate."

April continues. "All dogs will be weighed and blood drawn before the trial begins. The four will be fed your agent in their feed daily and on day seven, all will be weighed and blood drawn and labeled, their bodies examined as illustrated in the protocol, and all information recorded. This procedure will be carried out for three weeks."

Simon adds, "The dosage is based on the formula you gave us, which extrapolates the dose from the human mice study to the weight of each dog. The blood samples drawn from each dog at the end of the week will be labeled, and given to Dr. York for study. Weekly reports, excluding the blood studies, will be written from the research notebooks and ready for you and Dr. York at the start of the following week, and the gross examinations on each dog you and Dr. York perform, will be added later, as well as the telomere studies performed by Dr. York."

"That's correct. Let's get started."

Chapter 8

McGraw strolls the Circle M at sunrise, slowly drinking his coffee and ending up in the barn to visit his equine friends, TR (Texas Rodeo) and Majestic Lady. He opens the stall door of Majestic Lady, Holly's favorite horse, and rubs a hand along her neck and side. He tells her that tonight he's going to ask Holly and Dusty to come and live with them permanently. "What do you think of that, Lady?"

Hearing Holly's name, Majestic Lady neighs her approval. "You've missed Holly, haven't you, girl?" Majestic Lady neighs, again. "She'll be here soon."

On his way out, McGraw nearly collides with Whitey coming in to do his chores.

"Oops. Sorry, Noah. This is becoming our routine lately."

"My fault, Whitey. Got so much on my mind that I don't watch where I'm going."

"You have anything special for me to do?"

"No. I was just in to tell Majestic Lady some good news.

Whitey frowns. "What's that?"

"Tonight, I'm going to ask Holly and Dusty to come live with us."

"You mean for good?'

"Yep."

"That's the greatest news. It's much livelier around here when those two are with us. And now maybe you won't be so quiet."

"Quiet?"

"Yeah. Quiet. I know you miss having them here especially since you and Ms. Holly are so close. You won't admit it, but you miss her not being here."

"You're too smart for your britches, Whitey."

"Oh, I thought you were going to say, "Bless your heart."

They laugh because down south, saying "Bless your heart" to anyone means several things: expressing genuine sympathy but sometimes it can be an insult that conveys condescension, derision, or contempt.

"You know me better than that, Whitey. I was going to say, I know how you and Dusty really hit it off." McGraw raises his right hand. "I'm still wearing the bracelet you guys made for me."

Whitey nods. "He's my buddy, too, Noah."

"I know. Well, I gotta go. Still must buy Dusty a book for his birthday, and he'll love my surprise." He starts to head to the house and stops. "Hey, Whitey. Why don't you come with ma and me?"

"Oh, man. I'd love to but got lots to do here. Anyway, it's for you all."

"Can't convince you, huh?"

"I'll have lots of time with them when they come. You go and have fun."

"Okay."

McGraw remembers what Dusty said the last time he gave him a book. It was when he moved them back home form the Circle M after McGraw recuperated from his gunshot wounds.

"You know I like the books you give me. But I want more than books."

Knowing what's coming, McGraw asks, "What's that?"

"I want to live with you. I want you to be my dad."

McGraw now will be able to give him his wish.

Dusty runs to the front room, hops on the couch, pulls the curtain back from the window, and looks out. "I thought I heard McGraw's pickup. I can't wait to see him and Anna Marie. Boy, it's been a long time."

"Wait a minute. It's still too early. Come and help me set the table."

"What are we having?"

"One of Anna Marie's favorite dishes."

"What's that? You act like it's a secret."

She laughs. "No, honey. One of Anna Marie's dishes she taught me while we were living with them is in the oven. It's chicken and dumplings, McGraw's favorite."

"Did you make Anna Marie's biscuits?"

"Sure did. And we have veggies in the fridge."

"Sounds good. I really like Anna Marie's homemade biscuits," he says, as he goes into the dining area and prepares to set the table with their best dinner plates, silverware, and cloth napkins that he removed earlier from the cabinet against the wall over the counter.

Holly enters the dining area. "Dusty, the table looks great. Thank you, honey."

"Mom?" he says as he gets out the water glasses and places one by each plate.

"Yes. What is it?"

"I… I…"

"What, Dusty?"

"You know how much I like McGraw, right?"

"Yes, I do."

"I… I…wish he was my dad."

"I know, son."

Anna Marie is in the passenger seat of the sky-blue RAM 3500 pickup with her son, Noah, heading to Holly's. She hasn't said a word since they left the ranch, just stares at his Stetson and his handsome face.

"Mom, what's wrong?"

She shrugs. "Nothing, really."

"Come on. Something's bothering you. You've been looking at me ever since we left the ranch."

"Oh, well. You caught me."

He smiles.

"I see you have a package here," she says, holding it up. "Another book for Dusty?"

He nods. "What does that have to do with anything? This is his birthday."

"Noah, you know that book is not going to satisfy Dusty."

"What are you trying to say, mom?"

"You know darn well what I'm saying."

"No worry. That's not the only thing he's getting for his birthday. He'll love what else I have for him."

"You do? Where is it?"

"It's a surprise."

"Care to reveal it to your dear mother?" She smiles.

"Don't try that, mom. You know it doesn't work any longer."

They laugh.

"I hope it's the surprise I'm hoping for."

"You'll find out soon enough."

He maneuvers the pickup into a middle-class neighborhood with brick homes, trimmed lawns lined up in military formation along the curbs. Mid-sized to full-sized SUVs are in the driveways. Holly's driveway leads up to the garage next to the house with a large front window. This home is part of a divorce settlement from her ex, a real estate developer, who decided one day he had enough and left. Couldn't stand for her being away so much doing police work, when he wanted her around to interact with his clients, hoping to make his business more successful. But they have now made up and he's changed his life.

McGraw pulls up in the driveway next to Holly's Jeep Grand Cherokee, reaches for the small package and says to Anna Marie, "Wait up, mom. I'll come around and help you out."

"Have you forgotten I drive this thing? I can manage."

He steps out and meets her at the front of the pickup, and they walk around the curved sidewalk to the door.

"I hope Dusty won't be disappointed," she says.

"I'll guarantee you this will be the best night of his life."

She leads the way. Before she can knock, the door opens and Dusty flies out, almost knocking Annie Marie back into Noah.

"So glad to see you both," he says hugging Anna Marie, laying his head against her waist. "Missed you so much."

"Missed you too, son, and so has TR."

"How is TR?" he says, looking up at her.

"Waiting for you, son," she says.

She releases him and he almost jumps up on McGraw.

"Whoa, howya doin,' little buddy?"

"Better now, seeing both of you. How come it's been so long? I was thinking you all forgot me."

"No way." McGraw says, raising his right hand. "Look, I'm still wearing the bracelet you and Whitey made for me."

"Cool." He grabs Anna Marie's hand and pulls her into the house.

McGraw closes the door with the heel of his boot.

"Mom, Anna Marie and McGraw are here."

Holly comes from the kitchen, wiping her hands in her apron. She smiles at her guests. "So glad you could come, Anna Marie. Haven't seen you in a while."

"It's been too long, honey. How can I help?"

"Dusty, show McGraw to the dinner table while Anna Marie and I get the food ready." They move into the kitchen.

Dusty takes Noah's hat and sets it on the coffee table and leads him into the dining room. "You can sit by me," Dusty says, as he pulls a chair away from the table.

"I'll wait for the ladies before we sit," McGraw says, placing the package by his plate, and stands behind the chair. Dusty fixes his eyes on the package.

"It's my job to fill the water glasses." He walks into the kitchen for a pitcher of water, returns and fills the glasses. Holly brings the chicken and dumplings and sets the bowl on the pad in the middle of the table, while Anna Marie brings in the veggies.

Holly pulls out a chair next to her for Anna Marie to sit, then returns to the kitchen for the hot biscuits and fixings.

"Please, let's all sit," Holly says.

"Oh, boy. One of my favorite dishes, chicken, and dumplings with hot biscuits," McGraw says. "Are these biscuits from maw's recipe?"

Holly nods. "You have your mother to thank for this. She taught me some of her best recipes when we were at the Circle M," she says, as she places her napkin on her lap.

"Mama's the best," McGraw says.

She slaps him on the arm and says, "Stop it, son."

Dusty says, "McGraw, are you going to say Grace?"

"I'd love to."

After a brief prayer of thanks, Holly begins serving the chicken and dumplings while Anna Marie passes the veggies and biscuits. Throughout the meal, Dusty keeps glancing at the package next to McGraw.

When everyone had finished, Holly rises and says, "I have a surprise for our birthday boy."

She goes to the kitchen and brings out a large strawberry cake with eleven lighted candles and sets it in the middle of the table.

"Let me help you clear the table," Anna Marie says.

Once they make room, Holly and Anna Maire stand by their chairs and begin singing happy birthday to Dusty. McGraw stands and joins in the chorus. When they finish, Dusty blows out his candles.

Holly hands Dusty a wrapped gift.

"What is it, mom?"

"Open it."

He rips off the paper and opens the box, lifting out, colorful name brand, Wireless Earbuds. "Oh, boy. Thanks, mom. Just what I wanted." He rises and gives her a big hug.

Anna Marie signal McGraw with her eyes to do something.

"I noticed you eyeing this package, probably wondering what's in it," he says, handing it to him.

"I know it's a book." He tears off all the paper and finds a hard back cover of Ray Bradberry's, "Fahrenheit 451."

"That's a very interesting book, Dusty. It's about the burning of books. That's all I'm going to tell you. Once you read it, we'll talk about it like we always do.

"Thanks, McGraw. You know I like the books you give me." He pauses, looking down at the book, then jumps up, grabs the book, and darts out of the room.

Anna Marie looks at Noah. "You had another surprise for Dusty. Aren't you going to tell him what it is?"

"I was about to when he darted out of the room."

"Let me go get him," Holly says.

Minutes later, the red-eyed eleven-year-old came into the dining room with his mother, looking down at the floor.

"Dusty. McGraw has something to tell you," Anna Marie says.

"Dusty, I remember when I was here last having dinner with you and your mom, you said you wanted to live at the Circle M and that you wanted me to be your dad. Right?"

Dusty wipes his eyes. He frowns. "Yes."

"Well, I have another surprise for you."

"What" He looks up with wide eyes. What is it?"

"You know that your mother and I are engaged to be married."

"Yes."

"Well, I want you and your mom to come and live with Anna Marie and me at the Circle M permanently, and it would be my honor to be your dad."

Silence filled the room.

Dusty darts to McGraw and throws his arms around his neck. "That's the best birthday present, ever."

Anna Marie is all smiles.

Holly winks at McGraw. She moves her lips, saying, "Thank you."

Chapter 9

Blood samples of all dogs drawn before the start of the experiment were given to Jess York. She found that all dogs had telomeres that were short, which was an indication of advanced aging.

At the conclusion of the first week of treating the dogs with RapTOR, they showed some change in their skin and in their ability to stand. Their eyes weren't so sad looking. Their blood study, performed by Jess York to measure their length of telomeres, uses the flow-FISH test developed by a Canadian researcher. There is a little change seen in the telomeres of the treated dogs compared to the Lab control.

The researchers are showing guarded excitement after the second week over the improvement in the dogs' standing—not as wobbly—and less watery eyes. There telomeres are beginning to lengthen. As expected, the telomeres in the control dog, the Lab, appear to be shortening. A sign of aging.

Jess says. "Hey, why the sad face, M&M?"

"I was…oh, you know, I was just expecting more improvement," Michael says. He pauses, slipping into deep thought.

"M&M? Hello. Come back to earth. What's going in that mind of yours?"

"We're almost there. I can feel it," he says.

"Well, you should be happy, for heaven's sakes. A lot of good things can happen in another week."

He holds up a hand. "I'm thinking." After a pause, he says, "We need to increase the dosage. And if we must, we can test longer."

Michael turns and calls out to April and Simon. "We need to talk," he says.

"Are you sure?" Jess says. "By how much?"

"I believe we should increase RapTOR by one-fourth of the total dose."

Jess shrugs. "I guess." She pauses. "Yes, it wouldn't hurt to see what happens."

"You called, Dr. Mordecai?" Simon asks.

"We've decided to increase the dose of RapTOR by one-fourth of the total for the next week."

Simon and April look at each other. "But what about toxicity, sir?" April asks.

"That won't be a problem. It may also help us determine the MTD (maximum therapeutic dose)." MTD is the highest dose of a drug that does not cause overt toxicity over a specific time period. "We will want to look for toxicological endpoints: especially looking at liver function."

"Yes, sir."

The third week of treatment had demonstrated encouraging signs of a greater increase in telomere growth. As Jess and Michael were walking toward the animal room to examine the dogs, Jess was telling him, "We're on the right track, M&M. The telomeres of the four have grown so much more with the increased dosage. RapTOR is working."

When they enter the animal room, they find the four treated dogs standing erect, tails wagging, and they begin to bark when they see the two investigators.

"How are you guys doing?" Michael says as he taps on each cart as he walks down the line, carefully observing them. They bark louder and circle in their carts. The sickly Lab is down in cart 5.

April comes from the other side of the table and says," Dr. Mordecai. I'm afraid we're going to lose the Lab. Is there anything we can do?"

Michael stares at the sickly animal whose sad eyes are begging for help. "Yes. We have enough data and we don't have to use the Lab any longer as control. We've acquired enough information from her. I want you and Simon to begin to treat her immediately. I believe we can save her. It will also tell us if our final dose is effective.

"Oh, that's such good news, Dr. Mordecai," April says. "We're on it."

Chapter 10

The day that Dusty has been praying for has finally arrived. He and his mom, Holly Roark, are waiting in an empty house for McGraw to take them to the Circle M. Dusty is so excited that he nervously walks back and forth at the curb, looking for the sky blue 3500 RAM pickup.

With Anna Marie's help, it only took her and Holly several days to pack all the key items for Whitey, the ranch hand, to take to the ranch in a U-Haul. The rooms of furniture and appliances were sold, and some items were left for the new owners. The house sold in two days, and the new owners were eager to move in. Holly carries two suitcases to the door.

Dusty runs to her. "He's coming, mom. McGraw is here."

"Okay, okay. Let's go." She wheels their suitcases outside the door.

McGraw pulls his truck up close to the garage, reaches over and shuts off *Somebody I Used to Know*, playing on his favorite country and western music station, slides out and adjusts his white Stetson. Dressed in a starched white shirt, jeans, and his seven-hundred-dollar Lucchese boots with exotic square toes, he meets up with Dusty. "McGraw, where have you been? I want to see TR."

"Hold on, partner. TR will be there. He's not going anywhere. Let's help your mom and we'll load up and get going, okay?"

"Okay, but let's hurry. I've been waiting all morning."

Holly locks up, puts the key in the security box the realtor placed on the door, and turns to greet her two men.

"I believe we're ready," she says.

McGraw grabs the suitcases, noticing Holly looking at the house. "One last look?" he asks.

"Just a lot of memories here," she says, "but now I'm looking forward to our new life. I'm ready."

"So am I," McGraw says.

Holly and Dusty follow him to the pickup. He places the suitcases in the trunk, opens the driver's door, and hops in. Holly slides in next to Noah. Dusty slides in after her and pulls the passenger door shut.

"Well, you'll have a welcoming party waiting for you at Circle M."

"Who? Who, McGraw?" Dusty says.

"You'll see."

Dusty leans forward in his seat looking out the window. "Can't you hurry," he says.

"You want me to get a ticket?"

"Aw, McGraw, you and mom are the police."

"You don't want McGraw to break the law, do you, Dusty?" Holly says.

"Aw, mom."

She turns to the cowboy. "He's just excited."

"I can see that."

They laugh.

Minutes later, McGraw pulls into the driveway of the Circle M.

"Look," Dusty says, "there's Whitey with TR and Anna Marie waiting for us." He opens the door before McGraw comes to a complete stop.

"Hold on, Dusty. Wait 'til I stop."

Dusty hops out and runs to Anna Marie, hugs her, and then Whitey. He turns to TR. "Howya been, my friend." The horse neighs and Dusty knows it's time to hop on for the ride. "Help me up on TR," Dusty says to Whitey. Once on his horse, Dusty takes off.

McGraw and Holly are watching.

"He's sure glad to be back. Never saw him so happy," Holly says.

"That's what I like to see," Noah says.

They open the car door and slide out, walking around the pickup where Holly hugs Anna Marie and Whitey.

"Thanks for helping Dusty, Whitey. He really likes you as much as TR."

They laugh.

"We're buddies," Whitey says.

"Let's get to the house out of this sun. I got cold lemonade in the fridge and then we can get you settled in your rooms," Anna Marie says.

"Thank you," Holly says.

"Can I help you with the suitcases, Noah?" Whitey says.

"I got 'em."

"Then I'm gonna keep an eye on Dusty," Whitey says as he heads for the barn.

McGraw pulls the suitcases from the pickup and walks up the flagstones to the two-story white frame antebellum. The German Shepherds, Prince, and Tucker, bark up a storm as McGraw approaches the door.

Standing on the porch, Holly waits and turns to Noah. "They always know when you're coming."

"Sure do."

Chapter 11

Jess and Michael are reviewing the data from the completed 3-week study. Michael ponders over the results when Jess says, "Wow! The data look great. Telomeres have grown, animals' skins are tight and they're able to stand and move around. Their arthritis has improved and the dose is non-toxic. We can't ask for anything more."

He doesn't respond. "Michael. Did you hear me? What do you think?"

He turns to her. "It's all great, but I'm concerned that Corey will find something for us to do that will prevent Biogen from applying for clinical trials. I just know it."

April comes running from the animal room to Jess and Michael. "Drs. Mordecai and York, come quick."

"What's up?" Michael says, as they rush to the animal room.

April says, "Look. The Lab is standing and is playful. The drug has worked. Oh, she's so much better." April is in tears.

Michael and Jess look in at the Lab. She barks and turns in circles.

"Oh, my. It's a miracle, Michael," Jess says.

"Hi, girl. Howya doing?" He reaches in and pats her and she licks his hand.

"Simon. Rush over to Dr. Keller's office and tell him to get over here as soon as he can," Michael says. He turns to Jess. "He has to see this."

Minutes later, Keller comes rushing into the animal room. "What's happening here," he says. "What's wrong?"

Jess says, "Nothing. This was our control dog who was about to die a week ago. Michael decided to treat her with RapTOR and look at her now."

"I just finished reading your 3-week animal study and I have to say, I'm really impressed." He moves over to the Lab's cart. "She sure looks fine. Congratulations."

"Does that mean Biogen can now submit paperwork for clinical trials?" Michael asks as they leave the animal room.

"I'll take it up with our scientific committee, which is the first step," he says. "You know the protocol."

"But that'll take weeks. You know how they drag their feet, reading every damn little detail. Isn't there another way we can expedite this? Don't you want Biogen to beat the other Biotech companies to the anti-aging market?"

"Of course I do. I'm just as eager as you both are. Once your data are thoroughly reviewed, they'll approve your request, and then I'll submit the application to the FDA. Just be patient. I'll keep you in the loop."

"But Corey. I know you've seen all the TV drug commercials with all the horrible side-effects. When they read the list of side effects of all the drugs, it blows my mind. It's a wonder that the FDA approved any of those drugs. In our case, we haven't found one side effect with RapTOR."

Corey says, "I know your frustration, Michael, but my hands are tied. I'll move it along just as fast as I can," and he walks out of the lab.

Aw bullshit! Corey, you jealous bastard, you're purposely dragging your feet.

Once Corey is out of the lab and Michael heads to his desk, Jess says, "Hey, M&M." He turns to her. "What?"

She shrugs, as if she doesn't want to say what she feels she must tell him. "Michael, I don't want to upset you more, but during our last meeting with Corey, he told me to keep an eye on you." She pauses apparently looking for his reaction. "As your friend, I couldn't go along with that. Just wanted you to know."

He shakes his head. "That's Corey. But thanks. You're a jewel, Jess." He reaches for his backpack and walks towards her.

She says, "I know you're upset, but try to let it go. I'm sure the committee will approve RapTOR when they see the data."

Michael shrugs. "It'll take months. I know Corey too well," he says, slipping into a fit of rage. "I gotta get the hell out of here, Jess."

Chapter 12

That early evening, sitting at his desk in his home office, drinking three finger Scotch on the rocks, Michael is pumped up over the success of his anti-aging compound, RapTOR, but anger overwhelms him every time he thinks about Corey preventing him from receiving his rewards when they could beat the other biotech companies to market. He downs the scotch in one big swallow. The rage that overtook him when he left Biogen was so intense that during the rush hour, he almost ran into the back of a car that slowed in front of him. All he could think about was the fantastic results from his anti-aging drug and how it was being deliberately held up. He rises, moseys over to the liquor cabinet in the corner, and fills his glass again, neat.

What good is it to have a miracle drug and not get it to market? Corey's my roadblock.

Michael returns to his desk and sits, feeling unsteady. He takes another swallow of his scotch, leans forward, gazing at the painting on the wall, and racking his brain on what to do. He could kill him and drop him in East Lake? No, that wouldn't work. The cops could trace him back to Biogen. Everyone in the lab will tell them how he and Corey were at each other's throats.

No matter what I do, the cops are going to trace Corey back to Biogen.

He finishes off his scotch and twirls the glass as he thinks. Minutes later, the glass falls to the floor and his body collapses forward with his head ending up on the desk. Michael slips into a trance. A vision appears.

He sees Corey Keller in his red Corvette convertible racing along the

Interstate, trying to escape a black SUV that is ramming his back bumper. After several strikes to the bumper, the Corvette arcs in the air as it shoots off the road, like out of a cannon, eventually slamming to the ground, creating a trench as it scrapes the ground and finally crashes into a large Oak tree, throwing Corey out of the convertible. The person behind the wheel of the black SUV stops, hops out and surveys the scene. Corey is dead.

Michael groans as he begins to stir, gasping for air. His eyes open. He pushes himself backwards in his chair and wipes his mouth with his shirt sleeve. He rises and braces himself against the desk for a few seconds, then walks to the little frig for a bottle of water and slowly returns to his desk, sits, opens the bottle, and gulps down all twelve ounces. He takes a deep breath and exhales.

What the hell just happened? He inhaled deeply. *That was a vision on how to get rid of Corey, and I'm that person behind him in the black SUV. That's a good plan, but I must be careful, it will require careful planning.*

Chapter 13

The next day, Michael drives around Atlanta neighborhoods looking for a car with a for sale sign in its window, positioned on the front lawns. He thought it all through last evening after his vision.

Corey lives north of Atlanta on several acres in a large white-frame house. He's divorced and his ex has their two small children but she is seeing another man. Michael has been at his home once before Corey's divorce to attend a Christmas party, and remembers the area. He is following the plan given to him in his vision. He needs a car that cannot be traced.

After two hours driving around Atlanta, he spots a 2010 black Land Rover LR4 that has scratches on the body.

Someone didn't take care of it, he thinks.

Land Rovers are mainly good for off-the-road traveling, but it's a heavy car, weighing close to 6000 pounds, and should do the job. It's on the lawn of a house in southeast Atlanta. He gets out and walks over to the entrance, goes up four steps to the porch, pulls open the screen door and knocks on the door.

A large middle-aged guy with a round face, under six-foot, bald head, large arms, and a big nose with red spider web vessels, opens the door and steps out. He's wearing a black T-shirt with short sleeves that emphasize his bulging arms covered with tattoos around his neck, and snakes that cover most of both arms. On his right wrist is a blue cross.

"I'm here about the Land Rover for sale out there," Michael says, pointing.

"Five grand. That's final."

"Can I look at it?"

The big guy grunts and leads the way down the steps and onto the lawn, reaches into his back pocket and yanks out one key and hands it to Michael, and then moves to the front of the car as if to say, "You ain't going nowhere." Michel opens the door and looks inside as if he's really interested. Not bad.

"Lots of wear in here." The man only grunts, as if he gives a damn. "Someone must have gotten mad and took it out on this car," Michael says, trying to get the price down.

Again, the man doesn't say a word.

Michael starts it. The motor sounds okay. "Can we take it around the block?"

The man comes around to the passenger side, opens the door and hops in. "Head down to the road and turn right," he says.

After driving around for twenty minutes, Michael heads back to the house, pulls it into its original spot, and climbs out.

"It's in poor condition. I'll give you $3500."

The large man grunts and says, "What'd I tell you? 5Gs."

"I pay cash. On the spot," Michael says. "Take it or leave it."

The guy is silent for a few minutes. "You got the bread on you?"

"Is it a deal?"

"Lemme see the folding stuff, and it's yours," the man says.

Michael pulls out a wad of thirty-five, one-hundred-dollar bills. Counts it out in his hands but doesn't hand it over. Instead, he reaches for the key with one hand and holds the money in the other up in the air. They exchange a key for the cash.

"Title is in the glovebox," man says as he drops the key in Michael's hand. Michael nods—doesn't care about the title. No way would he put his name on it. He'll burn it. He hops into the Land Rover, drives off for home, and stores it in the garage.

The next afternoon, Michael waits in the Land Rover north of town in a grove of trees, assessing the traffic at the time Corey would pass through after leaving Biogen for the evening. Corey should have left work thirty minutes ago. He spots the red Corvette convertible traveling at a high rate of speed. Michael speeds after Corey from his hiding spot. It's no surprise to Michael that Corey has a heavy foot. Speed fits his personality, king of the road. Five miles out, Corey signals a right turn and travels two miles west where the road splits into a Y. He takes the road to the left and pulls into his driveway. Michael has surveyed the area for two days to assess the number of cars coming in both directions. and how heavy the traffic is around this time before the sun sets.

The next evening, Michael, dresses in a Frankenstein monster head mask to puzzle anyone who spots him. He doesn't realize how much of a thrill the mask gives him. It's like Halloween when he was a kid.

Even the authorities would have a hell of a time figuring out why I'm wearing this disguise.

Michael waits for Corey in the same spot where he waited the last two evenings. Looking through binoculars, he sees Corey zooming toward him in the red convertible. Michael revs up the Land Rover and shoots out after Corey as he passes. He catches up to him, and as in the dream he slams the back of the convertible. But unlike the dream, he doesn't have to hit him more than once. Corey doesn't even spin. Instead, he flies off the road like a bullet, crashes into a large tree, is thrown from the vehicle.

Just like the egotistical fool not wearing a seat belt.

Chapter 14

The next morning, Michael leaves home for Biogen around eight. He's watching the news on his cell as he enters his BMW and drives off. WSB-TV Chanel 2 is reporting a red Corvette convertible had crashed after leaving the highway at a high rate of speed last night and the driver—who hasn't been identified - was ejected from the car and is deceased. It was a one car accident with only one person involved. The identity of the person will not be released until the family is notified.

Michael pulls into his parking spot behind Biogen next to the vacant spot where Corey parked his Corvette. *He won't be needing that space any more*, Michael thinks.

He hurries around the building, darts through the entrance, signs in, and rushes up the steps, taking them two at a time. Jess is working in the lab at the hood with her back to him. He walks over to his desk without saying a word, wondering if she's heard anything about the red Corvette. She'd know it was Corey's, if she did.

Michael moves over to Jess and asks, "What are you working on?"

"Oh, I didn't hear you come in, M&M. I'm rechecking all our data to make sure Corey's has everything to give to the committee."

"We gave him everything, but it doesn't hurt to double check in case something has to be replaced."

As Michael walks back his desk, the CEO's secretary enters.

"Drs. Mordecai and York, Mr. Ruben would like for everyone to meet in the auditorium downstairs in fifteen minutes."

"What's it about," Jess asks.

"I wasn't told. Just asked to get everyone to the auditorium."

"Thank you," Michael says. *Here it comes.*

Jess frowns. "Wonder what's going on? We only meet once a year for our annual upward and onward speech," she says.

"Guess we better head down there to find out," he says.

They walk out of the lab and take the stairs to avoid the elevators where a crowd is waiting. Once down on the first floor, Michael and Jess walk straight to the west end of the building to the auditorium. All four entrances are open, and employees are piling in and taking a seat. The room is about half full when Michael and Jess walk down the aisle to sit in the front row.

Ten minutes fly by and the doors in the back are closed. Everyone is concentrating on the stage as a man in his early forties, dressed in an expensive blue suit, white shirt, and a bow tie, comes to the center of the stage from the side. Mr. Ruben is close to six feet in height, well-built, and has a full head of black hair. He's wearing horn-rimmed glasses and looks healthy. He taps on the microphone and asks if everyone in the back can hear him. It's an affirmative.

"One of our basic principles at Biogen" he says, "is our concern for our employees. We feel our workers are family members."

Michael whispers to Jess. "What the hell is he driving at?"

"God knows," she says.

Mr. Rubin continues. "We are saddened to report that one member of our family was killed last night in a one-car accident. Many of you don't know Dr. Corey Keller, but the police have informed us that he was driving at a high rate of speed, lost control of his car, ran off the road, and died in the crash."

There were moans, and several audible, "Oh, no!"

Jess gasps for air. "Oh, no. Poor Corey."

"Poor Corey? You gotta be kidding. You know how he treated us. I'm not sorry."

Rubin pauses to allow for this tragedy to sink into his audience.

Jess frowns at Michael and whispers, "Did you have anything to do with this?""

Michael acts hurt. He whispers back to her: "How could you even think that? You heard the report. He ran off the road and crashed."

“The police will be coming to interview all who worked with Dr. Keller. Please give them your full cooperation. That’s all for now. We will update you all via email.”

Everyone stood and headed out of the auditorium.

Michael says to Jess as they take the stairs back to the lab, “I imagine the police will find out that Corey and I didn’t get along.”

She says, “Lots of workers never get along, but they’re never accused of killing anyone. Anyway, nothing to worry about. As you said, he ran off the road at a high rate of speed.”

Chapter 15

That evening, Michael is in his office thinking about Corey and what Mr. Ruben said. Michael doesn't believe anyone saw him striking the back of Corey's car. Even if they did, they couldn't identify him in his disguise. They'd never find the car even if someone described it. It's in car heaven. Michael took it early this morning to the car crushing plant where he saw it crushed and sent off to a recycling center in Indiana. There it will be shredded and separated into small pieces.

He's breathing easy now when he hears his mother calling from the sunroom. "There's someone at the door, Michael. See if it's Dr. Rance Peters. He didn't come today. I really need my physical therapy."

Michael rises from his desk and heads to the front door. "I'll call Rance in the morning, mom," he shouts. "I think you got your days mixed up. He's supposed to come tomorrow."

When he opens it, Kendal Wilson is standing there with a beaming smile, red lips, and sparkling eyes set in a narrow face. Her dark glistening hair falls below her shoulders.

Is this a God thing? he thinks. *She's my answer.*

"Hi, Michael. Thought I'd drop by and visit with Gail. Is she available?"

"Oh, yes. Come in. She's in the sunroom."

Kendal moves in gracefully, as he closes the door and follows her through the house to where his mother is reading a book again.

"Hi, Gail," Kendal says. "Would you like a visitor?"

"Of course, dear," she says as she puts down the book. "It's always good to have such a sweet person like you here," she says, looking at her son.

That's a hint to Michael that she wants Kendal as her daughter-in-law. They've discussed it in the past, but Michael is noncommittal, even though they've been dating over six months, and get along well.

"Would you like something to drink?" Gail asks.

"No, I'm fine, thank you."

"Kendal, before you leave would you mind coming by my office?"

"Sure."

Back in his office, Michael closes the door and pumps a fist in the air, and shouts, "Yeah!" Kendal was his father's nurse and after he died, she went to work at the Jefferson Nursing Home. He moves to his desk, sits, and thinks about treating her patients with RapTOR. He knows she wouldn't agree if there are too many patients in the treatment group. Her supervisor could get suspicious. Won't need a control group or to draw blood. They'd just study the patients' skin, their strength, and their skill in walking. He and Kendal could work out the treatment protocol together, if she agrees.

An hour later, there's a knock on his door.

He rises and hurries around his desk and opens it. "Come in," he says.

"I haven't heard from you in over a week, is everything okay?" she asks.

"Yes, everything's great, except that the research director got killed last night driving his car so fast that he lost control and ran off the road."

"Oh, I'm so sorry. Did he have a wife and children?"

Why is she concerned about them? That's just like women. They want details.

"They're divorced and she has their two children."

"I feel so sorry for the family, especially the children."

Aw, bullshit.

"I got something to tell you. We've been busy as all get out. I'd like to tell you about it over dinner this Saturday night. Do you have any plans?"

She frowns. "No. This Saturday would be just great. I was beginning to think you had found someone else."

"What? No way. You should have known that I'm very attached to you."

"Just attached?"

"Oh, I'm sorry. That wasn't what I really meant." He pauses, looking into her beautiful dark eyes. "I consider you my girl."

"Just your girl?"

I'm not getting any place. She wants me to tell her that I love her.

"You're more than my girl. How long have we been going together? Six months? That means something, doesn't it? You're my sweetheart. Can I pick you up around seven?"

She smiles. "Sure."

He walks her to the door, and she stops before walking out, and looks back at him. "You seem different, Michael. I've never seen you this happy."

"I can't wait to tell you at dinner."

"I don't know if I can wait until then," she says, and walks to her car.

Chapter 16

The next morning around six-thirty, Holly Roark eases out of the house, trying not to disturb Anna Marie, who will be rising soon to work in the kitchen, and Noah, who will be taking his morning walk around the property, ending up with his two equine friends, Mystery Lady, and Texas Rodeo.

Holly hops into her white Jeep Grand Cherokee, which Whitey drove to the Circle M the day before Noah came to bring her and Dusty to the ranch. She backs out of the driveway and heads to Starbucks. Holly loves the early morning sunrise, as does Noah. It is the start of a new day, and in their line of work, the quiet time reminds them that life is okay and not all people are bad. It recharges her batteries so she can do her job.

She removes the holder with the two Starbuck coffees—Anna Marie only drinks tea—rolls out of the Grand Cherokee, bumping the door shut with her hip, and walks up the flagstones to the door. Before she can set the coffees down, Anna Marie opens the door in a house dress with a flour-covered apron, wiping her hands with a towel.

"Oh, I was hoping to return before you got up. Didn't want to wake you."

"No, sweetie, come on in. I saw you coming up the walk." She shuts the door and follows Holly into the kitchen.

"The biscuits are in the oven and breakfast is almost ready."

"Anna Marie. You're the best. I was wanting to return before you got up so I could help. You need to let me help you. I don't want to wear out my welcome."

They laugh.

"Oh, honey. You'll never do that. Noah and I love you and Dusty so much. So proud to have you both in the family."

They hug. "Thank you, Anna Marie."

"I guess Noah is with his two babies, Texas Rodeo and Mystery Lady."

"Every morning," Anna Marie says.

"Noah once told me that Mystery Lady would be jealous of any woman in his life, but the way she has taken to me, I don't believe that."

Anna Marie nods. "Don't you listen to that. I see how Lady takes to you."

"Do you think horses think?" Holly asks.

"Sure do."

"Well, I don't care, we're buddies, and she loves me. I think I'll go out and get my man," Holly says.

Anna Marie smiles and winks.

Holly takes the cups of coffee with her and heads to the barn. Before she gets there, her cowboy is coming out. She holds up a cup.

"Coffee the way you like it, half-caff with cream."

He removes the lid. "You know what I like. Thank you."

After a couple of sips, he plants a kiss on her. "That's for thinking of me."

"How could I not, you're my boss."

They laugh. "You mean, I'm your man."

"That too, I guess."

They laugh again.

"I'm gonna go in and give my Lady a little love rub. Back in a few."

Noah goes to the bench and sits, tilts his Stetson back, places one leg over the other knee and rests his left arm on the back of the bench.

"You look mighty rested there, cowboy," Holly says as she comes out of the barn. "Glad you are sitting for a while. We need to talk about something that I didn't want to bring up in front of Anna Marie."

Noah straightens up. "You look serious. What is it?"

"It's about Dusty."

"Is he not happy here?"

"Oh, no. He loves it here. He's asked me several times when were we going to spend more time with him. He knows our police work keeps us busy, but he believes we could find times to be with him more."

Noah finishes his coffee. "He's right. We've neglected our little man without realizing it. We thought, or at least I thought, he was so involved with Whitey and TR that he was completely happy. I assumed too much."

"Me, too," she says, "Let's seriously think about it. Maybe a weekend now and then."

"Sure. And maybe one evening during the week, occasionally."

Holly rises. "Great. Let's get some breakfast before we hit the road."

"I'm with you," he says as they head to the house.

Chapter 17

McGraw and Holly arrive in the homicide division a little after eight. He sets his Stetson on the side of his desk away from the aisle, and Holly sits at her desk and opens the computer.

Minutes later, Captain Norman Dipple, Chief of Detectives, comes out of his office and maneuvers with a purpose through the squad room. Roark watches every step the six-foot, ex-hockey player takes before calling out McGraw's name with a gruff voice. Dipple has the smile and face of actor Ernest Borgnine, whose acting career spread over decades beginning in the 50s.

"Got another one for you, cowboy," he says, throwing a folder on his desk.

McGraw glances over at Roark. She shrugs.

"A scientist from Biogen, a biotech company, was speeding, lost control of his car, flew off the road and crashed, killing himself. And in a convertible, no less. It's all in that folder," he says, pointing.

McGraw opens it.

"Wait a minute, Capt. Patrol can handle an open-and shut case. There's no mention of foul play. Why would we be involved?"

"Someone might have run him off the road. The back bumper was banged up, leading the super to think someone deliberately rammed the guy, causing him to fly off the road. Anyway, the Commish is good friends with the Biogen CEO, Mark Ruben, and he wants us to make sure all bases are covered. That's where you come in, cowboy. Check it out. It's all in that folder."

You said that already, Capt., McGraw thinks.

The Capt. pauses while his eyes glance around the room and then over to Roark, Kramer, and then Gomez.

"I'm pleased with the renovations we did in here last year," he says.

No one says a thing.

He turns and walks a few paces. Then stops and glances over the room, again.

"I see you've moved your desks around," he says, and then walks back to the Lion's Den.

"The big guy doesn't like what we did, does he, boss?" Gomez says.

"We have more important things to think about," the boss says, smiling.

They laugh.

McGraw has been the victims' avenging angel ever since he entered law enforcement, and his mission has always been to be their advocate. He never saw his job as just skill or craft. He reopens the file labeled "Dr. Corey Keller" and finds the officer's Incident Report (OIR). There's a picture of Dr. Keller, but not much to help in the investigation. No witnesses. Keller ran off the road around six-seven p.m. that evening. Some skid marks are reported that may be from someone ramming him two nights ago.

Could be old skid marks from someone braking, he thinks.

Minutes later, he picks up his phone and calls dispatch and asks for forensics to meet him at the site, then he picks up Keller's pic from the folder and goes to the crime board behind his desk and places it on the board and writes his name under it.

Roark comes up behind him. "Whatta we have?"

"Dr. Corey Keller," he says pointing at the picture, "a scientist that was research director at Biogen, a biotech company."

"Keller looks like a professor."

"Not much to go on in the OIR. No witnesses. It appears he was just going too fast and lost control."

"This isn't really for us, is it?" she says.

"You know the Chief. Once he gets the bug, he won't stop."

"You mean, once the Commish gets involved, the Chief bows on all fours."

McGraw nods as they laugh. He turns to Kramer and Gomez.

"Okay, everyone, let's meet at the table," McGraw says, as he picks up his hat and the folder.

Roark follows him to the table where Kramer and Gomez are sitting.

"We got this situation north of town where a scientist named Keller from Biogen, a biotech company—"

"—I've heard of them, boss," Gomez says, interrupting.

"Good. He was traveling at a high rate of speed and sped off the road in a convertible, crashed and was thrown from the vehicle, and died at the scene."

Kramer frowns. "Boss. That doesn't sound like a case for homicide. It's too cut-and-dry."

"Was there a perp that got away?" Gomez asks.

"No one knows. There are no witnesses," Roark says.

"The scene is going to be disturbed to no end with all the people trampling around on the grass and the M.E. removing the body," McGraw says. "We're going out there anyway to see what we can find and close this thing out. Probably nothing, but we must please the Chief," McGraw says. "Let's saddle up."

Roark looks at McGraw as they leave. "'Saddle up.' That's a new one."

"Well, the Marlboro Man is a cowboy, correct?"

"Sure is."

"Then, let's saddle up."

"Where's your cigarette?"

"Don't smoke."

"Okay, boss. I'm ready. Where's my horse?"

"Waiting outside."

They laugh.

McGraw and Roark hop into the black Silverado, the monster, and head north with Kramer and Gomez in an unmarked Impala following behind. A mile from the site, McGraw flips on the recessed strobes, pulls off the road, and stops behind the patrol car with its overhead lights flashing. Kramer and Gomez have their strobes flashing and pull in behind McGraw, who's the first one out and waits for his detectives. They head to the sergeant.

"Howya doing, Lieutenant McGraw?" He nods at Roark, Kramer, and Gomez.

"Well, thank you. I see the skid marks that were mentioned in the OIR.

"Yeah. The vic went off here and landed over there," sarge says, pointing, "ended up hitting that tree."

"I presume someone took pictures of these skid marks?"

"We have 'em."

"I didn't see 'em in the OIR."

"I'll see that you get them, Lieutenant."

"Let's walk over to the crash site," McGraw says. "No need to worry about any perpetrator's foot marks, if there was one, with all the people trampling the grass around here."

McGraw tells his team to spread out to see if there's anything that might help them determine if anyone else was involved.

McGraw and the sarge walk over to the thirty-foot oak.

"Dr. Keller was thrown out and landed over there, lieutenant," sarge says as he walks over to the spot that still had the red paint on the ground that outlined Keller's body.

"And the convertible's been impounded?"

Sarge nods. "We've gone over it with a fine-tooth comb. Nothing out of the ordinary."

"The OIR stated that the back bumper was dented, implying that someone may have rammed the doc off the road."

"Yes, it does. But who knows when it happened? It could be an old dent."

"A Corvette owner wouldn't drive around with a dented bumper," McGraw says.

"Never thought of it that way, Lieutenant."

"Who has his body?" McGraw asks.

"It's in the Emory Hospital morgue. The pathologist has gone over the body. His report should be released soon. The body hasn't been released yet. The doc's wife is the only family member claiming it."

"Dr. Keller. Not 'it,' Sergeant."

"Of course. I'm sorry."

"I'd like to see him,' McGraw says.

The sarge frowns. "You would?"

"Yes. Can you call it in and we'll head over there once we're done here?"

"Okay, Lieutenant," he says, and walks over to his patrol car.

McGraw slowly walks the area around the red-painted outline of the body and then walks a straight line from the tree to the skid marks on the road. The sarge seems puzzled at what McGraw is doing.

McGraw meets up with Roark, Kramer, and Gomez. "Whatta you guys think?"

Gomez is the first to answer. "Not a damn thing, boss. If there's anything, it's like a needle in the haystack."

Kramer says, "It's what we thought all along. The grass has been trampled and there are no scraps of anything that could help."

McGraw looks at Roark. "I agree with Kramer and Gomez," she says. "There's nothing here, not one piece of evidence."

"When a person travels at a high rate of speed and loses control, what happens next?" McGraw asks his team.

Kramer says, "They usually ride the edge of the pavement for an instant and then sail off the road."

"Most of the time they end up hitting something like Keller did," Holly says.

"But some spin and even flip over after flying off and don't go too far. Not as far as this guy did," Gomez interjects.

"You all are right." McGraw says. "Let's put it all in the proper perspective. Keller flew off the road, but why did he go so far and not overturn? Instead, he bounced off, scraped up a lot of ground before hitting the tree."

"He sailed off too fast to overturn," Roark says.

"That's right," McGraw says. "The force was great, causing the car to hit the ground and it didn't overturn. Why is that?"

"The speed had to be caused by someone ramming his backend," Gomez says.

McGraw remains quiet, looking at his team. "Anyone else?"

No one else answered.

"Gomez is right. Let's add this up. Keller didn't ride the edge of the rode and flip over because something hit him from behind and then he sailed off and landed flat and the speed caused the car to create a path before crashing into the tree."

"That's going to be hard to prove without a witness," Roark says.

McGraw nods and turns to Kramer. "I want you and Gomez to go to the station and go over the impounded Corvette. Talk to the mechanics, see what they've come up with. After that, track down the footage from the automated red-light cameras on the route we took to get here. You'll need to check what third-party company supervises the cameras. Maybe someone was following Keller. Give the footage the workover."

"Okay, boss," Kramer says.

He and Roark walk over to the Silverado. "We are going to the Emory Hospital morgue to view the body and get the pathologist's report to cover all bases."

Kramer and Gomez move to their car and head back to the station.

"What do you expect to find at the morgue?" Roark asks.

"Don't really know. Maybe the doc was on drugs or had been drinking. Who knows? The report will tell us."

"I see," she says as the sarge comes to them.

"Are you ready to go to the hospital, Lieutenant?" he says.

"Let's saddle up."

"Oh, that again?" Holly says.

"I like it," he says. "Something new."

"I like 'new'," she says, smiling.

Thirty minutes later, they pull into Emory Hospital midtown.

The sarge walks them down to the morgue to meet pathologist Dr. Bruce Carter. They walk into a large cold room where a body is covered with a white sheet. A tall slender man in his early sixties, thin white hair, long arms, and a cold smile, stands at a desk in the corner. Sarge introduces McGraw and Roark.

The doc doesn't seem too happy. McGraw thinks.

"I understand you want to see the body of Corey Keller, Lieutenant?" the doc says.

"Dr. Keller. Yes, we do."

"For what reason?"

Surprised at the question, McGraw says, "Because I want to."

The doc seems stunned. Slow to answer, he says, "That's good enough."

"This could be a homicide case. Do you have your report ready? I'd like a copy."

The doc doesn't say a word, returns to his desk, picks up a folder, comes to McGraw, opens it and says, "Here's a copy."

"Thank you." McGraw begins scanning it. "Did you do a tox study?"

"Only routine stuff for alcohol and drugs but no total screen."

"I see he had no alcohol or drugs in his body, doctor."

"That's correct. Did you suspect them?"

"Never know. We are very thorough."

"That's what I gather."

"Now the body, doctor."

The tall man dressed in white says, "Follow me." He walks over to the covered body. "I've been expecting you after getting the call and had the body placed here." He pulls back the sheet down to the victim's feet. The large Y incision down the front of Corey's chest made by the pathologist was visible.

There were gashes filled with dry blood on Keller's face. McGraw scans the body down to its feet. "Looks like his right arm is broken."

"And his left leg, and there are some internal injuries from being thrown from the car, hitting the ground and rolling some distance."

"Poor man," Holly says.

"That's what I wanted to know, doctor," McGraw says. "Thank you."

After thanking the doctor, McGraw, Roark, and the sarge left, returning to their cars.

"Did you get all you wanted, Lieutenant?" Sarge asks.

"Yes. Thank you. Appreciate your help."

"You sure are thorough. Now, I know why everyone at the station thinks 'You're the man.'"

"It's all team work, sarge," he says as he and Roark slid into the monster.

Roark says, "I've always known the man I'm going to marry is 'the man.'"

"Stop it," he says. "I'm just an ole cowboy."

"Oh, yeah. Tell that to the wind."

"Tomorrow we'll go to Biogen and question the scientists working with Dr. Keller."

"Better have the Capt. call the CEO," Holly says.

"Will do. We'll have him set it up so we meet with each one separately."

Chapter 18

McGraw and Roark pull into the reserved parking area behind Biogen headquarters this warm and sunny morning a little before nine. They step out of the Silverado and walk to the front of the glass building.

"Beautiful building," Roark says as they walk to the entrance. Don't know why I've never seen this structure before."

"Most of the times on the way to the station we're concentrating on our objectives for the day and rarely look around much. At least, that's what happens to me."

They proceed through the entrance and are met by a security guard standing by his desk. "Can I help you folks?" He stares at McGraw's Stetson.

"Yes, I'm Lieutenant McGraw and this is Sergeant Roark. We are from Atlanta PD homicide here to see Mr. Mark Ruben."

He glances down at his clip board. "Oh, yes. Mr. Ruben is expecting you. He's on two. You can take the stairs here in front or the elevators across the lobby toward the back. They open across from his office."

"Thank you. We'll take the stairs," McGraw says.

When they reached the second floor, an attractive woman in her early forties, slender-built brunette with well-kept hair, wearing an expensive blue suit, approaches them. Apparently, the security guard had called up to Ruben's office.

"Detectives McGraw and Roark?"

"Yes, I'm McGraw and this is my partner, Roark."

"I'm Elizabeth, Mr. Ruben's assistant. He's ready to meet with you. Please follow me."

She leads them through an outer office that is apparently hers, to the one in the back. The door is open and the gentleman standing behind his desk is a man in his early forties, black hair, wearing an expensive gray suit, blue shirt, and a bow tie. Mr. Ruben is close to six feet in height, well-built, and with a rosy complexion.

"Detectives. I'm Mark Ruben. I heard that the famous cowboy detective would be paying us a visit."

McGraw thinks, *the Capt. called him.*

"You just met Elizabeth, who has arranged for you to meet with everyone in the lab under Dr. Keller's supervision individually as requested. She has a sheet with their names and times. We've set you up in our conference room to interview our researchers as you requested."

"I'd like to ask you a few questions, Mr. Ruben," McGraw says.

"Sure…please have a seat," he says, pointing to the leather chairs in front of his desk.

McGraw realizes, *he was about to call me cowboy again.*

"Can I get you both something to drink?" Elizabeth says.

"I'm good," Roark says.

"No, thank you," McGraw says.

Mr. Ruben takes a seat behind his desk. "How can I help?"

"Just a few questions. How long had Dr. Keller worked for Biogen?" McGraw asks.

"About twelve years."

"And how respected was he?"

"I don't know what you mean."

"Did you consider him one of your top employees?"

"Most definitely. Corey was an outstanding scientist and a great director of research. It will be difficult to replace him."

"Would you say he got along with everyone?" Roark asks.

"I'd say most of the time. You must realize in science there's always disagreement, differences of opinions, and interpretations of results. But in the end, the resolution brings us closer to achieving our goals."

"When did you last talk to him, Mr. Ruben?" Roark asks.

"The day before he went missing, we were discussing Dr. Mordecai's new anti-aging drug, which has proven to be very effective. Corey was excited about it, pushing very hard to get Michael Mordecai's new drug through our science committee here so our data and application can be reviewed by the FDA for clinical trials."

"What can you tell us about Dr. Keller's wife?" McGraw asks.

"They're divorced. Ella moved away two years ago and has their two children, a boy and a girl."

"Do you know if their divorce was amicable?"

He frowns at McGraw. "You're not suggesting his wife had anything to do with Corey's death?"

"Just asking."

"The divorce was on agreeable terms," Ruben says.

"So he lives alone?" Roark asks.

Ruben nods. "But it's my understanding he was seeing someone."

"Happen to know her name?" McGraw asks.

"No, I don't. Elizabeth can provide you with Dr. Keller's personal information. I believe since this is police investigation, we can release his personal information. Correct, detectives?"

"Yes," McGraw and Roark say in unison.

"One other thing, Mr. Ruben," McGraw says, "do you know of anyone that might want to harm Keller?"

"No one, sir. He was well-liked here and as far as I know, even in his personal life."

"Thank you, sir," McGraw says, rising. "You have been very helpful."

"Anything we can do to clear this up, please let us know. We've lost one of our best, and we're willing to help in any way we can."

"That's very kind of you, sir," Roark says.

The detectives follow Elizabeth to the outer office. She goes to a filing cabinet against the wall behind her desk and opens the top drawer, reaching in for a folder.

"I had copied Dr. Keller's personnel file in anticipation that you would be needing it."

"Thank you. Very efficient," McGraw says.

She smiles, looks at the wall clock. "Mr. Ruben had me formulate a time line for you to meet the people who work in the Director's research lab. That would be: Dr. Michael Mordecai, Dr. Jess York, and two technicians. April and Simon. Here's the schedule," she says, handing the sheet to McGraw. "April should be in the conference room on four at the present time, I'll take you up there."

The detectives follow Elizabeth to the elevators. They ride to the fourth floor. When the doors open, they step out and walk about twenty feet to their right. The door to the Conference Room is open and a young lady in her thirties is seated at a long conference table. Elizabeth introduces April and excuses herself.

"I'm Lieutenant McGraw and this is Sergeant Roark," he says, as they sit facing her. He removes his Stetson and places it on the table. All the while the female tech is eyeing him, and licking her lips.

"No need to feel uneasy," McGraw says. He looks at her without saying a word for a few seconds. She seem somewhat distracted.

"You know about the unfortunate accident of Dr. Keller."

She nods, exhibiting nervousness. "Poor Dr. Keller."

"What was the relationship with everyone and Dr. Keller?" Roark asks.

April frowns and was slow to answer. "What do you mean?"

"Did everyone work well together?"

"I'd say yes, most of the time."

"What do you mean, 'most of the time'?" McGraw asks.

"There were times when Dr. Mordecai and Dr. Keller got together, they didn't see eye-to-eye on our work. The arguments were about the testing we do in the lab. Dr. Keller always wanted more tests. That's all."

"How about the other times?" McGraw asks. "Did they agree on things?"

"Yes, but we're used to Dr. Mordecai's way. You know, some scientists have funny ways."

"Do you think anyone here would want to harm Dr. Keller?"

"Oh, no."

"Thank you. We appreciate your help," McGraw says.

The young lab worker rises and leaves in a hurry.

McGraw looks at the sheet Elizabeth provided, and the other tech, Simon is scheduled. Seconds later a young man in his thirties comes in.

"Hello. My name is Simon, I'm one of Dr. Mordecai's tech. I believe it's my time according to the schedule."

"Yes, it is," Roark says. "Come in and please have a seat in the chair opposite us," she says, pointing.

Simon is close to six-foot and slender with blonde hair. He moves in and takes a seat. He seems a little less nervous than April. After introducing themselves, the detectives begin asking the same questions to Simon as they did April. They learn that he worked in the lab a few years longer than April and really enjoys his work, and that both Dr. Jess York and Dr. Mordecai are great people. Neither does he know of anyone who would wish harm to Dr. Keller. When McGraw and Roark finish the interview, they check the schedule and noticed that Dr. York is next.

She enters and the detectives stand and introduce themselves to her.

York takes a seat at the head of the table to the right of McGraw and Roark.

"Dr. York, how long have you and Dr. Michael Mordecai been working together?" Roark asks.

She frowns. "About ten years. I thought this was about Dr. Keller's unfortunate accident."

"It is," says Roark, "but we want to get a handle on the group that works in your lab. What is your role in there?"

"I'm an MIT Ph.D. trained in genetic engineering."

McGraw and Roark look at each other.

"Michael and I have been working on anti-aging compounds for months and he discovered an exciting agent that we had finished testing and were waiting for Dr. Keller to run all the data through the Biogen Science Committee so an application can be made to the FDA for clinical trials."

"What was the relationship between Dr. Keller and Dr. Mordecai?" McGraw asks.

"I don't know what you were told, but Michael and Corey, Dr. Keller, argued over moving Michael's agent more rapidly through our science committee. Michael felt Corey was dragging his feet and he had to put some pressure on him. And yes, that caused heated arguments. But then they'd cool down."

"Do you know of anyone who might want to see harm come to Dr. Keller?" Roark asks.

"No one."

"Where were you night before last from six to nine?" McGraw asks.

She frowns again. "Am I a suspect?"

"We must ask. It's routine."

"Working here until nine."

"Can anyone verify that?" Roark asks.

"The night watchman. We sign in and out."

McGraw looks at the sheet in front of him. Dr. Mordecai is the last one to be interviewed. He looks up at Jess York.

"I'd like to see your lab. Dr. Mordecai is next to be interviewed and I'd like to see what you all do in that the lab. Can you accompany us there?"

"Certainly. It's just a few doors down the hall."

Roark frowns at McGraw.

McGraw reaches for his hat but doesn't put it on. They rise and head to the lab. When they enter, they find the two techs are at Dr. Mordecai's desk, apparently giving him an update on what took place in the interview room.

Dr. Mordecai rises and walks over to McGraw. The techs rush to the back of the lab.

"I'm Dr. Mordecai," he says with emphasis on the Dr.

Dr. York introduces the detectives to Michael. "They would like to see the lab and then have a talk with you, Michael."

"Okay. Follow me."

He and Jess lead them around the lab showing and explaining what each piece of equipment is used for in their work and who does what in the lab. Dr. Mordecai shows them the animal room where the dogs were and explains briefly the worm, rat, and dog experiments used in his work.

"Very interesting work. You both should be congratulated," McGraw says.

"Thank you," both Michael and Jess say in unison.

"Can we visit with you in the conference room?" McGraw says.

"Certainly." He leads the way to the room a few doors down from the lab. They enter and Michael sits at the head of the conference table.

"How can I help you?"

"What is your background?" McGraw says.

"I'm a Harvard Ph.D. in genetics with a year postdoc training at Stanford."

"Impressive," Roark says.

He smiles. "I think so."

"What was your relationship with Dr. Keller?" McGraw asks.

"He was the director and my boss."

"I mean, how did you guys get along?"

He sighs. "I guess I could get a little impatient with Corey when he didn't move as fast as I thought he should."

"In what way?"

"He wasn't quick about pushing my work through committee. I'd pressure him to kick it up and he'd get mad at me and then I'd get mad. We'd blow off steam, and then we'd quiet down. That's all."

"Other than that, was he easy to get along with?" Roark asks.

He nods. "He was. We only saw him in our meetings and don't know how he interacted with others here."

"Can you think of anyone who'd want to harm Dr. Keller?" McGraw asks.

"Oh, no. No one here."

"Where were you night before last from six to nine?" McGraw asks.

"Oh, everyone's a suspect," Michael says. He laughs. "That's from watching TV. To answer your question, I was home working in my office."

"Were you alone?" Roark asks.

"No. My mother lives with me. She can verify that I was working at home like I do every night."

Rising from his seat, McGraw says, "That's all for now. Thanks for your help. We'll get out of your way so you can get back to work."

"Any time, Lieutenant."

Michael walks them to the door. In the hall on the way to the stairs, Roark asks McGraw. "Why did you want to see the lab? How does it fit into the picture?"

"Everything does. I wanted to get a feel for what is so important in the lab that one of them might kill Dr. Keller."

"Wouldn't knowing the arguments over the drug Mordecai discovered be enough?" Roark asks.

"Not for me. I need to get into their environment, into their heads, to think like them. I'm not saying anyone here did Keller. It's hard to believe anyone would kill after discovering something so important to their company and for our elderly. Drugs are discovered every day, but I don't know of anyone killing over them."

"Mordecai seems pretty excited over his discovery," Roark says, "but Keller did seem to go against him."

"Might be a motive for Mordecai. But according to CEO Rubin, Keller was really working hard on Mordecai's behalf," he says.

"So, you don't think York or Mordecai had anything to do with Keller's death."

"I didn't mean to imply that. You know everyone is a suspect until we clear 'em. I just have this feeling about them," he says.

"What about?"

"There's something about this place that seems too picture-perfect. No bumps."

As they begin descending the stairs, McGraw slips on his hat.

Roark says, "I never thought of it that way."

When they reach the lobby, McGraw says, "We need to check on something." He leads the way over to the security desk.

"Hello, again, detectives," security guard says, "can I help you with something?"

"Yes. Do you have the sign-in-and-out sheets for researchers that work here at night or who stay late?"

"Yes, sir. For what dates?"

"How about the last seven days."

"Sure thing." The guard reaches for a clip board and hands it to McGraw. "That's the list. I was about to file it away."

McGraw studies the names and glides a finger down them, then hands the board back to the guard. All the while the guard is staring at him.

"Thank you."

"You're welcome, detective. Have a good day. And, sir, I like your hat."

McGraw smiles. "Thank you."

As they move out the door, Roark says, "You were looking to see if Jess York worked late the other night?"

He nods. "She did."

They amble over to the Silverado and take off for headquarters.

Chapter 19

When McGraw and Roark enter the squad room, he tells her to try and reach Kramer and Gomez. "And while you're at it, see what you can find on Jess York and Michael Mordecai in case Elizabeth didn't give us everything."

McGraw places his Stetson on the desk and heads for coffee. He takes a couple of swallows and says, "I really needed this," as he passes Holly's desk and sets the cup on his desk, then ambles over to the Lion's Den to see the chief. Dipple's door is closed and McGraw knocks.

"Enter!"

McGraw opens the door and sticks his head in. "Got a moment, Capt?"

"Grab a seat," he says. McGraw sits in the chair facing the Capt.

"What did you learn at Biogen?"

"Nothing much. Interviewed Drs. Mordecai and York and their two techs. They all told the same story. Too perfect. Wouldn't put it past them preparing what to say when they found out we were coming to interview them."

"And what was their story?"

"That everyone got along with Corey Keller except at times Michael Mordecai and he used to get into some heated arguments over Mordecai's new drug."

"Sounds like two big egos going at it."

"That's what we think." McGraw pauses a couple of seconds. "Only thing…"

"Yes, what is it?" Capt. asks.

"Something doesn't ring right. Whenever people give statements that seem too perfect, maybe even rehearsed, I get the feeling they're hiding something."

"Understandable. What's your next step?"

"I don't know unless something turns up. We have very little evidence at this point. We went over to the crash site, and then to the morgue to see Dr. Keller's body and talk to the pathologist. He did a tox study and there was nothing in Keller's system. The crash scene was contaminated. Too many footprints. We found nothing. I'm bothered, though, about how Keller's car flew off the road. We're investigating the possibility of someone ramming him from behind."

"Well, stay on it. You're heading in the right direction with this investigation. Keep me posted."

McGraw rises and walks to the door. "Will do, Capt."

When he returns to his desk, Holly reports that Kramer and Gomez are on their way back to the station. McGraw sits and opens Corey Keller's personal file Elizabeth provided for them. Moments later, Kramer and Gomez enter the squad room, walk up to the boss, and place the tapes from the red-light surveillances on his desk.

"Boss," Kramer says, "we didn't find anyone following behind Keller. We reviewed the tapes ten times."

"There's one thing, though," Gomez says.

"What's that?" McGraw asks.

"It's crazy. There was a guy wearing this head mask, driving a Land Rover along the same route that Dr. Keller covered, but he wasn't tailing him as far as we could tell."

"What kind of head mask?" McGraw asks.

"The best we could tell, looked a little like the Frankenstein monster in the movies," Kramer says.

"You mean one that fits over the head?" Roark asks.

"Yep," Kramer says.

"How appropriate. Didn't the monster turn on his creator, Dr. Frankenstein?" McGraw says.

"What are you driving at, boss?" Roark asks.

"Mordecai turning on Keller," McGraw says.

"Are you suggesting Mordecai rammed and caused Keller's death?"

"Just flashed into my mind. An assumption, that's all," McGraw says. "I do remember, however, Sherlock Homes once said: 'When you have eliminated the impossible, what remains, how improbable, must be the truth.'"

"So, Sherlock, what you are saying—"

"—Just that Mordecai is high on my list," he says, interrupting her.

"Maybe the masked man was really going to a party," she says.

The boss turns to his junior detectives, "If the masked man is our guy, you can bet it's a stolen plate," he says.

Roark adds. "And the Land Rover should be damaged in front."

"You guys try and locate that Land Rover, call all the body shops, and ask if it's in there getting repaired. I'm afraid if he's our guy, the Land Rover is long gone. If he's not our man, then the Land Rover will have a legit license plate and we'll know who the masked man is."

"Will do boss," Kramer says. He and Gomez return to their desks and open their computers.

McGraw shouts over to his junior detectives. "I nearly forgot to ask. What did you learn about the Corvette?"

"Oh, sorry," Kramer says. "Nothing. It was clean."

"No alcohol or drugs," Gomez says. "Clean as a whistle."

"Just what I thought," McGraw says. "Thanks."

"There are three Land Rover dealers: one in north and one in south Atlanta and one in Buckhead," Kramer shouts.

"And there's a couple dozen auto repair shops in the city," Gomez shouts.

"Well, why are you guys telling us?" Roark asks. "You know what to do. Do you want us to hold your hands?"

"Yes, your highness," Gomez says.

Everyone laughs.

An hour later, Gomez jumps up from his desk. "Boss, the license plate was stolen. Mask man might be our guy."

"And no Land Rover is in for repair at the dealerships," Kramer says.

McGraw rises from his desk and walks to the center of his group.

"We can be sure of one thing: the Land Rover is long gone. The masked man is our number one suspect, but how do we find him? We need evidence."

"It's gonna be tough," Roark says.

McGraw goes to the crime board and writes *Masked Man,* and below it, *Keller's Killer?* He stares at what he wrote, then adds a question mark after the wording, because without evidence, they can't be sure he's the killer.

McGraw calls out. "Kramer, Gomez. Get me a picture of this masked man off the tapes and put it on my desk."

"Will do, boss," Gomez says, walking to the front, where he picks up the tapes, then he and Kramer move into the side room, which has their equipment.

An hour later, Gomez and Kramer walk up to McGraw's desk.

"We have the pic of the masked man," Kramer says, placing it in front of the boss, who stares at it.

"The mask sure does fit over his head," Gomez says.

Roark rushes over to have a look. "Ugly beast," she says, returning to her desk.

McGraw says, "It definitely looks like the Frankenstein monster." He goes to the crime board and tapes it under *Masked Man*. "If we just had a physical description. Good work, guys."

"Thank you, boss," the detectives say in unison as they walk back to their desks.

After studying the pictures of Keller and the masked man, McGraw goes to his desk and begins scribbling the names of *Keller* and *Mordecai* over and over on a yellow pad.

"What's going on Noah?" Holly asks. "You seem to be on another planet."

He doesn't answer. "Kramer and Gomez," he shouts," still scribbling.

"Yes, boss," Kramer says as he and Gomez approach his desk.

"I want you to tail Dr. Mordecai and more importantly, try and get us a sample of his DNA."

Kramer and Gomez look at each other. "Boss," Gomez says. "That could take days."

"Maybe not. Let's give it a shot, at least for a while. You have all the information we have on him."

"Sure thing, boss," Kramer says. "We'll shoot over to his work and see what develops."

"Mordecai usually leaves work around six or seven," McGraw says, as he rises and walks over to Holly.

"I think this is one of the evenings where we can spend some time with Dusty."

She looks up from her computer surprised. "It is?"

"Yes. We're at a standstill and it would be good if we took a break from everything.

"Well alright. I'm ready," she says, as she shuts down her computer.

Chapter 20

The next morning McGraw pulls the RAM pickup into an open spot in front of McAteer's coffee shop around eight. The sun is bright this warm morning, but comfortable. He reaches for his Stetson and slips it on, climbs out, walks to the entrance, opening the door for an elderly couple, who stares at the cowboy. The wife smiles and thanks him.

McGraw tips his hat, and says, "You're welcome, ma'am."

The smell of coffee and banana waffles attack his nostrils. He looks around and spots his Italian buddy, and former partner Zamperini, Zee for short, sitting in their favorite booth in the back drinking coffee, and he appears to be eating waffles. Noah never liked sitting towards the front where the patrons—many of whom are cops—are loud and used to come to their booth to strike up a conversation with Zee and him.

McAteer's is a hangout for the men and women in blue, since Shane was one of them; they opened this coffee shop when he retired. He and his wife, Ruth, are busy behind the curved counter serving coffee and waffles to the uniforms sitting on the barstools. Ruth, a slender blonde is in a white uniform, waves at McGraw. He tips his hat. Shane, like Zee, is much older than McGraw. He chose Zee as his partner instead of Shane, who went with another detective. Both retirees were great detectives.

The cops at the counter notice McGraw and one shouts in a playful manner, "Howya doin', cowboy?" Another said "There's The Marlboro Man," and another said, "There's the D that talks to his vics." Then everyone burst into laughter. McGraw just tips his hat. "You guys are just jealous."

Zee had told Noah that The Marlboro Man epithet stuck to him because he's cool, calm, and has his act together, just like the cowboy on the horse who used to be on the billboards around town, advertising Marlboro cigarettes before smoking became bad for you. The homicide detectives at the APD would swear that cowboy McGraw has some special talent for solving crimes. They believe the dead speak to him, the way he goes about processing a crime scene.

Shane wipes his hands on his white apron, nods as he ambles over to the register to take McGraw's order.

"Good to seeya, McGraw. Howya been? And how is my favorite lady, Anna Marie?"

"We're both fine."

"Whatta you having?"

"Just a skinny latte for now."

"Got some warm cinnamon rolls. Your favorite."

"Not this time, Shane. Thanks."

"Suit yourself. But I'll wrap one for Ms. Anna Marie."

"Thank you. That's very kind of you. She'll appreciate that."

"Bring her in some time. Ruth would love to visit with her."

"Will do, Shane."

McGraw carries the latte and cinnamon roll to the condiments stand against the large window facing the street, adds cinnamon and vanilla to his coffee, then moves down the aisle between the rows of black table tops, walking to the back. The place is packed as usual. Neatly dressed suits, many are texting or reading things on their cell phones, while others are typing at their laptops.

There goes our civilization, McGraw thinks as he passes them.

Noah hasn't seen his partner since he finished the Tongue Collector case, but they talk at least once a month. Zee comes from a large Italian family in New York and goes there quite often. He is munching on a large banana waffle with lots of syrup, nearly running off the plate. Noah slides into the booth opposite Zee and sets the cinnamon roll and latte on the table in front of him, removes his Stetson and puts it on the red leathered seat next to him, then reaches for his coffee and removes the cover, all the while eyeing his ole partner.

"You do know all that crap you're eating isn't good for you, right?"

The Italian, who resembles Tony Soprano (James Gandolfini), looks up with a mouth full of food, and says, “Will you ever quit the bullshit? You know I’m going to live to be a hundred. Let me enjoy my feast.”

“Okay, okay.” he says, holding up his hands, palms outward. “But I’m only concerned about the health of my best Dago friend.”

“Do your Dago friend a favor and cut the shit.”

They laugh.

“Okay, let’s have it,” Zee says.

“What?”

“The details. What’s happening?”

“We’ve closed the Jack Carter case.”

“You mean The Tongue Collector?”

“Yes, we’ve talked about most of it.”

“How did it go with burying his old lady? I know you weren’t too happy about that.”

“It’s just I had to reconcile my feelings and forgive her for what she did to Jack.”

“Good to hear. Forgiveness removes the load,” Zee says. He pauses, pushes his plate to one side and takes a drink of his coffee.

“I have some good news you’ll approve of.”

“What’s that?” Zee asks.

“Holly and I are engaged, and she and her son Dusty are now living at the Circle M.”

Zee slaps the table. “Best damned news I’ve heard in a long time. Congratulations. It’s about time you asked that pretty thing. I was worried you were going to lose her. If I were your age, she’d be mine.”

McGraw shakes his head. “In your dreams. She wants a real man.”

“I guess you think you’re that guy.”

“What do you think?”

“Okay, okay.” he says, holding up his hands. “I’m happy for you both. Tell that sweet thing I’m sorry she got away from me.”

They laugh. “I will.”

McGraw takes a couple drafts of his coffee. “I’m facing a troubling case I’d like to run by you.”

Zee squirms in his seat, finishes off his coffee. “Now, that’s what I want to hear.”

"The chief gave us a case involving a scientist at a Biotech Company called Biogen—"

"—I've heard of them."

"Well, one of their top scientists died in a one-car accident. He flew off the road in a convertible, hit an oak tree, and was found dead about twenty yards from his vehicle."

"Not having your seat belt on will do that to you," Zee says jokingly. "This guy probably had a high sense of self-importance. Why do you think he was driving the convertible? Ego. Even though their kind are well-educated, they don't have an ounce of common sense. Blinded by their pride."

"I've learned about that kind of psychoanalysis." McGraw pauses, drinks some of his coffee. "What I'm trying to get at is this. I didn't think it was a homicide case at first, and told the Chief that, but he insisted we follow up because the Commish is good friends with the CEO of Biogen."

"Aww. That political bullshit. But now something has changed your mind. What is it?"

"We secured the red-light surveillance tapes along the route the scientist took to his home. In those tapes we saw something very unusual. A man in a Land Rover, dressed in a full head mask of the Frankenstein Monster."

"You're thinking he ran the scientist off the road and was dressed that way so as not to be recognized."

"Yes."

"He could have been going to a party," Zee says.

"You're playing the devil's advocate, my friend. I like that."

"Have you ruled out that notion?"

"What do you think? The license plates were stolen and the Land Rover has vanished."

"I'd say he's your man, but you don't have much to go on. There is one thing in your favor, though," Zee says.

"What's that?"

"There's more to this guy than meets the eye. You rarely have a killer go to the trouble of dressing up like he did to kill someone. He could have run the guy off the road and never been identified by the vic because he's dead. You know the killer surveyed the area before he acted, to figure out how many cars came and went, so he wasn't worried about someone recognizing him. Then why did he go to all that trouble masking up?

Because he's a monster like the mask he wore."

"You mean emotionally, he feels like a monster." McGraw says.

Zee nods. "And he'll strike any time he doesn't get his way. Anyone standing in his way will suffer the consequence."

"So, you believe for some reason he's not done."

"Yes, and you must determine why that is."

"We thought the perp might be a scientist at Biogen based on the theory that the type of person victimized determines the type of his killer. In this case, a scientist is killed, so the killer might be a scientist, but we have no evidence."

"Then stay on it until the evidence proves otherwise," Zee says.

"I'm thinking we need some DNA evidence from suspected parties."

Zee nods. "That's a start."

Chapter 21

This is the second evening Gomez and Kramer are parked in the visitors space next to the Biogen building, waiting for Dr. Mordecai to appear. The boss sent them on this mission to collect the doc's DNA, and were told he normally leaves work between six and seven every evening. The first evening Mordecai left around six and went straight home and never left.

Kramer looks over at Gomez and says, "I've been thinking partner. What are we doing here? Don't you think it's a little too early in the investigation to get Mordecai's DNA when there's no evidence tying him to anything? To me, it's all speculation on the boss's part and a waste of time."

"Not really."

"You don't? I'm surprised. Getting his DNA this early is only based on the hypothesis that Mordecai being a scientist and Keller a scientist, that he might have killed Keller."

"You're forgetting that the boss leaves no stone unturned. He doesn't overlook anything that could possibly help in solving a problem. I never heard him say that Mordecai did it. He thinks he might, so he needs to have the doc's DNA on file, just in case. The boss always follows the evidence. He didn't tell us to arrest him, did he?"

"You're right about that."

Kramer looks at this watch. "It's almost seven. He should be coming out soon, and I hope he goes somewhere. I'm getting tired of stretching my neck."

"Does baby need some lotion on his precious neck?" Gomez says.

"Cut the shit. Here he comes."

"Man, such a handsome dude to be a killer," Gomez says.

"What did you just tell me? Now you're calling him a killer."

Where's your evidence?"

"Touché."

They laugh.

"Cool it. He's just hoped into his red BMW," Gomez says, as he backs out and races out of the parking lot, heading north. "Man, this guy has a heavy foot."

They reach the Chastain area and Mordecai pulls into the driveway of a million dollar one-story white stone house that covers several acres, surrounded by lots of greenery. In the front yard are an assortment of twenty-foot trees.

Gomez slows passing the house and turns around in the cul-de-sac and moves back to the house next to Mordecai's and stops.

"Man, this is a beautiful place. Big bucks," Gomez says.

"According to M's profile, he makes big bucks at Biogen." Kramer says.

"I'm going to call in and update the boss," he says, opening his cell. "Okay, boss, will do."

"What did he say?" Gomez asks.

"Stay on him."

The sun is about to set this June evening.

"Maybe he's not going any place again," Gomez says. "I'm getting hungry."

"Me too. Hopefully he's going to go out for dinner."

"Hey, you might be right, here he comes. Man, he's all dressed up."

They watch as he hops into his BMW, backs out, and speeds away heading north. Gomez races after him. Mordecai pulls up to this condo and stops. Once out of the car, he walks up to the door and knocks. It opens immediately.

"I'm ready," Kendal says with a huge smile, closes the door, and locks it.

"Wow! You look beautiful."

She looked surprised. "Thank you."

Kendal is in a red dress that fits close to her slender, thirty-year-old body, with long chestnut hair shining like her red lips, and milky white skin. Her eyebrows are dark as are her long black eyelashes. She is about his height.

Very sexy, he thinks. *And smells good, too.*

He reminds himself not to overdo his compliments. She's capable of seeing right through him. They walk to his BMW. He opens her door as she slides in.

"Wow. She's a looker," Gomez says. "I'd take her home to mama if I weren't married."

"She wouldn't give you the time of day."

"Have you forgotten that I'm smooth with the ladies?"

"That'd be the day." Kramer says.

"This is going to be interesting."

While walking around to the driver's side of the BMW, Michael realizes something.

Oh, no. I bet she thinks I'm going to propose tonight.

"I'll have to play this one very *carefully*. He would be willing to get engaged if it gets him what he wants—RapTOR to market. They could get engaged for a while and then he could dump her.

The valet parks Michael's car and they enter the foyer of the Pitcher's Mound restaurant. A large, gold-framed painting of a lean black man in a Braves uniform, posed in a pitching stance on the mound, is hanging on the wall. The headwater approaches them. "Good evening, Dr. Mordecai, your dad's table is ready," he says as he escorts them through the dining area, passing a row of tables covered with white linen, to the one in the corner, against the wall under a row of framed pictures of celebrities that extends the length of the wall. Kendal doesn't sit. She walks down the row of pictures, examining them closely. The main attraction is the slender ballplayer, standing shoulder to shoulder with fans, some taken in the ballpark and others in the restaurant. Movie stars and politicians aren't excluded. All pictures are of the same size except for the one in the center—Moose accepting the Cy Young Award from the Baseball Writers Association of America. He is smiling, ear-to-ear.

Michael noticed Kendal's fascination with the pictures. "You a sports fan?" he asks as she comes to the table to sit.

"This is great! Yes, I love baseball. I heard about Moose. And what did the waiter mean when he said this was your dad's table?"

"My dad was one of the first contributors to this restaurant. He also helped Moose get this place through a few of his patients that were in the business world. Dad loved this place."

"All the time I worked for your dad, I never knew."

The waiter approaches. "Are you ready to order any drinks, "Dr. Mordecai?"

"Yes, Matthew. But first I'd like you to meet my friend, Kendal Wilson."

He nods, and says, "Pleased to meet you, ma'am. Is this your first time with us at the Mound?"

"Yes, it is, Matthew. Very impressive place."

"Thank you. We think so."

Mathew opens a cloth napkin and places it on Kendal's lap.

I think to get Kendal on board I'll have to propose to her even though I don't have a ring. This must be good. I got to think this one through. Don't want to be too insincere. First, I need a little wine.

"Matthew, we'll have a bottle of my favorite Cabernet Sauvignon to start, please."

"Certainly, sir."

Another waiter brings a menu and places it in front of the two patrons.

Kendal looks over the menu, while another waiter places a basket of bread in the middle of the table and then fills their water glasses.

"I thought we'd have wine and talk some before we have the meal. Is that alright?"

"Yes, of course," she says, setting her menu to one side. "I've been wondering all week about what has made you so happy and now so jumpy."

"Jumpy? Happy, yes, but not jumpy." *I must be careful. This proposal thing has made me nervous.*

Kendal places her napkin on the table and rises. "Excuse me while I go to the powder room."

"Of course," he says, rising.

Kramer and Gomez enter the Pitcher's Mound. They look around and spot the doc sitting alone toward the center of the room at a table against the wall. Kramer notices several empty tables near them.

"Waiter, may we sit in that area?" Kramer asks, pointing and hoping they aren't reserved.

"Yes, sir. Please follow me."

The waiter places them a couple of tables away from Mordecai and his date, which gives the detectives a good view of them. Another waiter brings menus and fills their water glasses.

"The boss is going to pay for this," Gomez says.

"We'll make sure of it."

Kramer orders cod and Gomez has spaghetti.

"Look," Gomez says. "That beauty must have gone to the ladies' room. She's just now getting back to their table."

"Good," Kramer says. "That gives us time to eat some of our meal and strategize."

"Strategize? Wow! Big word. You must have gotten some smarts just being in this place."

"Cool it taco head."

"Ok, tell me this. Since you're so smart, how do we get the glass out without being seen by the wait staff? They're everywhere."

Kramer smiles. "Great question. But I have an answer."

The waiter brings their food. "Can I get you gentlemen anything else?"

"No thank you," Kramer says.

"Enjoy," he says.

After the waiter leaves, Gomez says, "Okay, let's have your answer."

"We eat half of our food and then ask for carry outs. Since there will be two, I'll ask for a bag to put them in."

"Very good, Mein Lehrer."

"Oh, so now it's not Kraut head, it's 'my teacher.' You've come up in the world."

"Don't overdo it. I just learned it for your benefit."

They laugh.

"Ok, back to our plan," Gomez says. "When we go over to their table, I'll snatch his glass and bag it and as soon as we get back in the car, I'll put it in the forensic bag for the ME."

"However, we still must determine how we're going to get the glass," Kramer says.

Kendal returns to her seat, and smiles at Mordecai.

Matthew brings two glasses and a bottle of red wine in a shiny brass bucket filled with ice and sets it next to the table. He begins opening the bottle, pours two glasses, and hands them to Michael and Kendal.

Michael lifts his glass and says, "Cheers," then takes a couple of swallows.

She responds, "Cheers," holding up her glass, takes a drink, all the while eyeing Michael over the glass.

"Now for what has me excited. I've developed a new anti-aging drug that I've named RapTOR, and we just finished a 3-week dog study and found that it helped them immensely. It increased the lifespan of the animals, which means it could increase the lives of humans."

"That's wonderful. No wonder you are so happy."

"But we are faced with a big challenge. All that is left is doing the clinical trials in humans."

"That's good, isn't it?" she says.

"Yes, but it takes a long time, and there are many hurdles to overcome. I want Biogen to beat these other pharmaceutical companies to market, but my director has been my stumbling block."

"What do you mean? I don't understand."

"I'll explain, but first I'd like to take you to the lab after we eat to show you the dogs and explain a little more about my work. I think you can be part of it."

"Me? Be part of it? How?"

"I'd like to leave that for when we go to the lab. For now, I have something I'd like say." He pauses.

Be careful.

The next several minutes he takes several big swallows of his wine to stall until he gets his thoughts straight.

"You were about to say," Kendal says, placing her wine glass next to her plate after consuming half of it.

"You and I have been going together now for over six months, right?"

Her eyes brighten and she's smiling. "Over six months."

"Well… I…think maybe it's time we got serious about our relationship. Don't you?"

She fidgets with her wine glass. Seconds later she says, "Yes, I agree. Where is this going?" She lifts her glass and consumes the rest of her wine, and the waiter, who is standing close, is quick to fill her glass.

Michael pauses again, and lifts his glass and downs all his wine. His glass is refilled. He reaches for her hand and takes a deep breath. "I know this isn't very romantic, but I'm going to do it anyway."

Her eyes sparkle. "What are you trying to say?"

She knows what's coming. "I'd like for us to become engaged."

She frowns and stares at him for a moment. "Are you saying you want to marry me?"

"Yes. But I wasn't planning on asking you tonight, but when I saw you standing at your door, something came over me. You looked so beautiful. I knew right then that we had to get engaged. Does that sound corny?"

"Corny? Oh, no. What took you so long? I've been waiting months for you to ask me to marry you."

"Like I said. It just hit me, and I knew we were meant for each other. But I don't have a ring."

"That's not important for now, but you better get me one, though, ASAP."

They laugh.

She reaches for her glass and takes a couple more swallows. "I have to confess that I've been attracted to you ever since we met in your dad's office."

"I felt the same way but didn't want to be pushy, and then my work got in the way."

"Are you ready to order?" Matthew asks.

Mordecai looks up at Matthew. "Yes, we are." He turns to Kendal. Let's order so we can later go to the lab."

She nods. "I'm famished."

Kramer and Gomez notice that the couple is doing more talking than eating.

Kramer has eaten half of his food, but Gomez is still at it.

"The food here is great," Gomez says, as he finishes his half as planned, then pushes his plate toward the center of the table. Kramer waves to the waiter an asks for carry outs for two and a bag.

"It looks like they might be finishing up soon," Gomez says, "and we gotta move fast to get his glass before the waiter cleans the table."

"I'm thinking I need to shield you so you can grab his glass," Kamer says.

"We're lucky there's no one at these other tables," Gomez says.

"Maybe I can bump into him while you snatch the glass, but his date might see you."

"I don't think so," Gomez says. "Being a gentleman, he'd let her step in front of him, leading the way out."

"Wait a minute," Kramer says. "This is too easy. Look around. What do you see?"

"Nothing. What am I supposed to see?"

"What luck. The waiters are busy up front and no one's back here. All we must do is for you to walk behind me, and then snatch his glass as we walk past their table."

"They're standing up. Let's get over there," Kramer says.

"Wait!" Gomez says. "Give it a minute until they walk away from the table. We can't screw this up."

Seconds later, Kramer says, "Now!"

They rise slowly, not to draw attention and move over to M's table with Gomez behind Kramer. As they walk past the table, Gomez grabs M's glass and bags it. The detectives walk out nonchalantly and leave the restaurant. In their unmarked police unit, Gomez bags the glass in a forensic bag.

Chapter 22

Michael rolls the red BMW into the well-lighted parking lot at Biogen and pulls into a parking place closer to the building. He opens the door for Kendal and they stroll over to the entrance. The glass building is brilliantly lighted, and the stairs and lobby are visible from the street. Michael must use a key to open the smaller door next to the main entrance. Researchers use this door after hours. Michael places his picture badge on his suit coat lapel.

The night watchman is at the security desk. "Good evening, Dr. Mordecai," he says as he takes a picture of his badge. He's used to Michael working late in the lab at night.

"How are you, Cyrus?" Michael asks. "This is my fiancé, Kendal Wilson. She's never seen my lab."

Kendal smiles. Apparently, she liked being called Michael's fiancé.

Cyrus nods. "Please to meet you, Ms. Wilson. He pushes the log book to the edge of the table and hands her a pen. "I need for you to sign in, please."

"Nice to meet you, too, Cyrus," she says as she signs the book.

Michael leads the way to the bank of elevators in the back.

"This lobby is impressive," Kendal says. "Such expensive furniture and those oriental rugs. So beautiful."

"Biogen tries to impress," he says.

When the elevator doors open, they step in, and he pushes the button to the fourth-floor.

"Fiancé?" she says in his ear. "I liked the sound of that."

"That's who you are now," he says.

She squeezes his arm.

The doors open and they step out into the hall.

"Wow. I'd hate to pay the electric bill for this place," she says. "Are all the lights always left on."

He nods. "One of Biogen's requirements is adequate security. There are other security personnel in a special room watching the monitors, besides Cyrus. You just don't see 'em. There's so much going on in here that Biogen is careful about keeping anyone from slipping in to steal our secrets."

"I saw the security cameras as I was signing in."

He nods. "Yes, they're all over the place."

They head down the hall to his lab. "All the scientific information is locked up somewhere. Even I don't know where it's kept, and don't care."

He pulls out his keys, opens his lab door, and they enter. "I had to sign a confidentiality agreement, which prohibits me from revealing any of our secrets except when specifically authorized."

"How about the computers on the desks over there?" she says, pointing. "Are they secure?"

"Yes."

"I didn't realize your lab was so large."

"This way," he says, as they move past several benches, turn, and walk between two benches to the animal room. When they enter, the dogs begin barking and circling in their crates.

"Oh, my, you're so pleased to see us, aren't you," Kendal says, in a voice like she's talking to an infant child. "They're beautiful animals, Michael."

"Oh, I hate it that they are penned up like that." She turns to Michael. "Do they ever get out for a walk?"

"Simon, one of our techs, takes them out of the building for an hour every afternoon. We're working to get Biogen to release them so they can be adopted now that our experiment is completed. But we haven't gotten permission yet from the big shots."

"They all look so healthy. I was expecting them to look different."

"You mean, sickly?"

"I guess so. I've never seen experimental animals, so I wouldn't know what to expect."

"They look healthy because of my compound, RapTOR. Come here.

I want to show you something." They move to the table against the wall. Michael opens a photo album. In it are a series of pictures of each dog before and after treatment. "We started treating them over four weeks ago," he says. "This first section is before treatment." He lets her ponder on them purposely before flipping through the sections one at a time.

"Oh, my. The poor things look so pitiful." She started tearing up.

He flips to the second week. "Note here how they are beginning to look much, much better."

"But why does the black Lab look like it's dying."

"Because she was our control animal and didn't receive any of the drug." He turns to pictures taken some time after the 3-week study had been completed. "Look at her now."

"They all look so healthy. Even the Lab."

"That's because we had accrued enough data on our new compound that we were able to start treating the Lab after three weeks so she wouldn't die."

"I can see now why you are so excited about your drug. Can we call it a drug at this stage?"

"I'd say we can. I'm very excited about it but I have a big problem."

"What's the problem?"

"You may not know, but there are many pharmaceutical companies working on anti-aging compounds. I believe I'm a step ahead of them and want RapTOR to make it to market before they do. But to do so, my drug must go through clinical trials and my director was dragging his feet on the application for a new drug with the FDA. Also, the Biogen bureaucracy slowed it down even more before the FDA would receive the application. It's going to take a long time before we can go into clinical trials." He pauses looking into her eyes. "Now here is where you come in."

"Me?"

"Yes, you." He pauses.

"Let's go out to my desk. I want to tell you more."

"First. Can I pet the Lab?"

He pauses. "I…I…think it'd be okay. But I'd feel better if Simon were here. Just a minute."

Michael goes to the crate and opens the door and slowly puts his hand in, talking to the Lab in a soft voice. "How you doing, girl?"

He pats her on the head and then she licks his hand.

"I think now she's ok for you to pet her. I wanted to make sure she wouldn't bite your hand off." He laughs.

Kendal slowly reaches in and pets the Lab saying, "Yes, girl, you are so sweet; yes, you are," she says, talking like she's speaking to an infant. The Lab is licking her hand and pawing it playfully.

After a few minutes, Michael closes the door.

"I hope these poor things find owners," Kendal says.

"We'll do our best. Now let's get out of here."

At his desk, he pulls Jess's chair over to his and Kendal sits.

"You've seen the before and after treatment of the dogs in our 3-week study. The results are fabulous. Now here is what I'm proposing. I'd like for you to join me in testing my agent in humans. The drug is very safe and is ready for clinical trials. You could become famous if all turns out the way I think it will."

"I don't understand. You just said Biogen is already moving your drug in the system," Kendal says.

"Yes, but the system slows things down. You know how bureaucrats can be. So much paper work and committees to review everything. It will take months, maybe a year. I don't want these other biotech companies to beat me to market. The competition is furious. We've been working for a decade on several projects and now we finally discovered an agent that can extent life and maybe prevent diseases like cancer."

"What did you mean, I could help?"

"Please listen to what I have to say before you say anything, okay?"

She nods.

"Ok. Here it is. How many patients do you attend to daily?'

"Six."

"Great! We wouldn't need any control because we used one in the dog experiment and we already know about telomere growth so no blood needs to be drawn. What is needed is only a capsule of my drug to be given daily at the same time for six days with one day off for each week. You will only need to pay special attention to their skin and mobility. What do you think? Can you help me?"

"I don't know. I wouldn't want anything to happen to my patients."

"Nothing will happen. I can guarantee it. We've done all the testing and have developed a safe dosage. There shouldn't be any problem."

"'Shouldn't be.' You said, 'shouldn't be.'"

He shrugs. "Poor choice of words on my part. There will, and I emphasize, there will be no problem."

"Could it interfere with the meds I give my patients?"

"No. It has a mechanism that no other drug on the market can interact with it."

"What kind of mechanism?"

Oh, shit. What a bitch. "RapTOR inhibits a protein known as mTOR. Your patients wouldn't be on any drug that has the same action."

"Well... I...need to think this through. Without FDA approval, we're breaking the law. I could go to jail."

"Nothing to worry about. Who is going to find out? My agent is very safe and there will be no problems."

She shakes her head. "Why don't I need a control patient? I remember a clinical trial that I was involved in during my nursing career. It was essential to have a control patient."

"We had a control dog in our experiment and recorded all the data, which was great. So, we won't need controls in our human testing. At this point, all I want is to accumulate enough data on humans so we can add all the data to the application Biogen will submit to the FDA."

"But will the FDA accept your data if done without their approval? You could go to jail."

What's up with this bitch?

"I believe it will be after the fact, and I may only get some kind of misdemeanor offense, Frankly, I don't care. I want to show Biogen and the FDA that RapTOR is an effective, safe agent for anti-aging. Biogen may be reluctant, but I'm positive with all the other competing companies working on anti-aging compounds, Biogen will put it in the application. I know it. They will state that the data were performed outside their facility without their knowledge, but since RapTOR has demonstrated such effectiveness against aging, it might also prevent certain diseases in the elderly, and that they felt it would be a disservice to the public not to make note of the experiments in the application."

Staring at him with a frown, she says. "I can't believe it means so much to you that you'd be willing to go to jail?"

He nods with raised hands, and leans in to her. "Just let me run through the protocol with you." He sits back up straight in his chair. "Do you give your patients meds in the morning?"

"Yes. All six get meds around nine o'clock."

"Okay. Listen up. You can give my capsule every morning to all six with their other meds. That way they won't know. But it should be given at the same time daily."

"That would be no problem."

"Then you'll keep an eye on them for six days in the week for three weeks, to see if they can get up better from their chairs, or walk better, and if their skin shows improvement. You will record all noticeable changes in each category that I'll put in the research notebook that I'm going to give you, and on the seventh day of each week, you and I will meet and go over your entries. How does that sound?"

"I guess it will be okay, but not having FDA approval really worries me."

"Just keep thinking. If we succeed, that means FDA will approve Biogen's application for clinical trials much quicker. That's my goal. Please help me."

Silence for several minutes.

"Okay. I guess I can do it."

"Wonderful. Let's get out of here."

On their way home, Kendal doesn't say a word.

They are near her condo when he asks. "What's wrong?"

"I was thinking."

"What about?"

"Did you take me to the Mound, and drink all that wine, and then ask me to marry you on the spot, just to weaken me so I would agree to help you test your drug?"

Whoa. She's smarter than I figured.

"No way. I can see where you're coming from…and I don't blame you for feeling that way. I've thought about taking you to the Mound for some time, but have been so busy with the dog experiment. One thing about me, when I get in an experiment, I don't do much of anything else, but eat, sleep, and work the experiment. You can ask my mother. She and I have discussed my relationship with you."

"You have. With your mom?"

"Yes. She thinks the world of you and told me I've been neglecting you. She's right and I'm sorry. I was going to ask for your hand in the traditional way later, but you looked so beautiful sitting there in the Mound, I lost it. I wasn't thinking. The words just blurted out. That's why I didn't have a ring."

He pulls up into her drive and she turns to him. "Would you like to come in for a night cap now that we're engaged?" she asks.

"I'd love to."

They walk up to her condo, and she opens the door. As soon as Michael closes the door, Kendal pulls him into her arms for a ten-second kiss. "Thank you for an enjoyable evening. I love you," she says as she grabs his hand and pulls him into her bedroom for a night to remember.

Chapter 23

Monday morning at seven, Kendal walks into the Jefferson Assisted Living Center, enters the locker room, changes into her whites, then walks out on the floor to prepare the meds for her patients. She oversees three men and three women, all of whom are in their eighties and have private rooms on the first floor. The rooms of the three men are across from those of the three women, which makes it convenient for Kendal to usher her med cart through the hall near their rooms and to check on them often in her 10-hour shift, during which time she helps other nurses on the first-floor wing. She is very friendly with her patients and takes time to chat with them and when not too busy, she'll sit for a brief visit, or wheels them outside, weather permitting.

Michael went to the lab last evening while his lab workers were gone, to prepare doses of RapTOR for Kendal's six patients she will treat for three weeks in his first human trial study. She has informed him that the six are three men and three women, all in their eighties. For this clinical trial he must prepare a total of thirty-six capsules per week for three weeks, which comes to three bottles of 36, which will take a night to prepare. Not being a pharmacist, he has no skill in filling capsules. Nevertheless, it should be no problem to get the three bottles ready for her to start treatment the following Monday.

He and Kendal have agreed to meet the next evening at her condo for a meal she's preparing, and to discuss the protocol, at which time he will provide her with the capsules and a research notebook.

The next day Michael arrives at her condo around seven-thirty with a bottle of wine, a briefcase, and the small box filled with capsules of his new drug. She opens the door wearing an apron and looking disheveled. She blows the hair out of her face.

"Hope you're in for spaghetti and Italian meat balls?"

"Sounds great. Can I help with anything?" he says, as he enters.

"The table is set but you can toss the salad and open that wine. I can use a glass. Not good at this cooking thing, but everything should be ready shortly."

"Take your time." He sets the wine on the counter, the box on the dining room table, his briefcase on the coffee table in the next room, and returns to the kitchen. "Sure smells good." He looks in a drawer for the corkscrew. "Not that one." She pulls out the one next to it.

"Here you go," she says, handing it to him.

Michael reaches in the cabinet above for two glasses and fills them with wine.

"Here. I think you need this," he says, handing her a glass of wine.

"Do I look that bad?" she says as she brushes her hair to one side of her face.

"Maybe a little over-heated."

They laugh.

She takes a couple of big swallows, and exhales. "That does the trick."

After working the salad, Michael carries it with his wine glass to the table in the adjacent dining area.

She yells, "Have a seat."

There are two place settings with water glasses next to the plates. He sets his wine glass down, pulls out a chair, sits, and begins sipping his wine.

Kendal brings a bowl of spaghetti covered in red sauce in one hand and a bowl of meatballs in the other and places them on the table, pulls out a chair and sits.

"Let's dig in," she says as she passes the spaghetti bowl to him. "I have some special Italian bread that a friend said went with this meal." She removes the cloth cover and hands the platter of bread to Michael as he hands back the bowl of spaghetti. He places a piece of bread on his plate and sets the platter down.

"What's in that box next to you?" she asks.

"It contains the bottles of capsules of my drug, one bottle of 36 caps for each week to treat your patients. We'll discuss it after dinner."

She nods.

"You've done well," he says. "This is really good."

"Thanks. I didn't know how it was going to turn out. Cooking isn't my strong suit."

After they finish eating, Kendal tells him he can go to the den and she'll bring coffee and they can begin their meeting. He rises, picks up the box, goes into the den and sits on the couch next to the coffee table. Minutes later, she comes in carrying a tray with two cups, a goblet of coffee cream, and a carafe of steaming coffee. She sets the tray on the glass coffee table.

"Your coffee with a little cream," she says as she hands him the cup.

"Yes, thanks."

Kendal pours herself a cup, then moves to the couch and sits next to him. He takes a couple of drafts of his coffee.

"Hmm. Great coffee."

She nods and smiles. "I'm glad we're having this meeting, Michael," she says as she takes a swallow of her coffee. "I… I…I'm getting cold feet. I've bonded with my patients and if anything happens to them, I'd never forgive myself."

Shit! How many times do I have to console her?

"Now, Kendal, we've talked about this. I wouldn't want anything to happen to them, either." He pauses looking into her sad eyes. "Kendal? Are you listening?"

She blinks and says, "What?"

"I assure you that my agent is nontoxic and has no side effects. Otherwise, I wouldn't ask you to treat them. And there's another plus. It will not interact with any of their meds."

"I don't know. It's just the feeling I have."

"Please. Think about the good it will do for them. They will be healthier, more agile and feel younger. Wouldn't you want that for them?"

"I guess so." She pauses. "I guess since you put it that way." Kendal stares into her coffee cup but doesn't take a drink.

He reaches into his pocket and pulls out a small velvet box, slides off the couch and kneels before her. He opens the little box and a beautiful diamond ring shines in the light. "I love you. Will you marry me?"

Her hands fly to her mouth, stunned. "You remembered."

"I said I would. I never break my promise."

Easy. Don't overdo it.

"Oh, Michael. Of course, I'll marry you."

He takes the ring from its box and guides it along her ring finger.

As he rises, she reaches and pulls on his arms. He falls on the couch next to her open arms. They embrace and he plants a five-second kiss on her, thinking she should be ready to participate now.

"Do you want to continue with the protocol or finish your coffee first?"

"No, I'm feeling better now. I'd like to know what I should do."

He reaches for the briefcase, opens it, and removes a notebook and a file with the protocol.

He hands her a copy and explains that she will begin treatment on Monday and will administer one capsule daily to each patient for six days, excluding Sunday. She reads along, as he tells her she'll make daily notations on each patient in the research notebook, and every Sunday she will summarize the week's observations, and then they'll meet in the evening to go over her comments on each patient. She continues to read as he recites that the entire experiment will run for only three weeks, and what she needs to look for, and to record her findings in the notebook. He reaches for it and hands it to her. She opens it and frowns.

"I've never done this before."

"No problem." He shows her how to arrange seven pages for the first week for one patient, and how to record her observations.

"Any questions?"

She nods. "Let's see if I have this straight. For the first week, I'll have seven pages for each day of the week—Monday through Sunday—for each of my six patients, and then the same for the second week and so on."

"Yes, you'll enter on each page the time you administered the capsule, and make sure it's the same time every day, and then on Sunday you will summarize your observations. If something unusual happens during the week, you can add it on that day of the week. You must get everything down. Is all that clear?"

"Yes, it is. I now feel better since you explained it so well. Just wanted to make sure I knew what to record."

"You'll do well."

He finishes off his coffee and rises with his briefcase.

Kendal holds up her ring finger. "Can you stay?"

I better keep her happy, he thinks.

"Of course."

Chapter 24

Monday morning, Kendal arrives at work for her early morning shift. She hides two bottles of RapTOR in her locker and the third one in her white coat pocket. She walks out of the locker room to the first-floor wing where her patients are housed. She reports to the nurse supervisor at the nurses' station for any special duties. She is needed on the west wing to help the other nurses with four new patients that are arriving this morning.

She finishes working in the west wing around nine o'clock and heads to the south wing and removes one of the empty med carts in a row against the wall, pushes it to the med closet, where she fills it with the day's supplies and the morning meds for each of her six elderly patients. When finished, she closes the door, wheels the cart into the hall, and stops next to Mr. Wilke's door. She opens the three med packets for him into a small plastic, transparent cup, then reaches into her pocket for the bottle of the new drug and pours out 6 capsules on the cart, one for each of her patients, and places the bottle back in her pocket.

She enters Wilke's room and says, "Good morning, Mr. Wilke. How are you feeling today?" He is sitting in a wheelchair still in his robe and close to the window on the other side of his bed, looking out into the courtyard. His bed is in the center of the room, a leather recliner is close to the entrance next to a beside cabinet, and an apartment refrigerator is against the opposite wall next to the bathroom door. Only one picture is on the wall. It is over the head of his bed, a portrait of Ronald Regan at his desk with the American flag in the background.

"Nice day for getting some sun, Mr. Wilke."

He doesn't answer. She moves his walker over against the wall.

"What's wrong, sir?"

"My children haven't been to see me in a week. That's the way it is. They forget you once they put you in this place."

"Oh, I'm sure they'll be here. I know your daughter has her hands full with three teenagers and your son told me he must go out of town sometimes in his work. Maybe he's out of town this week. Mr. Wilke."

"Maybe," he says.

"Let's take your meds and then later I'll take you outside in the courtyard for a little sun. Would you like that?"

"Yes. You are very kind. Thank you."

"Here are your meds," she says, turning the cup over in a shaking hand, reaching for the water on his bed tray, and filling the glass.

He throws the meds into his mouth and washes them down with the water she carefully hands him. "Thank you."

"You're welcome, sir."

He's eighty-nine, her oldest patient, with a slender body, just a couple of hairs sticking up on the top of his head, and thick gray eyebrows. His gaunt face is wrinkled, with sad eyes, and the doctor has prescribed meds for his tremors. She takes the glass, fills it again and sets it close to where he can reach it. His bony hand reaches for the glass and moves it closer to him.

"I'll come back after finishing with my other patients and take you out to the courtyard, Mr. Wilke," she says as she walks to the door.

"That'll be fine, Missy."

She laughs to herself. *He never remembers my name.*

Kendal moves the cart next door to Mr. James' room, who is in his early eighties, and with a pleasant demeanor. He's rather frail, but able to get around with his walker.

"You doing ok, Mr. James?" she asks as he sits in a chair by his bed to take his meds.

"Yes, better than yesterday. Had a hard time peeing, but a little better today."

She nods. "You've had that for a little while. The doctor has added an antibiotic to take care of that." The medical director along with the nurse practioner come once a week to review the condition of all the patients on her wing.

"Thank you, sweetie. I don't like that burning feeling."

Mr. James is of average height and body and always smiling.

"Do you want to get some sun this afternoon? I'm taking Mr. Wilke."

"Oh, no. He's too much of a sour puss. Maybe another day."

"You don't have to be near him."

"That's ok. Maybe tomorrow."

"Ok, but you'll miss seeing Jane Morris." She's the youngest of Kendal's six patients and a pretty grandma type. She is very pleasant, and they all get along with her.

"Well, if Jane will be there, I'm game."

"I thought you would. I'll be back later today."

Kendal goes to the cart to get the meds for her third male patient, a retired university professor of chemistry, also in his early eighties and withdrawn into his own world. She's a little apprehensive about giving him RapTOR. *Hope he doesn't question the fourth dose.*

"Good morning, Professor Allen."

He's sitting in his leather recliner reading a classic. She can see the title but asks. What are you reading, professor?"

"*Crime and Punishment* by Dostoevsky."

"Here's your meds." She pours them into his hand.

"It's all crap, but I'll take them anyway," he says with a gravel voice. He swallows them without examining them. He's more interested in being left to his reading.

Professor Allen is a wiry old grump who can be repugnant at times. He is thin-framed and not very tall, thin-faced and wrinkled but is in fair health. He never smiles.

"I won't bother you further, sir."

"Cut the 'sir' crap."

"Oh, I'm sorry. You like professor."

"You got that right. I earned it."

Oh, yeah. You arrogant jerk.

"I'll leave you to your heavy reading, *professor,*" she says with emphasis, as she moves into the hall and across to the rooms of her three elderly ladies.

The first one is an eighty-year-old pretty grandma, Jane Morris, who has difficulty walking and is confined to a wheelchair. She is a favorite among the nurses and the other patients.

Kendal enters the room but doesn't see her. There is a noise in the bathroom. "Are you ok in there?" Kendal says, standing outside the door.

"Oh. Is that you, Kendal?"

"Yes, ma'am."

The door opens and Jane wheels herself out of the bathroom.

Jane is a little over five feet, is a little beefy around the middle, but nice-looking, takes special care of her hair and uses plenty of makeup.

"How are you today, Mrs. Morris?"

"Oh, honey. Call me Jane. I guess it's med time," she says, wheeling herself to the bedside tray to get a glass of water, and then holds out her hand to receive her meds. "Got an extra one in here, I see."

Kendal is taken back, but quick to think of what to say. "It's a vitamin."

"Oh, that's good," Jane says, as she places them into her mouth and washes them down with the water. "Doesn't hurt to take a good vitamin."

"I'm moving the gang out to the courtyard this afternoon. Are you game?"

"You bet. They can't do without me."

They laugh.

In the next room is Brooke Harvey, an eighty-five-year-old, who is quiet but friendly. She has a full head of white hair and round face, does well using her walker, but can't go far. She loves to read romance novels, and sticks close to her room. She has five children and fifteen grandchildren, all of whom come to see her, and at times her room is packed. She uses a walker, gets around easily on her own, and doesn't like anyone helping her.

In the third room is, Catherine Sinclair, a retired schoolteacher in her early eighties, round shouldered, short gray hair, narrow face with some creases. Catherine is very independent and doesn't like anyone helping her, even though she needs it.

She has a visitor. Her great granddaughter, Blakely, who comes quite often. Catherine and she enjoy reading together.

"Can I interrupt you for a minute to give you your meds, Catherine?"

"Of course, dear." Blakely moves to her grandma Gigi's side. Blakely doesn't call Catherine grandma, just Gigi.

"How are you, Blakely?" Kendal asks as she hands the cup with the meds to Catherine.

"I'm fine, thank you. Gigi and I are reading a good story."

"Do you like reading?"

Smiling, she nods and says, "My great-grandpa also reads with me."

Catherine reaches for a glass of water on the side table and takes her meds.

"You are a lucky girl, Blakely," Kendal says.

Blakely nods with a big smile. "I know."

"Catherine. I'm taking everyone out for some sun this afternoon. I'm sure you'll want to come."

"Only if Blakely can go with me."

"Of course, dear."

Catherine looks at Blakely and smiles. "Then count us in."

Blakely nods at Gigi.

After the first week of treating her patients with RapTOR, Kendal is feeling more comfortable administering it. There are no signs of ill effects, and she notices some changes in the attitudes of all her patients. They appear more alert. Even old grumpy Professor Allen seems to be less grumpy. After the second week all subjects are beginning to walk better and four of her patients have a reduction in swollen joints. She's seeing smoother skin in all of them.

After three weeks, Kendal and Michael are meeting this Sunday afternoon in his home office to go over the three weeks of data. They are excited about the best results yet. Much more improvement in wrinkled skin, swollen joints, gait, and attitude of her patients.

"I need a larger sample of subjects in my clinical trials," Michael says. "Do you know of anyone else that works in a nursing home that we might approach?"

"There is an acquaintance of mine in nursing school, Emily Joyce, who works at New Haven Nursing Center. She might be interested."

"Can she be trusted?"

"I think so. The only way we can find out is to meet with her."

"That's a possibility. Let's do it. I must find more subjects."

The next day, as Kendal is preparing for work, she gets a call from the head nurse that Mr. Wilke has died. "I'll be right over," she says, dropping her cell on the floor. "Oh, no," she shouts, as she flops on her couch. *Poor Mr. Wilke.* Seconds later, she takes a deep breath, picks up her phone, and calls Michael.

"Michael, Michael. One of my patients has died. I just got a call that it's Mr. Wilke. I'm scared to death. Do you think it could be from your drug?"

"He's the eighty-nine-year-old guy, right?"

"Yes. Oh, Michael, I'm afraid."

"Get hold of yourself. How was his overall health?"

"He had a bad heart but was on meds and doing very well."

"It can't be RapTOR. It doesn't affect the heart. His heart just gave out."

"Do you really think so? You're not just saying that to make me feel better?"

"No. You've seen the results. Anyway, my drug would not cause any death."

"What if they perform an autopsy and a tox study. Would they find RapTOR in his system?"

"No. And his medical records should show his heart was weak. I'm sure the medical director will declare death by heart failure, and there won't be any autopsy."

"I'm heading over there right now to check on things," Kendal says.

"Call me immediately, once you learn what the medical director has decided."

"Okay. But I'm scared to death."

"Listen. You've got to get hold of yourself. You must keep your composure, so they won't expect anything."

"What if they talk to the other patients and find they've been given another med?"

"You're giving them too much credit. Most patients never think about what is given to them. They just take what they think the doctor orders."

"Yeah. That's true. I gotta go. I'm heading out the door now."

Chapter 25

Kendal races to the Jefferson Assisted Living Center. As she approaches the entry to the parking lot, she slams on the brakes to make the left turn into the area, parks against the building, bails out of the car and runs to the front of the building. At the entrance, remembering what Michael said, Kendal stops, takes a deep breath, and tells herself to calm down. She walks through the sliding glass doors as they hiss open and hurries to the ladies bathroom, where she throws water on her face and grabs a paper towel from the metal dispenser on the wall. She looks in the mirror.

I must be careful not to show any nervousness. She takes several deep breaths and heads to the first-floor wing.

The medical director, the head nurse, and two other nurses are huddling outside the nurses' station.

I wonder what they're talking about.

The head nurse points toward Kendal. "Here she comes now."

"Have they removed Mr. Wilke?" Kendal asks.

"Not yet," the medical director says. "We're waiting for the family. We were just looking at your reports. Did Mr. Wilke complain of any pain in his chest, or arm, jaw pain or shortness of breath yesterday?"

"No, sir. He was fine when I left him last night sitting in his recliner."

"He was receiving meds to keep his heart strong. We've determined he died of heart failure. That will be cause of death," he says.

Whee. What a relief, Kendal thinks.

"May I go in and see him, doctor?"

"Sure. He was your patient."

Kendal slowly moves to the room, opens the door, and enters. The LPNs have cleaned him up and he's covered with a white sheet, except for his head.

Poor Mr. Wilke. He loved his children but seemed so unhappy at times when they didn't come. I hope he went peacefully.

She moved in next to his bed and stared at his face. A wave of peace came over her. "You were always so kind, Mr. Wilke. I will miss you. I tried to make your stay here a little better when your children couldn't come. I pray you are in a better place with no pain. May God bless you, and may you rest in peace."

She turns and walks out of the room to the nurses' station. Mr. Wilke's daughter and son are coming through the hall toward them.

The medical director ushers them into their father's room. Kendal knows what they are discussing. The doctor will tell them what their father died of. She is thankful there will be no autopsy even though Michael knows nothing would be revealed. Kendal was hoping RapTOR would have kept Mr. Wilke alive.

His body was improving, but his heart must have been too weak all along.

I'm glad the study is over. Michael should be pleased; he has enough information for a good start.

Kendal calls Michael and gives him the good news that there will be no autopsy, and she's heading over to his house.

Chapter 26

Gail, Michael's mother, answers the door. "It's Kendal."

"Hi, Gail," she says as she enters. "I'm surprised to see you and not Michael."

"I was just in the kitchen making me some tea when I saw you pull up." She closes the door and wheels herself into the kitchen. "Would you like some tea?"

"No, thanks," she says as she follows Gail into the kitchen I won't be staying long."

"I know you and Michael have been very busy lately. Don't know much about it. It's like pulling teeth to get anything out of him." She reaches for her cup of tea and takes a couple of drinks.

"Yes, we've run a small clinical trial with his drug on some of my patients."

"He just gives me bits and pieces of what he's doing. But it seems important from what I gather."

"Yes, it is. His drug has proven very successful in my patients. Now he wants to get many more patients to continue his study."

"I see. Thank you for that. It's more than Michael has told me. He hides in his office most of the time."

He's such a loner, Kendal thinks. "I got some good news."

"You have? What is it, dear?"

"I don't know if I should be telling you or wait for Michael." She pauses. "If I tell you, will you not say anything until he tells you? I think he wants to be the one."

Kendal could see the widening of Gail's eyes. "As you wish. What is it?"

"Michael and I are engaged."

"Oh, my," Gail says, clapping her hands. "I've been waiting for this. You will make him a wonderful wife. I'm so happy." She reaches for Kendal with open arms. They hug.

"Please don't say anything to him. He'll get very mad at me."

"Oh, don't worry, darling. I won't say a word. I'm so happy."

"I'd better get in there before he starts screaming at me."

Gail's smile fills her face.

Michael is seated at his desk looking down on something and doesn't look up when Kendal knocks on the opened door.

"Are you asleep, Michael?" she says a little loud.

He looks up. "Hell, no. I'm trying to figure out where we're gonna get more patients."

"What about Emily Joyce?"

"I don't know. She works in the same environment type as you. Probably only has a few patients. We need many more, dammit!"

"Well, shouldn't we wait until we talk to her before jumping to conclusions? Let me know when you want to meet with her. If not her, she may know of someone else."

"I'll think on it," he says in a gruff voice.

"I see you're not in a good mood. It's been a tiring day, so I'm out of here. Let me know when you want to meet with Emily," she says as she walks out.

He hears Kendal saying something to his mother. Michael glances at the painting hung on the wall. He feels anger brewing in him.

The image of Donna Harvey, the matronly, middle-aged woman that takes care of his mother, flashes through his mind. Ever since she started working for them, he's been overly curious about why she drives a 15-seater van. Why would a single woman, or maybe a widow woman—he doesn't know—own such a vehicle? She's friendly, but mysterious, and only goes by Donna Harvey.

She said she has two first names. She's never revealed her last name, not even to my mother.

He rubs his chin. *I need to know more.*

Chapter 27

The next evening, after Donna Harvey leaves his home, Mordecai follows her to the east end of Atlanta, through a neighborhood with framed homes that must be over fifty years old and could use some paint. She pulls into the driveway that runs along the left side of a house to the back, she ends up at a wooden garage that needs its doors straightened. She parks and rambles out of the van carrying only her purse, and ambles up to the front, climbs up the stairs to the porch and steps into the house. The dwelling is a single-story, white frame with a large front porch, sits back about 20 yards from the street, surrounded by maple trees. Michael leaves his car and walks around the residence and notices windows close to the ground, exposing rooms in the basement area. There are several men in view eating at a table. Behind them are rooms, some with doors closed and others with their doors open.

The next day when Donna comes to assist his mother, Michael walks through the living room and calls to her, who is in the sun room attending to Gail. He is going to ask her what she does besides taking care of his mother. He thinks he knows, but wants to hear it from her.

"When you get a chance, could you please stop by my office?" She nods.

Ten minutes later, she comes into his office. "You need something, Dr. Mordecai?"

"Yes. Have a seat."

"I'd rather stand, sir."

"Okay. Good. I hope you don't mind me asking." He pauses. "I'm rather curious why you drive a 15-seater van."

"I don't mind. I'm proud of what I do." She moves in and decides to go ahead and sit in the recliner. "I feed and board homeless men through the support of my church. We clean up homeless camps by bringing the homeless men to my home. We had to renovate the basement area to room and board these men before we reached out to them. The church pays me to house and feed them until they can regain their health and strength, and for those that want to, I help find them work. Most stay with me for several weeks."

"What are the ages of these men?" Michael asks.

"Most are in their late 50s and mid-60s. The poor things are down on their luck. Some are veterans."

"How are they healthwise?"

"Many are sickly and undernourished."

"Would you mind if I visited with them?"

She frowns. "Why?" she asks, half-heartedly.

"I can help them regain their health with a new drug I discovered in my laboratory that is an anti-aging compound."

He believes he hit on anti-aging as something she'd be willing to do because it would go along with her goals—making the men healthy again.

"That would be helpful, sir."

"Maybe we can work something out together."

"What do you mean, Dr. Mordecai?"

"Would you mind if I came to your home and met with the men?"

"I'd have to talk with them first, but think I can convince them of the benefit of your treatment."

"Would it be possible for you to call me in the morning? I'd like to meet with them as soon as possible, but beforehand, I'd like to go over my protocol treatment with you so you'll know what to expect before we meet with the men."

"I'd like that. I'll call."

The next morning, close to eleven, Michael gets the call. She gives him her address, not knowing he had followed her home the day before.

He walks up the front steps to the porch of Donna Harvey's house and rings the bell. The door opens. A smiling Donna Harvey, dressed in a white uniform, motions for him to enter. She tells him that the men are cautiously interested. He is pleased to hear this, which plays right into his plan.

"Can we sit at the kitchen table and go over my treatment plan before we meet with the men?" He hands her a written copy of the 3-week study involving the single dose of RapTOR calculated for a 160 lb. male, and administered six days of each week, He reviews it with her at the kitchen table. He deliberately avoids telling her the actual dosage, but explains why they won't use anyone as a control.

They move to a door in the kitchen that leads to the lower level. He hears quarreling below as they descend the stairs. The men quickly turn and glance at them as they come down the stairs. The men continue to stare at them without saying a word, but eye Michael with suspicion as he walks among them. They do appear to be in their 50s and 60s, but look older, thin and have wrinkled skin.

"Okay, everyone. Please take your seats," Donna Harvey says.

The men sit in the two rows of folding chairs facing her.

"Men, this is Dr. Mordecai. He has something important to tell you."

"I want to thank you all for agreeing to meet with me. I believe Donna Harvey told you a little about my anti-aging drug, which is very safe and has no side effects."

He covers the 3-week treatment plan—to take a single capsule once daily for six days in each of the three weeks. He emphasizes that his med would make them feel twenty years younger. He and Donna Harvey will observe them at the end of each week. He re-emphasizes that the drug is very safe and can be taken with or without meals. One man, named Alan, around 50 years of age, stands up.

"Yes," Michael says.

"I'm not interested. I won't be participating." He pauses, looking at the other men that are waving for him to sit down. "I'm not gonna be your guinea pig."

The other men continue to look at him like he's crazy. "Why wouldn't you," several of the men said at once, "don't you want to feel young again and live longer?"

Alan shook his head. "No. I don't trust any experimental drugs."

Michael tried to convince him by stressing the wonderful outcome he could expect. Still Alan resists.

Donna Harvey takes Michael aside so Alan can't hear. "Alan was a corpsman in the Navy, thinks he knows it all, a real smart ass."

She tells Michael about Alan's nursing background, which he didn't do much with because he got so deep into drugs. He came to Atlanta as a traveling nurse, working at Emory hospital with her, but he got so deep into drugs, he couldn't keep the job and eventually became homeless. She's tried to help him.

"Is your treatment protocol FDA approved?" Alan asks.

"I have to first get more human data on my drug," Michael says, trying to reason with him.

"Not from me," Alan says. He looks at the other men. "You guys are crazy to let this jerk pump you with an unknown substance. It's not even a drug yet, until approved for such use by the FDA."

Michael moves close to Alan. "That's fine, Alan. What you are saying is true, but I have data from much testing in animal models that verify this substance does exactly what I've said, and has no side effects."

This guy is trouble. He could go to the authorities.

"Alan, I understand your reluctance. But you are not a scientist and I am. I have data from human experiments that prove my drug is safe. However, if that is not good enough for you, you can be excluded from the group."

"That's fine by me," Alan says.

"Does anyone else feel like Alan?"

"No way," most of the men said.

"Does anyone have any more questions for Dr. Mordecai?" Donna Harvey asks.

A few shake their heads and the others say nothing.

"Thank you," Michael says, "we will start treatment in a few days."

The next couple of nights after midnight, Michael works in the lab preparing capsules for the eleven volunteers at Donna Harvey's. The last night, he takes the samples to his desk and wraps them in separate boxes. He sits, thinking about his next plan of action. Each of the volunteers should have a physical and be checked for any health issues, but he'll skip those steps, as well as omitting a control group. If RapTOR proves successful as he thinks, FDA should approve Biogen's application to perform a placebo-randomized-double-blind study, but for now he needs much more data.

So far, it's working. He's excited.

People will not only live longer but they will live without health issues. Maybe I'll get the Nobel Prize.

He's feeling half-crazy with thoughts about how great he is. Then he frowns. He has a problem. He wanted twelve subjects but Alan had to be the thorn in his side. Michael slams his fist on the desk. "Can't have him influencing the other men or ratting on me to the authorities."

Chapter 28

Michael Mordecai begins supervising the administration of RapTOR to the homeless men this Monday morning. He watches as he instructs Donna to distribute the capsules and record the date and time for each man in the research notebook. She will observe and record any changes in the men daily, looking for attitude, agility, and skin changes, and Michael will come every Sunday to examine the men with her and go over her entries in the notebook.

After two weeks, the men are showing increased strength, smoothness of skin, and a better attitude. Michael meets with Alan in the den upstairs away from the other men.

"Alan, you're a cocaine addict, aren't you?"

"Who in the hell told you that? I'm clean."

"I guessed it from the scars on your arms."

Alan pulls his shirt sleeves down to his wrists.

"I can get you some. A little now and more later." He knows Alan will get hooked again and so does Alan.

Alan becomes quiet and looks away. "What are you trying to pull? I'm not that stupid."

Michael overlooks the comment. "If you participate in my experiment, you'll get some stuff now and more later." He knows Alan won't participate even if he accepts the offer. "What about it, Alan?"

"I don't know. It's bad stuff."

"I've heard it really makes you feel out of this world."

Alan just stares at him without a word.

What are you thinking, Judas? Michael thinks, remembering Judas' betrayal of Christ. *Because of you I've ended up with only eleven men.*

"It does make me forget my shit."

Michael reaches into his shirt pocket, pulls out a small, white square patch, shoves it across the coffee table. "Plenty more where that came from."

Alan stares at it for thirty seconds. His eyes are watering, and he licks his lips.

He's trembling. I got him. "Plenty more if you want it."

"I know what you're doing," Alan says. "You're trying to bribe me with snow, so I won't go to the authorities."

Michael fakes a surprise expression. "You're not that kind of man. You wouldn't tell anyone. You have morals."

He nods. "That I do." He grabs the packet. "I'll need more."

"As much as you want."

"When can you get it to me?" Alan says.

"How about tomorrow? We'll have to meet some place. I don't want anyone here to catch us."

"Okay. It's your call," Alan says. "Just get me more. Once on this, I'll need more."

"You got it. Can you call me tomorrow at around four at this number?" Michael writes it on a napkin.

I got you, you bastard.

The next day around four Michael gets the call from Alan, who is at East Lake in southeast Atlanta.

East Lake. My favorite spot. "What are you doing there?"

"You ask too many questions. This is where I used to meet my man. Bring me the stuff around seven?"

"How will I find you?"

"At the north entrance. I'll be waiting in the grove of trees. You can't miss it. I'll step out into the clearing when I see you coming. Blink your lights twice."

"No problem. I'll be there."

At seven, the sun hasn't set this summer evening. Michael pulls into the chat parking lot at the north entrance to the lake, driving a stolen blue Honda Ridgeline pickup. He turns on his lights, blinks them twice, and looks around. No other cars. No Alan. Michael picks up a box from the seat and his dagger, which he places inside his jacket pocket, hops out and walks to the grove of trees. He looks for Alan. Thirty minutes go by and no Alan.

What's up with him? he thinks. *Come on before someone comes in, you little shit.*

Suddenly, Alan appears from behind a tree and walks up behind Michael, carrying a small box.

Michael swings around. "What took you so long?"

"I forgot my syringe. I like to shoot up. Let's sit by that big tree," he says, pointing. He leads the way and sits with his back against the trunk, begins rolling up his left shirt sleeve and places a tourniquet around his arm. "Got a good vein here," he says to Michael, as he slaps it.

Michael opens the box and removes a small envelope and hands it to Alan. "There's more in this box."

Michael watches as Alan dissolves the powder in a large spoon filled with water. Then he asks Michael to hold the spoon while he heats the spoon with a cigarette lighter and then reaches for a large syringe, attaches the needle, and draws up the solution into the syringe. His hands are shaking but he's able to insert the needle into a vein and pushes in the plunger slowly, enjoying every second of it as he empties the contents into his arm. A couple more seconds pass and Alan's acting weird.

"Man, this is good stuff."

Michael pulls out his favorite dagger from the inside of his summer jacket and flashes it in Alan's face.

"Man, what…what? Holy, Jesus!" Alan's eyes are as wide as saucers. "No, no," he screams, too weak to fight him off. Michael makes his cuts into Alan's neck, loving every minute of his suffering. Alan's blood sprays on Michael's hands and jacket. The warm feeling from the blood excites Michael.

When he was twelve. Michael's father took him on deer hunting trips, which he loathed. He found looking at a deer through a dear rifle scope too impersonal. One minute the deer is looking over the valley, the next minute, a shot rings out, and the deer drops out of sight. Standing over the prey doesn't excite Michael, there's little blood, no noise, and its eyes are gazing into oblivion.

Unlike the deer, Michael likes to face his human prey, flashing his proud possession, the dagger with its shiny, curved steel blade, causing their eyes to dilate from the fear of impending death. Michael's excitement intensifies as he makes the first cut through the muscles in their neck, which tense and give way to the windpipe, air gushing out of the jagged hole, followed by spurting blood from the arteries within. Feeling the warmth from the blood bathing his hands, becoming sticky in the air, gives him a sense of superiority over the scum. Getting rid of worthless humans is the sport he now enjoys.

"You worthless scum," Michael says, as Alan falls over on the ground.

Michael carries him to the lake and throws him in and hurries back to the stolen truck, picking up the box, and the paraphernalia off the ground. He spots a man walking a dog in his direction. Michael quickly opens the driver's door, throws in the trash, grabs the Frankenstein mask, slips it on, hops in, and speeds off, passing the man with his canine friend.

Chapter 29

Two days later, a man with two sons, one fourteen and one sixteen, are fishing from a boat on East Lake. It was close to noon when the dad suggested they pull into shore and get something to eat. As they ease up to the shore, the sixteen-year-old boy stands up in the boat.

"Over there!" he says, shouting, as the boat approaches the bank. "That looks like a body!"

They move in a little closer. "It's a man, fully clothed," the dad says. "He's at the shore's edge, face downward." He reaches for his cell and calls 911.

Twenty minutes later, two patrol cars arrive. An officer begins wrapping yellow crime tape around trees close to the body, another calls in to Dispatch and describes the scene. While waiting for the detectives, the officers question the father and his two sons as witnesses to the crime scene.

"Did anyone touch or try to remove the body?" No was their response.

"How long was it before you called 911?"

"Immediately after we saw him," the dad said.

The sixteen-year-old says, "I spotted him first."

"Did you notice anyone else in the area?"

"No," they say in unison.

Two APD homicide detectives, Kramer and Gomez, arrive at the scene. They question the man and his boys again. Larry, the assistant M.E., arrives. The detectives walk the area, then call in their findings to Lieutenant McGraw.

Lieutenant Noah McGraw and Sergeant Holly Roark arrive at the scene about the same time as the forensic crew. Larry, the assistant M.E., has removed the body from the water and placed it on a tarp on the bank.

"He's got large gashes in the throat. Not much to go on out here," Larry tells the detectives.

McGraw and Roark slip on gloves and squat to look over the body.

"Were you able to determine time of death?" McGraw asks.

Larry shrugs. "Been in the water too long for me to give anything but a ballpark estimate. We'll know more once I get him in."

"These gashes in the neck seem to be the only sign of attack," Holly says. "No visible marks on the body, like he was trying to defend himself."

"None," Larry says. "Someone got to him before he had a chance to defend himself."

"Or he was probably unconscious when someone stabbed him," McGraw says. He went on to add, "Someone wanted him to bleed out."

"Hard to get an ID on a body in the water. We'll try to get one on the vic and run tox screens. Can I take him?"

Noah nods and tells him he'll be in touch with Nora Philips, the ME.

"What do you make of the cuts in the throat, Noah?" Holly asks. "I've never seen such gashes. Someone seemed skilled at doing this?"

"I don't think this killer is a doc," McGraw says, "if that's what you are suggesting. It could be very personal."

McGraw rises and begins walking an area ten yards from the shore, looking for whatever might tell him how this guy ended up in the water and where was he murdered. He's about twenty yards from the shore when he spots blood. Holly is behind him. The crime scene personnel have finished photographing the area and Chris is bagging blood samples.

"Lots of blood," McGraw says to Holly, pointing, as he continues into an area thirty yards from the lake shore to a grove of trees.

"He was hacked here next to the tree," he says as he squats to examine the spot.

Chris, the forensic super, bags a syringe and says, "Got a syringe here that apparently was used by the vic."

"A drug deal gone bad," Holly suggests.

"Looks like it," Chris says.

McGraw says, "We've never seen a syringe at a site where a drug deal went south. Someone was shooting up, and an argument probably ensued."

"Maybe two guys were half-crazy, fighting over the stuff, and the one who wanted it more won out," she said.

"But would he be in a condition to move the other guy or anything else?"

"You got a point, Noah."

McGraw begins scanning the area inch-by-inch. The grass doesn't reveal any footprints. He and Holly meet at the tree and look toward the parking lot. A man walking his dog comes toward them.

"Are you with the police?" he asks.

"I'm Lieutenant McGraw and this is my partner, Sergeant Roark. How can we help you?"

"My name is Will Deaver. Earlier today, I told a couple of detectives what I saw. I was walking Buddy here, like I do every evening around seven, but I also walk Buddy around noon, too, to get out of the house. I'm retired. Well, like I said, I saw this man shooting out of this parking lot at a high rate of speed. Funny thing, he was wearing a mask and what looked like blood on the front of him. I figured something bad happened when I saw all the cops around this place."

"What kind of car was he driving?" Holly asked.

"Blue Honda pickup. He probably saw me coming is why he shot out of here."

"About the mask?" McGraw said. "Was it a full mask or one like doctors' wear?"

"No, it was a head mask. Looked like the ones you'd wear at Halloween to scare the kids."

McGraw and Roark look at each other.

"So, it wasn't a mask looking like, maybe a U.S. president, or some Hollywood actor?" Roark asks.

"No, ma'am. Too scary. Had like bumps on it. More like the Frankenstein monster on TV.

"Did you notice the license plate?" Roark asks.

"No, ma'am."

"Anything else, sir?" Roark says.

"No, ma'am. Can't think of anything else."

"Thank you, sir," McGraw says, "you've been very helpful."

"You're welcome. Let's go, Buddy," he says to his doggy as he pulls on the leash.

"Well, well. Does the pickup driver ring any bells, Noah?" Holly asks.

"You wouldn't by chance be referring to the guy on the tapes?"

She nods.

"It's not out of the realm of possibilities."

"Who is this guy?" she says.

"It surely would help if we had a physical description," he says.

"I gotta say, he's pretty smart," Roark says.

Chapter 30

Early the next morning, McGraw and Roark arrive in the bullpen. The boss walks over to the coffee stand and finds the carafe empty.

He calls out, holding up the glass carafe. "Who's falling down on the job here?" Is it you, Gomez?"

He notices the frown on Gomez's face. "Boss, I didn't know that was my job." He rises from his desk, passes in front of Kramer and whispers to him, "That's your job, Kraut head."

"You the man, chipotle head," Kramer says, then smiles.

Gomez takes the pot from the boss' hand and goes to the sink to fill it with water.

"Boss, maybe you ought to think about getting a Keurig and coffee pods."

"And who would fill it with water? McGraw says with a smile.

All the while, Holly is watching. When McGraw returns to his desk with his cup filled to the brim, she whispers, "Since when is it, you're too good to make coffee?"

He winks at her and whispers back. "I like pulling his leg. When I came in, they had their heads down, pretending they're busy, I thought I'd shake things up a little for fun."

"You sure did shake Gomez up. You better say something to him. You know how sensitive he is, always wanting to please you. You made him feel like dirt."

McGraw takes a big swallow of his coffee standing behind his desk, then calls out, "Gomez. We need to talk."

Gomez hops up from his desk again, hurries up the aisle, passes by

Kramer again, who gives him a smile that says, 'You're in for it now.'

Gomez raises his head and twists his face to tell Kramer, 'Up yours.'

"Yeah, boss," he says.

"I want you to know I was just yanking your chain. I didn't mean to upset you. You know I appreciate all you do."

He nods. "I hope so, boss."

"I really do. You're a good detective." He turns toward Kramer. "Kramer, I want you and Gomez to know what good police work you both did getting Dr. Mordecai's DNA. Your story is one for the books."

"Thank you, boss," both Gomez and Kramer respond in unison.

"We now have Mordecai's DNA on record. The ME said she was impressed with you guys, too."

"And that's something coming from Dr. Philips," Roark says.

McGraw asks, Gomez. "Tell me, did you and Kramer find any credible witnesses at the lake?"

"I was about to bring you something very interesting after finishing my report. We talked to one witness, Will Deaver, who was walking his dog. He said he saw a man in a blue pickup flying by him and said the guy was wearing a mask and had blood on the front of him."

Kramer comes up front and joins in the discussion. "We had him describe the mask. It was like the guy in the tapes who was driving the Land Rover. This can't be a coincidence, boss."

"He might be the same guy," Gomez says.

"So, you both think the masked guy following Keller might also be the one at the lake?" McGraw asks.

Gomez shrugs. "It couldn't be a coincidence that another guy would be wearing the same kind of mask. Must be the same guy. One way to find out is to track the pickup."

"I don't know. You can bet the plates are stolen, and he's gotten rid of the truck by now," Roark says.

"Even if we find it, he probably stole it and the owner has reported it by now," Kramer added."

McGraw goes to the white board and writes:

Male vic in lake
Mask Man with blood on him is in a blue Honda pickup
Same Mask Man as one in Land Rover

"Did you want to say something, Sergeant Roark?" McGraw asks.

"Yes." She turns to Gomez and Kramer. "Was your witness a little guy with thin hair and dark eyebrows, and a big nose?"

"That's him," Gomez says. "Why?"

"We interviewed him, too. He told us what you are putting in your report."

"Well, I'll be damned. I wanted to impress you guys with our witness," Gomez says."

They laugh.

"You have," McGraw says. "Great work, you two. What if we didn't run into him? It's just that he walks the same path a couple of times a day is why we were lucky enough to meet him, too. He was probably on his way back when we met with him."

"I'll finish the report and put it on your desk, boss." Gomez says.

McGraw nods, as he starts to walk out of the pit. "I'm going down to the morgue."

Dr. Nora Philips, the ME, is leaning over the post mortem table working on the vic from the lake. The stitched Y incision made earlier from the chest down the front is visible. McGraw moves to the end of the table and watches for a moment without disturbing her.

"This is your vic, Noah. No water in the lungs. Gashes in the neck, but no other body wounds. He has some small veins and needle punctures in his arms. Most likely on drugs, and killed somewhere else and then dumped into the lake."

"How long had he been dead?"

"From the stomach contents, there were remnants of a lunch meal, hamburger meat and fries. He was killed sometime in the late afternoon or early evening. We'll treat this as a homicide and do a tox study, but it'll take 24 to 48 hours."

"Whatever it takes," McGraw says.

"Your vic is five-foot-five, 145 lbs., short brown hair, scar in the appendix area."

"How old would you say he is?"

"In his fifties."

"Do you have a pic of the vic?"

Nora turns toward her desk. "There's one on my desk that I had for you."

"Thanks." He moves over to her desk, picks up the photograph, and says, "We really need help IDing this guy."

"I'll see what I can do. His skin is loose, probably been in the water for a couple of days. The destructive effect of water complicates the chances of recovery, but since he was in the water under fifteen days, chances are good we can get prints."

"Sound great. Of course, there's always DNA," McGraw says.

"That's for sure."

"Appreciate your letting me know what you determine and when the tox study is done."

She nods. "About to have lunch and will get to it in about an hour."

McGraw thinks about why it takes so long to do a tox study as he walks back to homicide.

The recommended specimens for this vic will be blood, urine, gastric contents, bile, liver, hair, and vitreous humour from the eye, which take time to analyze. Blood is often the specimen of choice for detecting, quantifying, and interpreting drugs and other toxicant concentrations. Hopefully, this vic hasn't any decomposition, which can interfere with testing since the specimens may be difficult to analyze.

McGraw enters the squad room, posts the picture of the vic on the crime board, and writes under it.

LAKE VICTIM
Five-foot-five
Caucasian male
Weight – 145
Short brown hair
Scar in the lower right quadrant
Gashes in the throat
In his fifties
I.V. drug use

Roark, Kramer, and Gomez are watching him from their desks. He turns to Kramer and says, pointing at the pic. "Run this vic's profile through the missing CODIS and APAT and see what comes up. And Gomez? Run stolen pickups."

"ID'ing this guy may be tough," Roark says.

"We may get a break," the boss says. "Nora will try to get prints but she may have to resort to DNA."

Moments later, Gomez says, "Boss, two pickups were stolen in the last 72 hours."

"What areas were they in? It might help us to learn if the killer might be living there."

"Both vehicles were in southeast Atlanta."

Gazing at the white board, McGraw says, "Since Keller might have known his killer, let's assume for the sake of argument that the masked man is someone at Biogen who had it in for him. He drove the Land Rover, which he ditched. Now, let's assume we have the same guy now in a blue pickup. If he does work at Biogen, making the big bucks that we learned from the file Elizabeth gave us, he wouldn't live in southeast Atlanta, which means he deliberately stole the truck in that area to throw us off.

"All we have is a masked man that has killed two people. It can't be a coincidence that these crimes were committed by two different people with the same kind of mask. It's almost like he wants us to know it's he."

"So, you think someone at Biogen killed Keller and the vic in the lake?" Roark asks.

He nods. "It's only hypothetical at this stage. Unfortunately, we don't have a description of our suspect. He's only been spotted in a vehicle. And to add fuel to the fire, we don't have an ID yet on the vic in the lake."

"For now, our challenge is to figure out how this masked man, whoever he is, is connected to the two murders," she says.

"That's the 64-thousand-dollar question. Generally, we assume that the type of victim often reveals the type of killer," McGraw says. "Consequently, since Keller was a scientist, his killer might be a scientist."

Kramer calls out. "The vic's body description does not fit any of the missing persons in the databases."

"Okay, thanks," McGraw says.

Roark shakes her head. "Once the lake vic is ID'd, we might know how he was connected to his killer," Roark says.

"And we should be able to connect the dots." McGraw says. "For now, let's play a game. Let's assume someone at Biogen had it in for Keller. We don't have anything else to go on except to explore the areas in which the masked man might live."

"Scientists at Biogen make big bucks. We saw that in Mordecai's personnel file," Roark says. "I can think of several highfalutin areas they might live in. As starters, Brookhaven, Argonne Forest (very wealthy), North Buckhead, another affluent area, Peachtree Heights East, probably the safest neighborhood in Atlanta, Chastain Park, an affluent suburb, and Atlanta Station, another top-rated area."

"You'd have to make big bucks to live in those areas," the boss says.

"I could check those who worked with Dr. Keller," she says.

"That's a good start. And don't forget the CEO, Mark Rubin."

"Mark Rubin? You really think he had anything to do with Keller's death? He had nothing but praise for Keller."

"Praise could be a cover. Don't want to leave anyone out."

"Well, ok. You're the boss."

McGraw's phone vibrates on his desk. He looks at his wrist watch. Three-forty p.m. He reaches for the phone.

"Detective McGraw."

"Noah, this is Whitey. Dusty… Dusty…fell off TR—"

"—Is he okay?' McGraw says, jumping up.

"Don't know. He was unconscious when they took him."

"How'd it happen?"

"Dusty was trotting around the track and next thing I knew, he was on the ground. I heard a shot from somewhere and I think TR got spooked. TR loves Dusty, he just stood there trying to comfort the boy. We're now following the ambulance, to Emory Hospital."

Holly jumps up and rushes over to Noah. "Is it Dusty? What has happened? Tell me!"

"We're on our way."

"Noah! Tell me!"

"Dusty fell off TR and he's been taken by ambulance to Emory Hospital."

"Oh, no. My poor boy. Let's go!"

"Get hold of yourself. Whitey said he just got banged up," Noah says, stretching the truth so as not to traumatize Holly.

Noah grabs his hat and they run out of the building and hop into the Silverado. McGraw barrels out of the parking lot with the strobes flashing and the siren blasting. They make the fifteen-minute trip in five minutes, pulling under the canopy next to the ambulance covering the entrance to the ER. Holly hops out, races to the sliding glass doors, and rushes in to the nurses' station. "I'm Dusty Roark's mother, detective Holly Roark. They just brought him in."

The nurse looks down at her clip board. "Oh, yes, he's back in ER, and you can wait in the waiting room down the hall and to your right. There are signs."

"How can I find out who is treating him?"

"They will come out and call the family as soon as they can."

Noah comes up behind her.

"What did you learn?"

"We need to go into the waiting room until they come for us. Follow me."

They race down the hall, spotting the sign above the glassed-in room designating the waiting room. Anna Marie and Whitey are in the half-filled room, sitting in two leather chairs against the wall. They hop up when they see Holly and Noah.

"Have you heard anything?" Holly asks.

Whitey shakes his head, while Anna Marie hugs Holly and says, "Nothing yet, dear."

"So, he just slid off TR?" Noah asks, looking at Whitey.

"That's what I think. I only took my eyes off him for a minute and there he was, on the ground."

"Was he hurt bad?" Holly asked.

"I don't think so," Whitey said. "I'm thinking he may be bruised pretty bad and will be sore for quite a while."

"Can we get you anything, Holly?" Anna Marie asks.

"No thanks." Holly nervously walks around the room and stops at the glass door looking for the doctor.

"Don't you want to have a seat?" Noah says.

"I'm too nervous to sit."

Ten minutes later a six-foot man in his forties, dressed in whites, pushes the door open.

Before Holly can ask about Dusty, the doc calls out for the Smith family. Two adults and two teenagers jump up and follow the doc out of the room. Thirty minutes later, Holly goes back to the door and looks out down the hall, but sees no one. She decides to sit and closes her eyes. Minutes later another doc dressed in white comes in and calls for the Roark family. Holly is the first one out of her seat and rushes to the doc. "I'm Dusty Roark's mother. Is he okay?"

"He's going to be fine."

Now Noah, Anna Marie and Whitey have circled the doc. "I'm Doctor Adams. Dusty has large bruises on his right arm and leg. We did an MRI checking for a head trauma, and found nothing. He has been undergoing neurological protocol—"

"—When can we see him, doctor?" Holly asks.

"In thirty minutes. We've moved him to a room for observation to continue protocol. He should be released sometime tomorrow. Once he's settled in, the nurse will come to take you to him."

"Oh, thank you, doctor." Holly felt like hugging him, but thought better of it.

Anna Marie hugs Holly. "I've been praying for Dusty. Tomorrow, he'll be back with us. Thank God!"

"Yes. Thank God!" Holly repeats.

Thirty minutes have passed and a nurse comes in and takes the Circle M family up to the third floor. Dusty is in room 303, close to the nurses' station. Dusty is sitting up with bandages around both arms resting on the white cover over his body.

Holly rushes in and bends down to squeeze the life out of Dusty. "Oh, mom. I'm okay, but if you squeeze me any harder, I may be here longer."

Everyone laughs. "How is my little buddy?" Noah asks, pinching his toes.

"Feeling good, just sore all over, but the doc says it will go away."

Anna Marie moves in and gives Dusty her hug.

"Love you, grandma," Dusty says for the first time.

"Oh, my," Anna Marie says, placing her hands in a prayer fashion against her lips. "I love you calling me grandma, you sweet young man."

Holly looks at Dusty with such love in her eyes.

Whitey moves in and takes Dusty's hand. "I'm sorry you had your spill. It's my job to take care of my little friend. Can you tell us what happened?"

"I don't really know. I was trotting around the rink and before I knew it, I was falling off TR. It's never happened before."

"We're thankful that TR didn't stumble and fall on you, Dusty," Noah says.

"Aw. That will never happen with my TR."

"We should probably let you get some rest. I'll be here tomorrow morning and wait until you check out," Holly says. She bends down and kisses him on the forehead.

They all give him hugs and smiles, and tell him there will be a party when he comes home.

Chapter 31

Lieutenant McGraw enters the Pitcher's Mound Restaurant, owned by the celebrated Braves pitcher, Moose Johnson, Cy Young awardee, pictured throughout the best steak house in Atlanta. The dining area is filled with tables covered with white tablecloths, and many are lined up against the soft gray walls over which hang beautifully framed pictures of this famous pitcher taken with politicians, movie stars, and other VIPs. Moose accepting the Cy Young Award is the one that stands out in the center of the montage.

Noah spots his big Italian friend, Zee, seated at their table, which is against the wall in the center of the room, below the picture where Moose, with a big smile, is holding his award. McGraw moves to the chair below the picture, and sits facing Zee. The waiters are aware that this table belongs to the retired Detective Zee whenever he makes a reservation, or there will be hell to pay. The short pudgy waiter gingerly places a glass of Johnny Walker Red, neat, in front of Zee and a glass of Merlot next to McGraw's water glass and leaves.

"What's with the waiter?" Noah asks, taking a pull on his wine.

"The big Italian frowns. "What?" He downs half of his Scotch, and licks his lips. "Man, that's good."

"That poor waiter bowed down so far, I thought he was going to kiss your ring."

"C'mon, man, you're just jealous. Can I help it if I get more respect than you do?"

"That'd be the day. You deliberately put the fear of God in the poor guy."

He shrugs. "Can I help it if he knows I'm important? That's more respect than I get from you, Champ."

They laugh.

Zee finishes off his Scotch, and says, "Okay, enough of the bullshit. I'm hungry. You owe me a steak."

"In case you've forgotten, I paid that debt last time."

Zee raises his head. "Oh, yeah, I do remember now. Well, you won't mind paying again. After all, I'm retired."

Zee waves to the waiter two tables away. He rushes over. "Ready to order, sir?"

"Yeah. We need another round of drinks and bring our usual steak dinner," Zee says, handing him his empty glass. "I want mine with blood and my wimpy friend wants his cremated."

The waiter looks puzzled. "Just make it well done, "McGraw says. "I'm not a cannibal like my friend."

"Yes, sir," he says, reaching for Zee's glass and hurries off.

Noah shakes his head as he drinks the rest of his wine. "You better give the guy a big tip."

Noah spots the owner, Moose Johnson, talking to customers at the far end of the room. He likes to make his rounds greeting the patrons.

The waiter rushes back with their drinks. Noah thanks him. "Here comes the man," he says.

"Howya doin,' Zee?" Moose says, gently patting him on the shoulder. The big Italian looks up over his shoulder at the famous owner. They knuckle punch. "Doing good, Moose," Zee says.

"How's my former cook?" Moose says looking over at McGraw.

"Doing well, Moose."

Noah, his mother, and Holly have worked in Moose's food kitchen, called Home Plate. It's a brick building in the poor section of town that serves lunch and dinner to about 100 homeless people. Noah had to slack off when he got heavily involved in the Tongue Collector case.

"Tell Ms. Anna Marie and Ms. Holly I miss them, and anytime they'd like to help at Home Plate, they're always welcomed."

"I will and maybe when things calm down, we may take you up on that," Noah says.

Moose smiles. "Gotta circulate. Seeya later."

Both Zee and Noah smile and salute him by holding up their drinks.

"Okay, Champ," Zee says to Noah as he takes a big waft of his Scotch. "Since you aren't buying my steak, let's get down to business. I can see something's bothering you, again."

"A couple of things. Day before yesterday, Dusty gave us a scare. He was trotting around the ring on the property, fell off his horse, Texas Rodeo, and was rushed to the hospital. He's fine but ended up with bad bruises on his right arm and leg and he's very sore, but we're thankful that he didn't have any head injury."

"And thankful that that horse didn't fall on him," Zee says.

"For sure. That would have been catastrophic. He's home now doing great."

"Good to hear. I've known for some time how close you are to Dusty, giving him books that would enlighten his mind." He takes another drink of his Scotch and then says, "Okay, what else is bugging you?"

Noah takes a drink of his wine and begins describing his two homicides. "I have a masked man who killed two people. He ran a scientist named Corey Keller off the road, causing his convertible to overturn and hit a tree, and was thrown out. Keller was the research director at Biogen, a molecular biology company."

"Stupid scientist. I've heard of Biogen."

"The second vic is a male whose body ended up in East Lake. We haven't ID'd him yet, but the same masked man was seen leaving the scene. It can't be a coincidence that these crimes were committed by two different people with the same kind of mask. It's almost like he's taunting us."

"What kind of mask is it?"

"Frankenstein Monster. Covers the whole head and neck."

"You're right. Usually, the killer doesn't wear a mask to hide his identity. It's used to inflict terror or for his own excitement. In this case, I'm sure he wears it because he gets a kick out of it. He's a show off."

Noah nods. "I agree."

"I'm sure you've discussed this with your team, but the question you have to ask is how the masked man is connected to the two murders," Zee says.

"We have. And I've suggested that the type of victim often reveals the type of killer," McGraw says. "Keller was a scientist, so is his killer a scientist?"

"You haven't ID'd your lake vic so you don't know his connection?"

"That's right," McGraw says.

"You know how I operate. I always begin with the three motives for murder: money, sex, and revenge. It appears your killer isn't killing for money or sex. So, revenge must be his mission. He's getting even with his vics by killing them because they have harmed or prevented him from accomplishing something important to him."

"Excellent. We must determine what's so important to our killer that he'd kill these two men for opposing him?" McGraw says."

Zee picks up his drink. "I'll drink to that."

Silence.

Zee is staring down at his empty glass. Noah knows his old partner is in deep thought. Zee looks up. "You've interviewed the people at Biogen?"

"We did."

"What did you find significant? Give me just the bare facts."

"We learned from one of the scientists, Jessica York, who works closely with Michael Mordecai in his lab, that he and Cory Keller went at it often in their meetings over the testing of Mordecai's anti-aging agent in the different animal experiments. She said Mordecai was impatient and wanted Keller to lighten up and not keep adding more tests for him to run so Biogen could beat the other pharmaceutical companies to market with his anti-aging agent."

"Well, you said the type of victim determines the type of killer. Keller was a scientist and Mordecai is a scientist. So, Champ. There might be a motive here. Keep an eye on this guy, Mordecai.

Chapter 32

This Sunday evening, Michael and Donna Harvey review all the data in her kitchen from the study of RapTOR on the eleven men. She has done such an excellent job of supervising the testing and recording data that he feels she can be trusted not to go to the authorities.

"I want you to know that you've done an excellent job supervising the men and the testing."

"Thank you, sir. The men are so much better. I'm so happy for them. Some want to find work."

"I'm very encouraged with this study," Michael says. "Especially since we didn't have any side effects from the drug."

"Will they need to continue it?" she asks.

"That we don't know." He pauses. "I wanted to ask you something. Would you be willing to continue to follow them? It would be very helpful in our study to know if they will continue to remain in good health or if they will recede to the way they were. Could you have them check in with you on a weekly basis to determine if the drug must be taken continuously? I'd continue your pay."

"I'd love that. The men are very easy to work with and since they feel so good, I know it won't be a problem to get their cooperation."

"Great."

He hands her an envelope with cash, rises, walks to the door, stops and turns around. "We can follow through with the results of the continued treatment when you come to the house to take care of my mother."

"Yes, sir."

Michael arrives home around eight that evening and goes into the kitchen to make coffee.

"Is that you, Michael?" Gail asks.

What now? Who in the hell else would it be? "Yes, mother. I'm having coffee. Want some?"

"No, thanks."

He takes his cup to his office, sits at his desk and takes a couple of swallows, then reaches for the phone and calls Kendal.

"Kendal, what are you doing?"

"I'm getting ready for work tomorrow. Why? What's up?"

"We've finished the study with the homeless men. I'm now ready to take on more subjects. Do you think Emily Joyce will meet with us?"

"I'll call and see if she is still interested."

"Can you try and reach her tonight? I'd like to meet tomorrow."

"I'll be in touch."

Michael finishes off his coffee, thinking about how slowly the testing is going. If he just had a large group, but for now he'll have to try for several smaller groups. He thinks about the six subjects in Kendal's nursing facility and the eleven homeless men, and shakes his head.

That only makes seventeen participants.

He slams his fist on the desk. "Shit."

The phone on his desk rings.

"Yes."

"Emily can meet tomorrow at Old Town Coffee Shop a little after three when she gets off work. That fits my schedule. How about you?"

"I'll meet you there at three." He hangs up and glances at the invoice for trading in his red BMW for a white caddy. He glances at the painting on the wall, the one with the dagger in the man's throat, and wonders if the cops have found Alan's body in the lake. No mention of it in the paper yet.

The little rat got what he deserved.

Chapter 33

The next day, close to three in the afternoon, Michael pulls his white caddy into an open parking spot in front of the Old Town Coffee Shop, steps out, and walks to the door. The aroma of strong coffee hits his nostrils as he enters. A path next to the wall leads to the counter and on his right is a large area with numerous tables and chairs. A guy in his late twenties, wearing a name tag with *Jimmy* printed on it, is grinding coffee at the order station, while a girl about his age is waiting on customers at the pickup counter. Michael places his order, pays for two medium caffe lattes, and steps over to the pickup station.

He turns around, sees Kendal entering behind him and waves for her to follow him to the table against the rough plastered wall, under a framed abstract painting that looks like someone got mad and threw several colors of paint on a canvas.

"I got our favorites," Michael says, as they pull out chairs from the table and take a seat. There's one chair left for Emily Joyce.

Kendal reaches for her coffee and takes a couple of swallows. "Thanks."

"What does Emily look like?" Michael asks, as he takes a couple of drafts of his coffee.

"See for yourself. Here she comes now." Kendal waves at her.

A fiery red head, six inches taller than Kendal, walks slowly toward their table. She is slim, fair skinned, wearing a blue sweater and black pants, and close to being homely.

"Hi, Emily," Kendal says.

Emily nods with little expression as she pulls out a chair and sits.

"This is Dr. Mordecai."

"Pleased to meet you, Emily," he says.

Emily only nods.

"How do you like your coffee?" Kendal asks.

"Tell Jimmy I want the usual."

Kendal goes to the counter. Michael stares at Emily over his coffee cup. She stares back at him. He takes a drink of his coffee, and says, "Kendal tells me you are interested in working with us testing my new drug."

She looks down and shakes her head. "I don't know." She pauses. "I haven't decided."

"Oh, is that right?" *You bitch. Playing us, are you?* "What will it take to bring you on board?"

Before she can answer him, Kendal brings Emily's coffee, sets it in front of her, and then takes her seat. Michael notices that she doesn't thank Kendal. Right off he's getting bad vibes about the redhead.

He says, "Would you like to hear what we've done with the testing of my new drug? If not, then why did you come?" He can feel her lack of enthusiasm and he's going to write her off.

"I've been thinking," Emily says. "I don't believe I can chance it at my work."

"I'm disappointed in you," Kendal says. "You led me to believe you were very interested."

"I'm only saying, maybe at this time."

Michael finishes off his coffee. "Excuse me while I get another cup." He walks to the counter to shed some of his anger, thinking that this bitch is playing him for more money.

I don't trust her.

He returns to the table with a fresh cup of coffee and sits. "Where were we?" he says.

Kendal says, "I think Emily has something to say."

"Is it money we're talking about?" he asks.

"I had a figure in mind, but on second thought I can't go through with it. My super checks everything I do and she's always on my back."

"I don't believe this," Kendal says, about to rise from her seat. "You've known all along about your supervisor, just like I know about mine."

"I know, but I'm afraid I'll slip up."

"Then what about Dennis?" Kendal asks. "Is he interested?"

"He's very interested," she says. "He really needs the money. Denny works at a Veteran's Home, has complete control over a dozen vets. His super stays mostly in her office."

"Can he be trusted?" Michael asks.

"Of course. He's willing to participate for the right amount of money," she says.

"I'd like to meet him," Michael says.

Emily reaches for her coffee and stands. "I'll call you, Kendal," she says, without looking at Michael, and leaves.

"There's something about that red-head's attitude. She's crafty. I don't like her, nor do I trust her. Mark my word. She's going to ask for money at one point, or she's going to the authorities."

Kendal frowns. "Wait a minute. You're not thinking they're in cahoots?"

"I most certainly do. They're playing us. Tell me more about her."

She hesitates. "Emily and I were just acquaintances in nursing school. We never hung out together. She's kind of a loner. I heard she had a rough childhood. An alcoholic stepfather beat her and her mother. I couldn't help but feel sorry for her."

Michael shakes his head. "She knows too much about us now." He inhales a deep breath. "She's trouble."

Chapter 34

Around nine-thirty that evening, Emily Joyce has just finished cleaning up after dinner when the doorbell rings. She wonders who it might be.

Probably Dennis, she thinks. *He's always in a hurry and likes to take charge.*

Emily moves to the door and opens it. Dennis is standing there.

"What do you want? We're not meeting until tomorrow."

"I couldn't wait. What did you tell Kendal and that researcher, what's his name?"

"Dr Mordecai. I told them what we discussed. I played hard to get and that you needed the money."

"Good. I'll try to get as much as I can. Got too many bills," he says.

"You spend too damn much money. That's your problem."

"Look who's calling the kettle black," he says. "And who's always asking me for money?"

"Don't I always pay it back?"

"Okay, okay. How much do you think this doc would be willing to pay me?"

"We didn't discuss money. They want to meet with us first. The stage is set."

"Are you going to participate, or are you chickening out?"

She feels herself frowning. "I'm still debating, but the money sounds good."

Her cell phone vibrates on the kitchen counter. She glances at the ID. "Kendal's calling me. What should I tell her?"

"We want to meet as soon as possible."

"Hi, Kendal. Yes, Denny is here and we'd like to meet with you and Dr. Mordecai as soon as we can." She looks at Dennis.

"Tomorrow afternoon at three?" Emily says.

He nods.

"Yes, we can make it. You're welcome. See you then." She flips off her cell.

"We're meeting at McAteer's Coffee Shop. Let's get our story straight. How much are you going to ask for?"

"A thousand."

"I wouldn't push him for more."

"I'll see how we get along."

"You need to wait until you get far into the testing before asking for more," Emily says.

"This doctor is looking for subjects to test his drug. He's not going through regular channels, like the FDA. This testing is on the shady side. So we can squeeze him, or maybe threaten him that we will go to the authorities."

Emily shakes her head. "No, don't try that. You don't know what he's capable of doing. This means a lot to him and he could get mean."

"I can handle him."

"You scare me, Denny."

"Just follow my lead and keep quiet," he says as he walks to the door and opens it. See you at the coffee shop tomorrow."

Oh, Lord, you scare the hell out of me, Denny. I'm not going through with this.

Chapter 35

Ten to three the next afternoon, Michael and Kendal are sitting in McAteer's Coffee Shop at a table in the back out of the way, drinking coffee, waiting for Emily and Dennis. Minutes later, the redhead enters with a nice looking, lean, and trim guy in his late twenties, dark thick hair, baby face, dressed in a blue shirt and jeans.

"This is my friend, Dennis," Emily says to Michael.

Dennis reaches for Michael's hand. "Pleased to know you, sir."

"Likewise," Michael says, noticing Dennis' dark eyes are full of uncertainty.

Emily says, "I think you've seen Kendal before, Denny."

Dennis raises a hand and nods. "Hi, Kendal."

Kendal smiles. "Have a seat, you two."

"Care for any coffee?" Michael asks.

"No, not me," Dennis says.

"I've had plenty," Emily says.

"Well, I presume you are interested in working with us, is why you're here. How much do you know?" Michael asks.

Dennis says, "All I know is, you're a research doctor that has developed a new drug that you want tested on people without them knowing about it, and you don't want anyone else to know about it, either, is why you are wanting us to help since we deal with patients."

"That's a good start," Michael says. "Let me explain more about what is behind this." He takes a swallow of his coffee. "I've developed an anti-aging compound that has shown to be very effective in all animal testing and in humans, and has no side-effects. The reason we want your help is that you work with patients who are in the age-group we're looking for to get data to prove further how effective my drug is. I'm seeking your help because my company is dragging its feet in the process of reviewing all the scientific research I've done before making application to the FDA for permission to do human randomized controlled, clinical studies. There are many other companies working on anti-aging compounds and I want to be the first to get my drug to market to help people. So, my thinking is: with your help, I can get much more data to convince my company to move faster on the paperwork."

"How long does it usually take your company to approve your stuff?" Dennis asks.

This kid is really interested, or he's playing me.

"Months, or even a year. I don't want to wait because so many people are dying from old age diseases. They can benefit from my drug and I want to help them. And to do so, I must beat these other pharmaceutical companies to market."

That should suck him in, Michael thinks.

Dennis stares at Michael for a few moments. "I see. I really like that, Dr. Mordecai. Helping people, I mean." He turns and looks at Emily and then back at Michael. "You can count me in, sir, because I like to help people, too. That's why I work with the vets." He pauses. "Only thing though, I'd like to be paid."

"How much are we talking about?"

"How long will the testing go on?"

"Three weeks."

"I'm thinking a thousand dollars is a fair price."

Michael pauses for effect, staring at Dennis.

"I think that's fair," Michael says. "But first I'd like to visit your facility and then meet somewhere to go over the testing protocol in detail."

"I can arrange that," Dennis says, "and then we can meet in my apartment away from the Vet Center."

Michael nods. "That's a great plan."

"Can I get the money up front?" Dennis asks.

"I can bring the money with me when I come to your apartment after I inspect your workplace."

"Good enough," Dennis says. "My shift this week is eight to four. I finish my meds around eleven. We can meet after that."

"What if I come before eleven and you can show me around and then we can go for lunch."

"I'd like that," Dennis says. "I may tell the staff when they see us together that you are my uncle from St. Louis. Is that ok?"

"Agreed." Michael turns to Emily. "What about you?"

"From what I've learned here and how Denny can show you around, I couldn't do that. My super is on the floor my whole shift and watches me at every turn. She's a witch." Emily sighs. "I wish I could help. I really need the money."

"When does your super go on vacation?" Kendal says.

"I don't know. I can't remember when she went last."

"Maybe you could break her leg. Accidently, of course," Michael says in jest.

Emily frowns.

"Oh, Emily, he's just kidding," Dennis says.

They laugh but Emily still looks puzzled.

Michael gets up as does Kendal. "I'll see you tomorrow morning, Dennis," he says as they step away.

"Yes, sir. Thanks."

Outside of the coffee shop, the traffic is heavy but only a few people walk past them. Dennis stops in the middle of the sidewalk, grabs Emily by the arm. "What's wrong with you?"

She pulls away from him and begins walking toward his car. "You get all the breaks," she says. "You really hit it off with the doc."

"When I heard he wanted me to help people with his drug, I really wanted in. For a moment I forgot about the money because I really like my vets. They're great people and maybe his drug will really give them a new lease on life."

She doesn't say another word until they reach his car. "I've never seen you like this. Caring for other people. You really do like what the doc wants you to do."

He nods. "Him wanting to help people got to me."

"Well, you're now in a good position to earn a thousand. I need to find a way to get some of his money, too."

"How are you going to do that if you're afraid of your super?" he asks.

She shrugs. "I don't know. But I'll find a way."

"You cautioned me about pushing the doc," he says, "Be careful how you go at it."

Chapter 36

Roark hangs up her desk phone.

"Boss, Nora has something for us on the lake vic."

"I'm on my way." He walks away from the crime board and out of the squad room. Dr. Philips is at her desk reading a file. There are no bodies under white sheets.

"You have something for us on the vic, Nora?" he says.

She looks up. "Sure have. I sent his prints and DNA to the FBI. A friend I know there helped me get results quickly."

"Appreciate that. What do you have?"

"For starters, the vic's name is Alan Borowitz, born in New Jersey, spent six years in the Navy as a corpsman, honorably discharged in Maryland, and after that, nothing. It's like he vanished. There's no record of him after his discharge."

She pages through the file. "The tox study revealed he had cocaine in his system, nothing else."

"Addict. Wonder why he came to Atlanta?" McGraw says, thinking out loud.

She shrugs. "I couldn't even guess. That's your department."

"Now that we have his name, we'll run him and see what surfaces. He had to be doing something here," McGraw says.

Philips hands him the file. "This is for you. Good luck on this one."

He reaches for it and says, "Thanks. As always, you have done more to help. Appreciate you."

She frowns as she stares at him for few seconds, and then says, "You're welcome."

McGraw enters the squad room, throws the file on his desk, and heads to the crime board. His team is watching. He writes the name *Alan Borowitz* above *Lake Victim*.

He turns to face his detectives. "Our lake victim is Alan Borowitz, he was born in New Jersey, served six years in the Navy as a corpsman and after being discharged in Maryland, he vanished. What we need to know is: why did he come to Atlanta and what did he do here?"

"He's not a scientist like postulated," Roark says. "So Keller's and Borowitz's deaths are probably not connected. Maybe they weren't killed by the same person."

"Wait a minute. Don't be so sure. Can't rule out a scientist not being the same assassin even though the two vics aren't connected," McGraw says. "What we need is more info on Borowitz to determine his involvement. Zee and I have discussed the masked man theory and concluded that he could have taken revenge on Keller and Borowitz because they tried to prevent him from accomplishing his goals."

Roark says, "Now our job is to find out what his goals were."

The boss nods. "Once we find out, we'll know what Keller and Borowitz did to go against the masked man."

"No record of Borowitz anywhere after he left the Navy," McGraw says.

"He couldn't just vanish," Kramer says.

Gomez says, "Don't corpsmen handle drugs?"

"I would say so," Roark says.

"What are you driving at, Gomez?" the boss asks, deliberately not telling them about Borowitz's tox study.

"The M.E.'s report says the vic had scars on his arms. Tells me he probably was into drugs."

Roark says, "That makes sense. He may have gotten into drugs and become homeless, which is why there are no records of his life after the Navy."

"What you say may be true," McGraw says. "Dr. Philips did a tox study, and he had cocaine in his system. So, it's a good possibility he was an addict. But what brought him to Atlanta?"

He turns to his junior detectives. "Kramer and Gomez, I want you both to run this guy down. Find out all you can on him."

Both detectives give an affirmative nod.

Chapter 37

This sunny morning around eleven, Michael pulls his white caddy into a visitor's parking space in front of the Eisenhower Veterans Center. The building is an attractive, one-story brick in a T-configuration, with pitched roofs, large windows on both sides of a canopy in the middle that covers a long concrete passageway to the glass-door entrance. The building is spread over several acres and appears to have many rooms. Under the front windows is a spread of flower gardens decoratively interspersed with greenery. Around the grounds in the front are thirty-foot shade trees.

Michael steps out, leaves his car, and walks up the passageway to the entrance. The glass doors slide open as he approaches and he enters a small lobby with a couch and two cloth side chairs resting on an oriental rug. To his right is a large window with an attendant whose head is a few feet above the sign-in counter, sitting at a desk. On his left is the administrator's office and directly ahead is a large seating area with couches, tables, and chairs. Many of the tenants are playing card games. Beyond them is a long hallway. He reports in at the window and is asked to sign the book, then asks for Dennis Murray. The twenty-something girl with chocolate brown hair lifts the phone and places a call. Five minutes later, Dennis is coming down the hallway toward him.

"Good to see you again, sir. Come this way," he says as they walk toward a few ladies playing bridge, who look up and smile at Michael as they pass and continue through the rug-covered hallway for about twenty yards. Dennis makes a left turn into a second hallway that ends perpendicularly in another one that runs to the left or to the right, forming a T configuration. Dennis makes a right turn, and they move past several rooms on both sides before entering an open area with a circular desk. Within are three ladies in white. Beyond the circular desk are more rooms on both sides of the hall.

Dennis stops at the desk and introduces Michael as his uncle from St. Louis to his supervisor and two nurses. After the pleasantries, Dennis says, "I'm going to show him around."

"We are quite proud of what we have here," his super says.

"I'm impressed so far," Michael says.

Dennis leads him to an area with a series of med carts. "I am about to give out the meds to the last of my patients," he says, "You may go along."

"I'd like that very much," Michael says.

Dennis pushes the cart through the hall to the first room on his right and they enter. A tall man who appears in his seventies is adjusting his TV with the remote, standing in front of it.

"How you doing today, Bill?" Dennis says.

"Oh, about the same. The pains never go away. Just must live with 'em."

"This is my uncle from St. Louis."

Bill looks Michael over for a few moments. "You're not one of those specialists, are you? I've had my fill of doctors. I'd just want to be left alone."

"No, sir. I'm a scientist that develops new drugs."

"I wish you'd find something for the damn aches and pains in my joints."

Michael glances at Dennis and smiles. "I got your meds, Bill," Dennis says, as he reaches for the water glass on the bedside table and hands it to Bill along with his meds.

Once finished, Dennis motions for Michael to head for the door.

"Nice meeting you, Bill," Michael says.

"Sure, sure. Me, too," he says not turning away from the TV.

Back in the hall with his cart, Dennis tells Michael that he has eleven men and one woman on this wing, and he's sure he can distribute the new drug with ease.

"I like the setup here. This is perfect."

"I'm ready when you are, sir," Dennis says.

"Can we meet tonight at your apartment? I must skip lunch."

"Sure thing." He pulls out a pad on his cart, tears off a sheet of paper and hands it to Michael. "Here's my address. It's not far from here."

"How about eight tonight?"

"That will work."

Dennis walks Michael through the halls, retracing their steps back to the entrance. "See you tonight," Dennis says.

Seven-thirty that evening, carrying his briefcase and a small box, Michael shouts to his mother that he's going out and will be back in a couple of hours. He walks to his Caddy parked in the driveway close to the garage door. Slipping in, he places the briefcase and box on the passenger seat next to him and backs out. Driving to Northeast Atlanta, he pulls into the well-lighted Avalon Apartments, looking for unit 101 on the first floor. He spots it and pulls into a parking spot, grabs his briefcase and box off the seat and steps out. He ambles up to the door that has a single light above it, knocks, and it opens.

"Come in, doc," Dennis says. "We can sit over at the kitchen table, if that's okay."

"Sure, anyplace is fine," Michael says as he moves in. The one-bedroom apartment has a spacious living room, kitchen to the right, and down a narrow hall is the bedroom on the left and bathroom on the right, with a washer and dryer against the back wall.

"Nice apartment," Michael says, "You been here long?"

"It's okay. About two years."

They move to the kitchen, pull out chairs and sit.

"Can I get you anything—water, coffee, or Coors light?"

"No, thanks. Let's get started."

Michael places the briefcase and box on the table and opens the briefcase, reaches in, and pulls out copies of the 3-week study.

Dennis reaches for the study. "What's in the box?"

"My drug you'll be administering."

Dennis nods. He begins looking over the protocol sheets.

As Dennis reads, Michael reviews the administration procedure involving a single dose of RapTOR calculated for a 160 lb. male and administered six days of each week with analysis each Sunday. Michael avoids telling him what the dosage is. He emphasizes that his med would make Dennis' patients feel twenty years younger. Dennis will observe them and record daily his observations in a research notebook that Michael reaches for in his briefcase. He re-emphasizes that the drug is very safe and can be taken with or without meals.

He tells Dennis since he can't be with him, that he must make every effort to be accurate and to record in the notebook the date and time for the daily administration of RapTOR for each patient for the six days in each of the three weeks. He will observe and record any changes in the patients every Sunday, looking for any changes in their attitude, agility, gait, or skin. Michael will come every Sunday evening to his apartment to go over his entries in the notebook.

"Do you have any questions?"

"I've never done this before. You need to show me how you'd enter information into this notebook."

"Sure." Michael reaches for the research notebook and opens it. He spends the next hour showing exactly how Dennis will structure the pages for each patient so he can enter the data for each day of the three-week study, along with his observations.

"Thanks. I think I can do it now."

"I know, you will get the hang of it once you do it for a couple of days. Just make sure you hide the notebook on your cart or somewhere where no one can ever find it."

"No problem. When will we start?"

"This Monday." He hands him the box. "There are enough doses for twelve patients in there for two weeks. I'll prepare more for the following week." He then reaches into the briefcase for an envelope and places it in front of Dennis.

"That's your money."

Dennis looks at the envelope for a few seconds and then reaches for it.

"Thank you, sir."

Michael rises and picks up his briefcase. "I'll call you Monday after five to learn how it went," he says, as he walks to the door.

"I see no problem," Dennis says. "If I need help, I'll go to my locker and call you."

Michael nods his approval as he opens the door. "You'll be fine, and expect a big change in your patients."

Chapter 38

Kramer and Gomez spend most of the day contacting dozens of homeless shelters in the city, asking if they had a resident named Alan Borowitz.

"No one I've called had him," Gomez says, turning to Kramer. "They never heard of him."

Kramer shakes his head. "Same here."

"The boss will want us to search the homeless camps," Gomez says. "You know what that means. Approaching them with caution. They could draw a knife on us."

"Yes. It's all how we approach them, making sure we remember our training. Not to scare them so they don't think they're in trouble."

"I know. "We'll say, 'You're not in trouble, we just want to talk.'"

"Great, you remember your training."

Gomez only grunts.

"We still have a couple more shelters on the list to call," Kramer says. "Maybe we'll get lucky."

"I hope so."

They continue the phone calls for the next hour.

"Kramer, Gomez," McGraw calls out from the crime board. "Any luck on Borowitz?"

"None, boss," Kramer says, "We're just finishing up."

McGraw removes Borowitz's picture from the crime board and walks over to his detectives. "Here's his pic," he says, handing it to Kramer. "I want you both to check all the homeless encampments."

Both detectives look at each other. “But boss,” Kramer says, “You know how many homeless camps there are under the bridges and overpasses?”

“Quite a few, I’d say. That’s why you’ll need to get an early start in the morning and hit ’em all. Take several days, if you must. Find out who this guy is.”

McGraw could see the disappointment in their faces. “You may find it interesting, using your training on how to interact with the homeless. Some are tight-lipped, but don’t let it get to you. Keep plugging along. Someone will talk.”

The Atlanta PD has adopted the Denver Police Department’s report, where they have identified several different groups of homeless individuals:

1. Chronically homeless Persons.

2. Persons who suddenly lost their jobs, divorced, or faced other unexpected events. These people are generally sane and rational, and usually don’t stay homeless too long.

3. Homeless persons because of their finances.

4. Young people in their teens or 20s, who go from community to community with no ties to the communities. Many don’t consider themselves as homeless. They resist services but will accept food.

The next morning at dawn, Kramer and Gomez are sitting in an unmarked black Dodge in front of a McDonald’s drinking coffee and looking at the list of homeless encampments they acquired from dispatch.

“The box of food purchased should help get these guys to open up and hopefully they won’t be afraid of us,” Gomez says.

“It should. Best that we start with bridges and overpasses on I 85,” Kramer says, sitting in the passenger seat looking over the list. “You know that DOT has put boulders where the homeless sleep to try and keep from having fires.”

“I know,” Gomez says, “but we should find some areas with homeless.” He drives off. “Here we go.”

Twenty minutes later, Gomez takes the ramp off I 85 and travels for several miles until he spots an encampment. He pulls off the road toward the center and onto the grass. They step out, taking with them the box of food. There appear to be around eight to ten men in the camp. Some are in tents and others in sleeping bags. There's a man sitting on the top of his sleeping bag leaning against a concrete pillar with his head down between his knees.

"Hello there," Kramer says. "Are you okay?"

The man looks up with apprehension in his face.

"We just want to talk," Gomez says. "You're not in any trouble."

"We have some food for you," Kramer says.

The man appears to be in his forties, long hair, unshaven, and could use a shower. He reaches for the box, takes out a sandwich, and devours it like he hasn't eaten in a week.

"What's your name?" Gomez asks.

Slow to answer, he says, "Richard."

"Richard, we are looking for a friend. His name is Alan Borowitz. Here's a picture of him," Kramer says. "Have you seen him?"

Richard is slow to reach for the picture. When he does, he takes his time, chewing his food a little before looking at the picture.

"Haven't seen him," he says, handing the picture back.

"His name is Borowitz. Have you ever heard that name?" Kramer asks.

"No."

"How long have you been here, Richard?" Kramer asks.

"Too long. Maybe a month."

"Do you need help from any of the services?" Gomez asks.

"Don't want anything to do with them," he says.

Kramer watches as Gomez walks over to another man who is just working his way out of his sleeping bag. Kramer follows him in case his partner needs help.

The man is holding the picture of Borowitz and is shaking his head. "Haven't seen him and never heard the name Borowitz."

Gomez looks at his partner and shrugs. "Let's see what the others have to say." After they've questioned everyone, they move out, walk to the car, and slide in.

"Guess Borowitz has never been in this encampment."

"On to the next camp," Gomez says.

After spending the entire day interviewing the homeless at nine different encampments, Kramer and Gomez decide it's time to quit for the day. When they are about to walk away, a tall man in his fifties approached them.

"I heard you talking about Alan Borowitz. Can I see that picture?"

"Sure thing," Gomez says handing it to him. "What's your name?"

"Benny." He stares at the pic and says, "Yeah. That's Alan. He was in our camp. I've been here the longest. These guys weren't here when Alan was with us. There are times the cops come and ask us if they can get us help. There are a lot of shelters in this town. I've been to several. Some are good and some are not. I don't like 'em. The help there act like they're better than us, and treat us that way."

"Sorry to hear that. Did you know Alan?" Kramer asks.

"We were in a shelter together once. He was on the hard stuff and finally got off. Then we came here."

"When did you last see him?" Gomez asks.

"About a month ago. We had been back from the shelter a couple of days when this lady who comes at different times to take anyone interested to her home for rehab. We heard she's very good."

"Did Alan go with her, Benny?" Kramer asks.

He nods.

"Did you ever see him again?" Gomez asks.

"Yeah, once. He was looking for the stuff." Benny shakes his head. "Bad stuff."

"Did he leave the woman's place?"

"Not really. Just looking for drugs but wasn't happy. Said some guy was treating the guys with something to make them feel younger. But Alan didn't want none of that."

"Did Alan ever say more about the guy? What he looked like?" Kramer asks.

"Naw."

"How about the woman? What did she look like and anything about her car?" Gomez asks.

"She's a kinda large woman, not very tall. The grandma type but not that old. She drives a 15-seater van."

"Did you ever hear what name she goes by?" Kramer asks.

"Donna something. It's two names but I only remember Donna."

"Would you know the year and make of the van?"

He shakes his head. "Sorry, I don't."

"If you don't mind me asking," Gomez says, "Why didn't you go with her?"

"One guy she helped told me if you go with her, you can't leave. She keeps 12 guys in her basement with pretty good facilities. He snuck out one night when her church people came to help."

"Why did he leave if she did them some good?" Kramer asks.

"He said she was too damn strict."

"Is that man in this camp?" Kramer asks.

"Naw, man. They don't stay in one place."

Gomez asks, "Did your friend ever mention what part of town she lives in?"

"The southeast side, I think."

"Thank you. Is there anything we can do for you?"

"How about some of that food you got there."

"Sure thing," Kramer says, reaching in and handing him two hamburgers and a peach pie.

"Here's a few dollars and my card," Gomez says, "If you think or hear of anything about Donna, please give me a call."

He nodded. "Thanks."

Kramer and Gomez walk over to the police unit and slide in. They sit for a few moments in silence.

"Gomez says, "We have a woman named Donna, who drives a 15-seater van and lives in the southeast part of the city. Takes 12 men to her home to rehabilitate them with the help of her church."

"That's some help," Kramer says.

"Who is the guy giving the homeless something to make them feel younger at Donna's place," Gomez says. "I never thought the homeless were given any treatment."

"Maybe they give them physicals and some over-the-counter stuff," Kramer says. "The boss will want us to call churches in Donna's area to track her down."

"If he asks, what will be our strategy in calling the churches?"

"For starters, we tell them we are looking for the lady who might be a member of their church, who helps the homeless and drives a van. If we get a hit, we tell them we are homeless and need help."

"That's good." Gomez says. "Since we're homeless and have no transportation, they'll probably want to pick us up."

There's a knock on the driver's side window. Gomez turns and Benny is standing outside. Gomez lowers the window.

"I remembered Donna's second name—Harvey. Don't know her last name."

"That's very helpful, Benny. Thanks," Gomez says.

"Oh. One other thing. Alan told me he was a corpsman in the Navy and came to Atlanta as a traveling nurse."

"That's really helpful," Gomez says. "Thanks." He raises the window. "Now we know why he came to Atlanta. What's next?"

"Let's go talk to the boss," Kramer says.

Chapter 39

Roark has finished the background checks on the Biogen researchers, Drs. Jessica York, Michael Mordecai, including Mark Rubin, the CEO, when she reaches for a sheet of paper in the printer and leaves her desk. McGraw is paging through the autopsy reports on Keller and Borowitz.

"Looking for a connection?" she asks.

"Don't know what I'm looking for. One guy is run off the road and the other is found in a lake with his body filled with cocaine and throat gashed. No connection." He looks up. "Whatta you have?"

"It doesn't help much, but here is what I've found. As we thought, the Biogen people make big bucks and live in the best areas in town. Mark Rubin lives with his wife and three boys in Brookhaven Argonne Forest. Jessica York lives alone in a home in Peachtree Heights East, and Michael Mordecai lives with his mother in Chastain Park."

"Did you know Mordecai's father was a neurosurgeon?" McGraw says.

She shakes her head. "It wasn't in the file Elizabeth gave us. Why the interest?"

"I heard about him through a church friend, but never went to him. The kind of man he was—had a reputation for being personable, and caring for his patients, had a great bedside manner."

"Many children don't follow their parents' footsteps," she says, "if that's what you're driving at."

"It's not that. I've been thinking more about Michael's personality. Children watch and learn from their parents. Most of the time the parents aren't aware of it. Something bothers me about Michael. He's nothing like his father. Remember how he introduced himself. 'Dr. Mordecai' with emphasis on the doctor part. I sensed he was putting up a front for us. Didn't you think his actions and reactions seemed too perfect?"

"Maybe a little narcissistic?"

"Little? How about cold within?"

"Boss?" Kramer calls out, as he and Gomez enter the squad room.

"They're back," Roark says.

McGraw rises and walks over to the center table. "Any luck?"

Kramer and Gomez pull chairs away from their desks and slide them to the table. McGraw and Roark pull up chairs to join them.

"What do you have?" McGraw asks, as he sits.

Kramer starts off. "We found this homeless guy who knows Borowitz. Recognized his picture and told us Alan went to a shelter. Borowitz is a druggy, got clean and then he went back to the homeless encampment."

Roark leans forward. "You mean he didn't get a job after rehab?"

"Nope," Gomez says. "According to Benny, the homeless guy, Alan came back under the bridge until a middle-aged woman named Donna Harvey picked him up with several others in her 15-seater van to take them back to her home where she has a rehab center supported by her church. Benny didn't go with Borowitz."

"Why not?" McGraw asks.

"Benny said she's too damn strict."

"Well, wouldn't she have to be with homeless guys so they'd follow her orders?" Roark asks.

Kramer shrugs, then leans back in his chair. "We learned from him that Donna Harvey housed 12 men in her basement. He thought Borowitz was still there. We didn't tell him he was dead."

"Boss, we know why Borowitz came to Atlanta," Gomez says.

"Okay? Let's have it."

"Benny said Borowitz was a corpsman in the Navy and came here as a traveling nurse."

Roark says. "So, that's why? I've been racking my brain to figure him out."

"We learned another interesting thing," Gomez says. "Benny said Alan told him some guy would come to Donna's giving the homeless men something to make them feel younger, but Alan would have no part of it."

"Boss? You have that look again. You onto something?" Roark asks.

"Many questions are flowing through my mind. Take the Mask Man as a starter. Why did he kill Borowitz, a homeless person? What was his motive? It must be different from that of Keller's, but must be related to his connection to Donna's place."

"So, you're saying the masked man could be the one administering something to the men?"

"Yes, and Borowitz must have known something more about him than just a person giving them something to make them younger, which got him killed. Lastly, this guy had to have fed coke to Borowitz before killing him, to shut him up."

Roark says, "Boss, maybe Borowitz threatened to go to the authorities."

"That's a good possibility."

"Do you think our killer is a doctor?" she asks.

"Only one way to find out."

Gomez says. "That means we gotta get into her place and find out what's going on."

"Too risky," the boss says. "Better for you two to follow Donna Harvey after she comes to her church, and then give her home the once over."

"Since our suspect has easy access to Donna Harvey's place," Roark says, "he could be spotted coming and going."

Kramer says, "Maybe he's a corpsman like Borowitz and works in a hospital or for some doc and assists Donna Harvey."

McGraw stands. "Great thinking everyone. But I don't think our killer is in the medical profession. The only way we'll find out anything is for Kramer and Gomez to call the churches in Donna's area. Tell them you need to reach her because you're homeless, and you need her help. Don't give out any more information, except what encampment you're in. Pick one before you make the calls. They may want to pick you up. Anyway, you'll know the church and you two can go there and keep watch for Donna Harvey."

"We'll start calling right away," Kramer says.

"I'll see what I can find on the 15-seater van," Roark says

An hour later, Kramer shouts, "I got a hit. Old Parkside Church. They wanted to pick me up to come to their service this Sunday."

"You need it," Gomez says.

"Look who's talking."

"Okay, guys. What'd you learn?" Roark says.

"The church secretary said Donna Harvey comes every Saturday for supplies."

"What's the plan, boss?" Gomez asks.

McGraw looks at him and then Kramer. "Go to the church and wait for Donna Harvey and follow her home."

"I knew that, boss," Gomez says.

"Well, why did you ask it, Chipotle pepper head?" Kramer says.

"For your sake, Kraut head."

"Okay guys. Back to work," Roark says, smiling.

Kramer and Gomez are parked in an unmarked black unit close to Old Parkside Church this Saturday morning around ten, waiting for Donna Harvey to come for supplies. Gomez is behind the wheel and Kramer is in the passenger seat. An hour passes.

"There's the white van," Kramer says, as it pulls up on the side of the building with a wide door and she hops out of the van.

"That's gotta be her," Gomez says. "She fits the description."

"Yeah. She looks tough."

"No wonder Benny didn't go back."

They laugh.

Donna Harvey ambles to the large door, opens it, and enters. Minutes later, two men help her load supplies into the van. When finished, she hops back into the van and takes off, Gomez following her at a safe distance. Twenty minutes later, she pulls into the driveway next to her one-story frame house. Gomez slows to a stop across the street as they watch six men help her carry supplies inside. Gomez moves past and at the end of the block, turns around and slowly moves to an open field next to Donna Harvey's and stops.

"What do you think?" Gomez says. "Should we take a look around?"

"That's why we're here," Kramer says. "To learn all we can."

They slip out and begin walking around the property. Kramer moves to the driveway and Gomez ventures through the open field close to the house.

He notices a couple of windows close to the ground and eases over to one side of the first window. He peeks in and sees a dozen or so men at tables playing cards and chess. The area looks clean and the rooms off to the side of the gathering area seem clean and neat. A fridge is near a small kitchen with a coffee stand on the counter.

The men seem happy, and the place is clean. Wonder if she is in the house cleaning business, Gomez thinks.

"Whatta you observing?" Kramer asks, as he comes up behind Gomez.

Gomez nearly jumps out of his skin. "For criminy sakes, you scared the living daylights out of me, Kraut head."

Kramer throws up his hands. "Sorry, man. I didn't mean to scare you. What's going on in there?"

"Look for yourself," Gomez says as he moves away.

"Interesting. The men seem happy enough," Kramer says. "Guess she does a good job taking care of them."

"I didn't see her," Gomez says.

Just then they hear the van backing out of the driveway.

"Let's hit it," Gomez says.

They race to the car, hop in, and speed away to catch up with her. Thirty minutes later. the van turns into the driveway of a swanky house in Chastain Park. She hops out, ambles over to the front door and enters.

"What's she doing here?" Kramer asks.

"She's dressed in a housekeeper uniform and carrying an apron. What does that tell you, big man?" Gomez says.

"It tells me you're a smart ass," Kramer says.

"I'm calling it in." Gomez opens his cell and punches in the number to Sergeant Roark.

"Sarge, we've followed Donna Harvey to Chastain Park area—"

"—Chastain Park?" Roark interrupts.

"Yeah," Gomez says.

"Wait a minute. I know that one. Hold on."

"What's up?" Kramer asks.

"The Sarge has me on hold. She didn't give me a chance to tell her it's Dr. Mordecai's home."

She returns and says, "That's Dr. Mordecai's residence."

"Donna Harvey is dressed like a maid and has gone into the house,"

Gomez says. "Kramer thinks there's a connection here."

"Hold on," she says. Seconds late she returns, again. "The boss wants you guys to come in, pronto."

"Mordecai. That's damn interesting."

"Why?"

"Because he is probably involved with her?"

"Why would you say that? She's just his maid. What do you think he's involved in?"

"The boss seems to feel Mordecai is up to no good. You know how the boss's sixth sense works."

"I know," Gomez says. "But we don't have anything on him that could tie him to her yet."

"You're probably right. But now maybe we do."

"Have you ever known me to be wrong?" Gomez says.

"Most of the time," Kramer says, and laughs.

"We gotta get back."

Thirty minutes later, Gomez maneuvers the cruiser into the APD parking lot. On the way to the entrance, they meet up with Larry, the assistant M.E.

"You guys been out screwing up crime scenes again?"

"No, we leave that up to you," Kramer says as Larry opens the door for them.

"After you, detectives," he says, as he waves them in, bowing.

"Whatta you want?" Gomez says. "You're never this nice."

"C'mon guys. You know I'm always nice. Don't forget you'd never solve a case without us."

"What do you want, a pat on the back?" Gomez says.

"Aw, be nice to him, partner," Kramer says. "He feels lonely, not able to talk to the stiffs in the morgue."

"Okay, guys. That's it. I'm not gonna be Mr. Nice evermore."

"Don't go away mad," Gomez says as he and Kramer head to homicide, laughing.

They enter the squad room.

McGraw is at the crime board writing the names Donna Harvey and Michael Mordecai on the board. He turns and looks at his junior detectives.

"So, Donna Harvey is also Mordecai's maid?" McGraw asks.

"Yeah," Gomez says. "Looks that way."

"This may be farfetched, boss, but he could be involved in some way," Kramer says.

"Go on."

Kramer shrugs. "I don't know, it's just how you think, boss. You mentioned earlier that Mordecai seemed too perfect and when Donna Harvey went to his house, I thought is there more to them?"

"Good thinking," McGraw says.

Gomez adds. "I have an idea that ties into that. Why don't we go up to her door after she leaves. Maybe one of the homeless guys will open it."

"That's possible. Someone must be in charge when she's gone," Roark says. "How would you approach him?"

"I'd say, 'I'm looking for Alan Borowitz,'" Kramer says. "'I'm his brother and was told he may be here.'"

"What if he says 'No Alan here?'" Roark says.

"Then I'll ask if he knows how I can reach him?"

Gomez adds. "Kramer could also say he heard Alan was treated for something there and did he know who treated him. Maybe we can be treated, too, and could he give us a name."

"Go for it. I think it's time, but only you, Kramer, go to the door," McGraw says.

Kramer looks at Gomez and raises his eyebrows a few times.

"That would be wise," Gomez says. "Kramer looks like Borowitz."

They laugh.

The next morning, Kramer and Gomez head out to Donna Harvey's house dressed in shabby clothing. When they arrive, the van is still in the driveway.

"Son of a gun," Gomez says. "I was hoping she'd be gone by now."

"I have this feeling," Kramer says.

"What feeling?"

Kramer shakes his head. "Something tells me this isn't gonna be easy, and it may take a while."

"You never know. We might get lucky and some good guy comes to the door and gives us what we want."

"What if the guy won't talk?"

"Then we go and come back another day and maybe a new guy comes to the door."

"You're forgetting how tight-lipped these homeless guys are. They trust no one."

"We'll, we're gonna find out. There she goes."

After the van is out of sight, Kramer hops out and goes along the sidewalk and up four steps to the porch. He knocks on the door. No answer. He knocks again. This time he pounds on the door.

Nothing.

He turns and looks at Gomez sitting in the driver's seat of the unmarked black car. Kramer shrugs.

Gomez motions for him to keep knocking.

Kramer pounds the door and after a few minutes, it opens and a brawny middle-age guy with thin hair that needs combing and a four-inch white beard, scowls at him.

"Whatta, you want?" he says irritated.

Kramer thinks the guy is upset because he had to get up from his game.

"I'm looking for my brother. His name is Alan Borowitz. I'm told he could be here."

"No! Him not here!"

"Do you know him?"

"Yeah. I know him at encampments. He here but left."

"Guess you don't know where he went?"

"Nope." He was about to close the door.

"Please. Just one more thing. Did you know the man that came here to give you guys something to make you feel younger? My brother told me about him, but didn't give me his name. I need to get some of that stuff."

"Him don't come here no more."

"Did he give you the medicine?"

"Naw. That before I came. The guys told me good stuff. I want some."

"So, he doesn't ever stop by?"

"Whatta, I say!"

Kramer holds up his hands. "Sorry. It's just I need some. I'm not in good health."

"You ask the lady when she come back. She knows."

"Is there anyone else here that took his medicine?"

"Naw. They gone. I go!" He slams the door in Kramer's face.

"Shit!" Kramer walks back to the car and slides in.

"I can tell from your body language; you didn't get anything out of that twerp."

"Nope. He talks goofy. Must be on something. We'll have to try again in a couple of days. Maybe someone else will open the door."

Chapter 40

Around seven-thirty this Monday morning, Dennis hurries through the passageway to the entrance carrying the small box with RapTOR. The glass doors open as he approaches and enters the Eisenhower Veterans Center for his morning shift, continuing down the hall to his locker. Today is the first day he will administer Dr. Mordecai's drug, and he's rather excited; especially to see how it works on old Bill, who he's taken a special liking to. Bill is a Vietnam veteran who earned a bronze star for bravery.

After changing into whites, Dennis reaches for a white towel from his locker and wraps it around the box and walks out and down the hall to the circular desk and reports in. He looks over the records of all his patients to check for any instructions or comments from the night nurse. Not much this time. Bill is still complaining about his pain, but the doc doesn't want him addicted to pain killers, so he's prescribed Tylenol. Dennis walks over to the row of med carts and slips the box under the first shelf, and then pushes the cart over to the med closet where he gets the meds for his patients. All bottles have the patients' names and room numbers on them.

After thirty minutes of filling the twelve individual vials with their meds, Dennis moves his cart down the hall where his patients are housed. He has six men on one side and one woman and five men on the opposite side. He stops the cart next to Bill's room and looks around. No one. He reaches for the box, opens it, pours out 12 capsules of RapTOR, one for each of his twelve patients.

Dennis carries two med cups into Bill's room, who is in his recliner half asleep. The TV is off.

"What's wrong with the TV, Bill?"

He looks up. "Oh, the damn thing has been acting up. Sound went off. It's like pulling teeth to get anyone around here to help you."

"Once I give you these, I'll take a look at it." He pours water into Bill's glass and hands it to him, and then pours Bill's meds into his hand.

"I appreciate it. My program comes on soon." Bill swallows his capsules. Dennis' patients never look at their meds, they just take what he gives them.

Dennis checks the TV and finds the problem is in the remote. Bill has pushed the mute button and didn't know it. Dennis shows it to him and explains if it happens again to push the button in the middle row and the sound should come back on.

"Thank you, son. You're the best."

"Need anything else, Bill?"

"Naw. I'm okay now. Thanks."

"Sure thing."

Dennis closes the door and pushes the cart across the hall to Maxine's room. He reaches for her cup of meds and adds one RapTOR.

Maxine is a seventy-nine-year-old nurse who served in Vietnam. She's the only women vet on his floor. She's thin and somewhat frail and slow, but has spunk, and is always very positive.

"How are you today, Maxine?" he says as he pushes his way into her room.

She is standing at the window looking out. Turns around and says, "Oh, doing okay as always. But better when I see you."

"Aw, you're sweet."

"You got my drugs?"

"Right here," he says, holding up the plastic cup.

She reached for her glass of water, holds out her hand, and throws them into her mouth and washes them down with a glass of water.

"Can I get you anything before I leave?"

She moves over and whispers. "Can you get me a chocolate ice cream cup?"

"For you, sweetie, anything. I'll be right back."

Dennis goes out to the circular desk area where there is a goodie stand for the patients. He searches through the cooler of vanilla, strawberry, and finds a chocolate cup. He enters Maxine's room with the cup of ice cream and a small spoon.

"Here you are, dear."

"You're an angel."

"That's what my mother always said."

They laugh. "Well, you know mothers are always right."

"I'll be on my way. Have a great day."

For the next several hours, Dennis finishes his rounds of meds with all his patients.

At the end of the first week, Dennis and Michael meet in Dennis' apartment on Sunday and review his research notebook and discuss the outcome of RapTOR. Dennis reports that he's surprised at the difference in his patients after just one week. They are in good spirits and seem spryer.

"I'm excited, doc."

"You should be. You are helping your patients, and your notebook is well maintained. Congratulations."

"I can't wait to see what happens next week."

"Just don't get impatient. You'll see wonders the next two weeks."

Chapter 41

For the next week, Dennis observes additional improvement in his patients, especially in walking and attitude. They seem more alert and happier.

On Friday of the second week, Dennis goes to his locker and calls Michael. "Dr. Mordecai, I couldn't wait until Sunday to tell you. I'm seeing great changes in my patients."

"Great news, Dennis. But be careful that in your excitement you don't forget and tell someone. Keep our tests quiet and go about your business as usual, making sure you record every detail."

"Okay, doc. But I'm really excited for my patients. They're family."

On Sunday, of the second week, they meet in Dennis' apartment again and go over the data.

"Dennis, these are excellent results. Your patients are demonstrating a better attitude, better dexterity, clearer skin, and much less joint pain."

"My patients are happier and feel so much better about themselves. They don't know what's happening to them. What will happen after next week, doc?"

"I'm going to let you discover that for yourself. I'm not supposed to prejudice the data by giving you any information."

"I see. That has something to do with your method of treatment, right?"

"Yes. We're not using any control group, but that's not necessary for what I want. The changes in your patients will be enough to get my drug through the channels I want."

Chapter 42

On Sunday of the last treatment week, Michael is reviewing all the data for each patient for the three-week study that Dennis has collected. He quietly turns the pages and is in deep concentration. Dennis sits at the end of the table in his apartment watching, wondering what Dr. Mordecai's thinking.

Finally, Michael looks up and says, "From your description of their sitting, standing, and walking, it appears RapTOR causes increased muscular strength."

"That's good, right, doc?"

"It's damn good, Dennis. We've seen it in other patients but not to this degree."

"What are you thinking, doc?"

"RapTOR is going to be a great drug for slowing aging."

"What's next?" Dennis asks.

"I need to test RapTOR in one more group. Do you think you can get Emily on board?"

"Don't know. She's not a strong person. Too easily manipulated."

"If we had twelve more patients, I could end my study. Do you know of anyone else that could help us besides Emily?"

"I have a friend at the Center who has the same type of job as me, but works in a different wing. I could approach him."

"When you ask him, don't tell him you've done a study with me. Just tell him that you know me and about my work at Biogen and you are looking for persons to help me in a new drug trial. If he's interested, then we must meet."

"I can do that. What about Emily?"

"I'll wait to see what you find out from your friend. By the way, what's his name?"

"Tommy Evans. He's very good at what he does. Has received awards from his section leader."

"This wraps it up for us. I appreciate all you've done, Dennis."

"Is there a finder fee, if Tommy decides to do the study?"

"You bet. I appreciate what you'd done. If Tommy comes on board, you'll get another big one."

"Oh geez, doc. That's great. Thanks!"

Chapter 43

Emily Joyce has been stressing all day in her apartment since she talked to creditors that have been hounding her for payments the last two days. She has maxed out two credit cards and is past due on payments to two lending agencies. She is still in her PJs feeling depressed and stressed out, while trying to relax on the couch. She is having trouble sleeping.

Why did they lend me the money? Those idiots knew my credit was bad. It's their fault for taking a chance with me. What am I going to do?

Her cell vibrates on the coffee table.

"Emily. This is Dennis."

"I know it's you."

"Hey! What's up with the attitude?"

"I guess you're calling to gloat over your work with the doc."

"Well, I thought you'd be happy to know the study ended good, and the doc needs another twelve patients. I told him Tommy might help. Doc Mordecai said I'd get another thousand if Tommy comes on board."

She snorts. "Damn you! You get all the breaks. I need some of that money."

"Not any of mine," he says,

"You jerk head. I meant some of the doctor's money."

"Hey, don't get on your high horse with me. I can't help it if you were too chicken to join us."

"Oh. So now you're big buddies with him?"

"What's wrong with you? He's a pretty good guy."

She disconnects and punches in Kendal's number.

"Hi, Emily. What's up? I'm about to hit the sack."

"I've been thinking about ways I can help the doc. I'm desperate. I really need to earn some money."

"I don't know how, Emily. If you can't participate in any study, Dr. Mordecai has nothing else for you to do."

Silence.

"Emily? You there?"

"Yes. I've been thinking. Biogen wouldn't be too happy to learn what Dr. Mordecai is doing, would they?"

"Emily! What are you saying? You aren't threatening us, are you?"

She sighs. "I was just thinking, it might be of interest to him, if his studies were kept under wraps."

"I don't like the sound of this, Emily. You aren't saying you'll go to the authorities, are you?"

"I just thought he'd be willing to pay out some cash."

"Emily. You sound different. What's wrong?"

She started crying. "I'm in a bad way. My bills have mounted up and now they're after me."

"I'm sorry, but I thought we could trust you. Dr. Mordecai is working to keep people forever young with his new drug."

"But isn't he going about it the wrong way? His company would be unhappy with him, I'm sure."

"I'll tell him what you said, Emily. But I can tell you, he won't like it."

"Tell him a couple thousand would be nice hush money."

Kendal hangs up on her.

Chapter 44

Michael, working at his desk in his home office, is shaken out of his thoughts about having Tommy join their group to treat his patients with RapTOR, when his cell vibrates on his desk.

It's Kendal.

"Yes. What is it?"

"You're not going to like this. Emily called threatening to go to Biogen or the authorities if she doesn't get two thousand dollars from you."

Silence.

"Michael, did you hear what I said?"

He's fuming. "I did. Just wait a damn minute. I'm thinking." After a few seconds, gaining his composure, he says, "I'll try and convince her to accept my offer."

"I don't know, Michael. She's adamant about two grand, and sounded a little crazy."

"Let me handle it, okay? I'll get back with you." And hangs up on her.

Seconds later, he jumps up in a storm of rage thinking about that bitch, Emily. Walks over to the liquor cabinet, pours himself a three-finger scotch, downs half of it, returns to his desk, and sits. He twirls the glass for several minutes, then finishes it off. He gazes at the dagger sticking out of the neck of the victim in the wall painting. Slowly, as in a dream, the man's face transforms into Emily's. Michael shudders and reaches into his desk drawer for his burner phone.

"Hello."

"Dennis. This is Dr. Mordecai."

"Hi, doc. What's up?"

"I understand Emily is distraught over not being able to participate in our project, and wants money because she feels she introduced you to us and if she doesn't get any money, she's going to the authorities. As you know we're working very hard to save lives with my drug, and need more time and more patients to test it further, but Emily is threatening to stop this project."

"She can be a pain, doc. It's an honorable thing you're doing."

"Since you both are more than friends, could you reason with her? I'm willing to pay her a thousand dollars."

"That's fair, doc. I can convince her. Don't worry."

"Tell her I'll bring the money tomorrow evening around eight."

"Sounds great. I'll call her now and get back with you. How do I reach you?'

"I'll call you. Do you think an hour would give you enough time?"

"It won't take that long. But you can call me in an hour."

"Thanks. You're a champ."

Michael heads to the liquor cabinet when he hears his mother calling him.

"Michael," his mother calls out. "Can you help me?"

"Not now, mother. I'm busy. "

I'm planning to kill someone.

"I need help, I've fallen."

Damn you. She always needs something.

He walks into the kitchen. Gail has slipped out of her wheelchair and is sitting on the floor. "I was getting ready to make me some tea and slid out of my chair."

He gets behind her, moves his arms under her arm pits and pulls her up into the wheelchair.

"Thank you, son. Would you like some tea?"

"I'm busy right now," he says in a gruff voice.

He hurries back to his office and flops into his high-back chair, reaches for the burner phone and calls Dennis.

"Good news, doc."

"What did she say?"

"She'll take the thousand but really wants two. She'll meet with you tomorrow evening at eight."

"Thanks, Dennis. I owe you."

Chapter 45

Michael rises early the next day and takes an uber to Bob's used car lot. He has the driver pull up to the curb where he steps out and slowly walks through the lot, stops when he sees a black Chevy Malibu in fair condition. At the far end of the lot is a small shack with one door. Out comes a short portly man in his sixties with gray hair and dark hard rim glasses, wearing a sport coat that he couldn't button around his bulging waist. After some haggling, Michael pays the man cash and drives out in the 2002 Malibu without signing any papers. When he's done dealing with Emily Joyce, the Malibu will end up where the Land Rover was taken, to the crushing mill.

Earlier on the way to Bob's used cars, Michael thought about going to Emily's apartment complex after getting a vehicle, to survey the area, but decided against it. Someone might spot him and remember the vehicle and he can't take that chance.

That evening coming out of his home, Michael looks up to the heavens, pleased that there is little moonlight.

I must be living right, he thinks.

He backs the Malibu out of the garage. It looked nastier parked in there next to the red corvette he just bought. He drives to the east end of Atlanta and flips off his lights when he enters Emily's apartment complex. Her unit is in the back where the only lighting in the parking area is dim, probably set to keep bright lights from entering the first floor windows. Thankfully, her unit is on the first-floor behind a flight of stairs that rises to the second level. He pulls into a space next to the staircase, shuts down the Malibu.

He looks at his trophy on the passenger seat—his dagger with a seven-inch curved blade, and a decorative handle made of natural bone and featuring a decorative hand-carved motif of a lion. The blade is made of stainless steel, famous for its sharpness and rust resistance. He paid $1500 for it at one of the gun shows he and grandpa Oscar attended. The genuine leather sheath lies next to it.

He reaches for the bone handle and puts the dagger in the special inside pocket of his sport coat. He's about to slide out when headlights flash over him as a pickup races around the corner of the building. He ducks down and waits a few seconds before lifting his head to look out the passenger window. The vehicle pulls in at the end of the building and a man and woman jump out and rush into the end apartment carrying what looks like pizza boxes.

Michael steps out of his vehicle, eases the car door shut, and stands close to the Malibu as he cautiously looks around. No one. Just a few lights coming from the first-floor units.

He moves to apartment 95 and knocks.

An eye appears in the peep hole.

The door opens.

Standing inside is Emily dressed in sweats. "Dr. Mordecai. Come in." She closes the door behind him. "You got the money?"

"Right here," he says patting the dagger in the inside pocket of his sport coat.

Emily turns her back on him and walks toward the center of the living room without saying a word.

Michael is seething.

Who do you think you are, turning your back on me? No one gets the upper hand on me. You little extortionist.

Quickly, he reaches for the dagger and moves in behind her. With his left hand, he firmly grabs her around the mouth but she bites his hand and struggles, scratching his hands and pulling on his hair.

Damn you. You aren't going anywhere.

He has a headlock on her and swiftly swings the dagger around and punctures her throat a couple of times.

This drives Michael insane. As she falls on the floor, he drops to his knees next to her body, and like a wild man, he stabs her several times. Blood spatter is over the couch and overstuffed chair close to the coffee table. Michael's hand is bleeding a little from Emily's bite. He puts pressure on it using his handkerchief.

He looks at the lifeless body lying on the floor in a pool of blood.

You got what you deserved. Bitch!

He slips into latex gloves, which he didn't put on earlier so not to draw attention. He looks over his clothes. Lots of blood on the front of him but he doesn't care. He eases to the door, dims the light at the wall switch, and slowly opens the door. He glances out but sees no one; slowly moves out and opens the trunk of the Malibu; reaches in for the large, black lawn bags and duct tape and returns to the apartment.

He kneels at the body and begins slipping Emily's feet into one bag, pulling it up to her waist. Then, he slips the second bag over her head and pulls it down to her waist where it meets the other lawn bag. He reaches for the duct tape and begins wrapping it around the body, sealing the two bags together.

With gloves there will be no latent prints on the tape, he thinks.

It took nearly all the tape to seal it the way he wanted it. Knowing her body would eventually give off gases, he didn't want her rising to the surface, so he punched holes in the covering with his dagger.

Michael looks around the apartment to make sure nothing is left to connect him to the place. Once satisfied, he pulls Emily's body to the door, opens it, and checks outside. No one. He lifts her body, carries it to the car, throws her into the trunk like a piece of trash, and eases the lid shut. He hurries back to close the door and darts back to the car. Once inside, he inhales a deep breath, feeling proud of himself.

Another one out of the way.

Michael starts the engine and drives out of the complex slowly so not to draw attention. He drives toward East Lake. Thankfully, it is pitch black out. Once inside the familiar park area, he follows the narrow road for a second time down to the shore. There's a little reflection of moon light on the surface of the water. He hops out and opens the trunk. He lifts Emily's body out, drops her to the ground and slams the lid shut, then rolls her to the edge of the lake and pushes her in. Back in the Malibu, he removes his gloves and reaches in the back seat for his Frankenstein mask and pulls it over his head.

Really no need for it, he thinks.

But he couldn't take a chance racing, out of the park into the brightly lit street, that someone might see him.

Chapter 46

Dennis arrives at Emily's apartment around seven for their dinner date, pulls into an open spot, slips out and walks up to her door. He is eager to learn if she accepted the doc's offer. He called several times during the day but couldn't reach her. He knocks several times. No response. He looks around but doesn't want to call out her name. He reaches into his pocket for the key she gave him and opens the door. The place is pitch black. He guides his hand in next to the wall and flips on the dining room lights.

"Oh, my God."

Stunned. He stands frozen in his tracks.

Blood covers the wool carpet and there's spattering on the couch and chair. Horror overtakes him as his mind races with visions of what could have happened. He tries to steady himself.

Something bad has happened to Emily.

He listens, fearing the killer might still be in the apartment. No sounds. Then he eases down the hall toward the bedroom, fearful that someone will jump out at him, but he must know if Emily is in there? He inhales deeply as he slowly opens the bedroom door, an inch at a time, fearful of what he might see. He flips on the light. The bed is still made. Nothing is out of place. He turns, terrified that the killer may still be somewhere. But where? He rushes to the door and steps outside.

He reaches for his cell, calls 911, barely able to speak. After several deep breaths, he's able to tell the operator his name, the address of the Millsaps Apartment Complex, and Emily's apartment number. He describes the scene, and reports his girlfriend missing. The operator asks if he touched anything or did anything that could contaminate the crime scene. He told her he only flipped on the living room wall light and walked down the hall and back outside. She told him officers are on the way, to stay put. He waits outside with the door open, shaking.

Poor Emily. Who did this to you? Surely not the doc, he's too kind.

Two patrol cars with strobes flashing race into the lot. Two officers bail out. Two other patrol cars with lights flashing enter. In minutes, the place is swarming with cops and the renters are popping out of their units like roaches, wondering what all the commotion is.

An officer approaches Dennis and introduces himself as Sergeant Williams and asks if he's Dennis Murray.

"I am."

The sergeant glances inside. "Did you touch anything?" he asks.

Dennis shakes his head. "Just looked in and saw all this. I walked around the blood to check her bedroom. I'm afraid for my girlfriend, Emily Joyce."

The sergeant doesn't say anything, concentrating on the scene.

"Look at this place, officer. Something terrible has happened to my girlfriend."

"When did you see her last?"

"Several days ago. Talked to her day before yesterday and made the date for tonight.

"Come with me. He places Dennis in the backseat of the patrol car with an officer standing by.

McGraw gets a call from dispatch. He frowns as he listens intently and writes down the information. "No body?" McGraw says. "Notify forensics to meet us there. We're getting a search warrant and then heading out there."

He turns to his team.

"Got a possible homicide at the Millsaps Apartment Complex with no body." He hands the slip of paper to Kramer. Get a warrant from Judge Virtue. You know the ropes."

"Yes, boss, we're on our way.

He looks at Roark. "Let's roll."

As they hurried out, Roark says, "'Let's roll,' again? You must love that."

"I thought you'd like it."

They laugh.

McGraw slides into the driver's side of the Silverado and Roark hops in the passenger side and they head out of the APD lot. At the Millsaps Apartments, they pull up to the yellow tape and hop out. Uniforms have locked down the scene and some are questioning a few renters, who gawk at the detectives as they walk up.

"How you doin', Detectives," the sarge says, as McGraw and Roark approach the apartment.

"We're okay, sarge," Roark says as she and McGraw sign in, and then head to the door and look in.

"Plenty of blood," Roark says.

The sarge says, "No body, lots of blood, the tenant is a 25-year-old named Emily Joyce. Her boyfriend, Dennis Murray, called it in. He's in the back of my patrol car. Said he came here for their dinner date and had only talked to her a couple of days ago. Someone must have really had it in for her. Of course, no one saw anything."

"That figures," McGraw says. "Thanks."

"You bet, Lieutenant."

Two forensics vans pull up. Workers hop out dressed in white protective uniforms with hoodies. Chris, the forensic super, leads the team into the apartment with all their equipment. Kramer and Gomez pull their vehicle in next to the vans and hop out. Kramer hands the warrant to the boss.

"Thanks. See what you guys can get out of the tenants on the first floor as a start."

They move through the uniforms who are talking to a couple and then begin their own canvassing, making their way through the gawkers asking them questions.

McGraw and Roark walk over to the patrol car. He opens the door, bends down to look at Dennis, who looks scared out of his wits, and is twisting his hands together.

"I'm Detective McGraw and this is Detective Roark. You okay?" he asks.

"I don't know. Someone has really hurt my girlfriend."

"When did you see her last?"

He's slow to respond. "We talked several days ago. We…we made plans to go out tonight." He wipes his face with his handkerchief. "She didn't answer my texts or my calls today."

"Did you guys have an argument?" Roark asks.

"No. No way."

"Do you know anyone who would want to harm Emily?" McGraw asks.

"She wasn't a very sociable person. Liked to be alone a lot." He sighs. "No, I don't know anyone who would want to do this to her."

"Can we call someone to be with you?" McGraw says.

"My father is on his way. How long will you keep me?"

"This is Detective Roark. She'll stay with you. We'll have to take you to the station."

"I guess from TV I'm a suspect. Those closest to the person, isn't that right?"

"We need to talk more," McGraw says, as he walks away. He hears the vacuum sweepers going in Emily's apartment as he walks over to it. Chris, the forensic super, can be seen through the open doorway.

The rule followed in every crime scene is: Do not touch, alter, move, or transfer any object at the crime scene unless it is properly marked, measured, sketched and/or photographed.

Chris greets McGraw. "Lieutenant."

"Chris."

"My guys are working the back rooms, and they've swept through this room and have finished bagging and cataloging all items. We've finished processing the blood, so you can come in."

"Thanks."

Roark comes up behind him. "I put Gomez with Dennis Murray."

He and Roark move into the living room. They see flashes of light in the back rooms coming from the photographers. The detectives walk the room looking for evidence that could tell them what took place. Was there a struggle? Blood spatter on the couch indicates the vic could have received several wounds.

Roark follows McGraw around the living room, gazing at the pool of blood. It's the largest room in the apartment, with a built-in bookcase on the left wall and an open kitchen to the right. The hallway leads to a bedroom and bathroom. Emily Joyce seemed to be an animal lover. She had elephant ceramics all over—in the bookcase and on side tables.

Elephants are large strong animals. Maybe they gave her strength, McGraw thinks.

"She sure loved elephants," Roark says.

"I get the feeling she was a little on the weak side," McGraw says. "Maybe the animals gave her strength."

"Oh, I forgot you had a few courses in psychology."

"Now, don't be a smarty pants."

"Oh, forgive me, bright one."

"Concentrate Sergeant Roark," he says, followed with a big smile.

"I guessed that's why we're here. Lots of blood for starters."

"Very observant, Detective Sergeant."

She punches him on the shoulder.

"Down to work," he says.

An hour passes and Chris says, "It's all yours, Lieutenant. We've completed our work here; so, you can play around like you always do."

"Do me a favor, Sarge. Thank your guys for trampling over the place and moving things around so I can't solve the case."

"Touché, Lieutenant."

They laugh.

McGraw and Roark begin exploring all the rooms.

"Tough without a body," Roark says.

"We'll have to rely on forensics," McGraw says.

Silence.

"What are you thinking, Noah," she asks.

"Doubt if forensics will find any other prints than those from Emily and her boyfriend."

"DNA is shed easily from the body and may be helpful," she says.

"I'm thinking blood evidence. The killer is probably a male, so if in the blood analysis they find a Y chromosome, found only in males, then our hunch would be correct."

"Oh, yes, that's a start," she says.

Chapter 47

The next morning, McGraw and Roark enter the squad room. He goes to the coffee stand as he does every morning. Last evening, he and Holly had discussed the Emily Joyce case, but nothing surfaced that gave them a lead.

At the coffee station the boss fills his Braves cup and looks over at Gomez, who is talking to Dennis Murray, whom he brought in for his nine o'clock follow-up interview. Gomez moves him into interview room one.

"Have a seat. Lieutenant McGraw will be here shortly. Would you like something to drink?"

"Can I have a Dr. Pepper. Not much for coffee."

"Sure."

Gomez returns with a can of Dr. Pepper. "Are you okay?" Gomez asks.

"A little scared about what's going to happen to me."

"Hey, man. As I told you. Nothing's going to happen if you're innocent."

"Thank you, officer," Dennis says, "for being nice to me." He takes a swallow of his drink.

"Do you have your cell phone with you?"

He nods and reaches in his pocket for it.

Gomez hands him a sheet of paper. "Sign this waiver allowing us to check it out. It's standard procedure."

After signing the waiver, Dennis hands his cell to Gomez.

Gomez steps out and sees McGraw coming from the chief's office. He walks over to him and says, "Boss, go easy on the kid. He's scared to death."

"I'm gonna skin him alive," he says, reaching for a yellow pad on his desk.

Gomez frowns. "Oh, boss, don't do that to me," he says, and then laughs.

Sergeant Roark reaches for the tape recorder and joins the boss as they go to the interview room.

Dennis stands as they enter.

"No need to stand, son," McGraw says. "Just relax and have a seat." Dennis looks at Roark who starts off telling him that its standard procedure to record interviews.

Dennis just stares at her. Takes another drink of his Dr. Pepper.

She flips on the recorder and states the date and time, then says, "Please state your full name and occupation."

"Dennis Charles Murray. I am a nurse working at the Eisenhower Veteran's Center."

"What is your relationship with Emily Joyce?"

"She is my girlfriend. We have been together since nursing school."

McGraw asks, "When were you two together last?"

"We only talked on the phone two days ago."

"Was she worried about anything or did anyone threaten her?"

"Not that I know of. As I told you last night, she didn't have many friends. Was raised in a bad family, went to live with her grandma when she was thirteen and stayed to herself."

"What do you mean she had a bad family?" Roark asks.

"Father a drunk, mother a whore and alcoholic. Father used to beat her and the mother. Just like on TV, a dysfunctional family."

McGraw looks at Roark and raises his brows. "We're sorry to hear that," McGraw says.

"Are her father and mother still alive?" he asks.

"Father is in prison and mother died when Emily was sixteen."

"Is there a grandma still living?" Roark asks.

"No, ma'am. Died last year. Broke Emily's heart. She was the only person that cared about Emily."

"Do you know if anyone in the apartment complex had anything against Emily?" McGraw asks. "Or did she ever say she had a run-in with anyone there?"

He shook his head. "Never had any problems with anyone." He becomes quiet. Finishes his soft drink. Looks down at his feet.

"Something you'd like to say, Dennis?" McGraw asks.

"Emily had money problems. She'd spend more than she made working at the Assisted Living Center. She was always behind on her bills and nagged me for more money and hardly ever paid me back."

"Did she get along with everyone at her work?" Roark asks.

"Yes. She's great with the patients but her supervisor is a holy terror, always on the nurses' backs because they are shorthanded, and the company won't hire more nurses."

"Do you think her supervisor had it in for her?" McGraw asks.

"Naw. She's a blow bag. Talks tough but is a weak kitten."

"Will you submit to a lie detector test and give a DNA sample?" Roark asks.

"Yes, ma'am. Whatever it takes for me to be ruled out as a suspect."

"We must verify everything."

"One more thing," McGraw says, "Give us some idea how Emily would have spent her days this past week."

He sighs. "She doesn't do much of anything. Goes to work, comes home, gets her clothes ready for the next day, same old routine. She reads a lot, loves mystery novels, but not much for TV. She really enjoys writing in her diary."

McGraw shoots a glance at Roark. *Diary*. "So, she doesn't entertain?"

He shakes his head. "As far as I know, I'm the only one that goes there."

"Yet, she had to know the person with whom she had the confrontation," Roark says.

Dennis shrugs. "I guess so."

McGraw stands. "Detective Roark will get you ready for the lie detector test and collect your DNA," he says, then opens the door and walks into the corridor and goes to the stairs in the back that lead to the lower level. The officer in the evidence room is behind a wire mesh, reading a magazine. "Lieutenant," he says jumping up.

"Josh, I'd need to check out Emily Joyce's diary and cell phone."

"Sure thing." He goes to the stacks, and seconds later, brings the items forward for McGrow to sign them out.

"Thank you."

He nods. "Your welcome, Lieutenant."

McGraw heads back to the squad room, walks over to his desk and sits.

Roark enters. "I've collected Dennis's DNA and he's now in for the lie detector test. What do you have there?"

"Emily Joyce's diary and her cell phone." He hands the phone to Roark. "Check the phone numbers, maybe she talked to the killer."

While Roark takes the phone to her desk, McGraw begins reading Emily's diary.

"Noah. Did you notice this cell has been smashed?"

"No. I didn't pay any attention to it. More interested in reading Emily's diary. Is it bad?"

"I can't open it."

"Call Kris in forensics, he has a guy that can do wonders with cells."

"Will do."

McGraw opens Emily Joyce's diary again. He skips most of the items not having any bearing on the case, until he comes to her entries about Dennis. She really likes him and admires what he does at the vet center. She wishes he would ask her to marry him. She gets mad at one point because Dennis won't lend her money."

"Noah," Holly shouts. "Have you gone deaf?"

He looks up, making a face. "What now? Can't you see I'm busy?"

"Well, excuse me, boss. Just reporting that I'm going down to forensics. Kris said they can help me."

"Well, go. You're a big girl now, and can handle it."

"I'm glad you noticed."

Noah smiles and returns to the diary.

"You're really enjoying that, aren't you."

Noah doesn't respond, just turns a page, and continues reading the entries. Emily and Dennis argue over money.

He's making a thousand dollars and won't give me any. *I'm going to find a way to get some of that money he's earning.*

The last entry gets McGraw's attention.

If I don't get any money, I'm going to the authorities.

McGraw thinks. *Who is she threatening for more money, or she'll go to the police? I must ask Dennis about this and where he made the thousand.*

"Gomez?" McGraw says. "Earlier you ran Dennis and Emily, Bring me up to date."

"Nothing that we don't already know, boss. I'll put the info on your desk."

"Go get Dennis. He should be done with the lie detector test and put him back in one. He trusts you."

"Will do."

Roark returns with Emily's cell. "Noah, that guy, Sam, is a real genius. He showed me the location of the cell towers that handled her calls, text messages, and the type of call and number dialed, and the number for an incoming call. That's more than I could take in."

"Who called her and who did she call the most?"

"The majority of the calls came from Dennis, and she made many to him. The only other calls were from and to a Kendal Wilson."

"Kendal Wilson? That's a new one. We'll ask Dennis about her. I have something else quite interesting to inquire about."

"What's that?"

"You'll have to wait. This time I want you to watch his body language when I ask him these questions. Sometimes it's better than a lie detector."

"I don't understand."

"You know the rule in homicide: Somebody always knows something. But are they going to come forward? We'll see what Dennis has to say."

Gomez has placed Dennis back in interview room once, again. He leaves when McGraw and Roark enter. Dennis rises a second time.

"Have a seat. We have more questions," McGraw says, as he places a yellow legal pad and a folder on the table.

Roark sets the recorder in front of her and says, "We'll record this session, too, Dennis." She begins by stating the date, time, and location of the session. "Please state your full name and occupation, again."

"Dennis Charles Murray, I'm a nurse at the Eisenhower Veterans Center."

McGraw removes two forms from the folder and slides one in front of Dennis, and holds the other one in his hands.

"What is this?" Dennis asks.

"Miranda. By law, I'm required to read your rights."

Dennis becomes pale looking at the form.

"I'm going to read these rights to you as required by law. You'll see on the form, there's a place for your name, date, and time. Please fill that in now."

Roark hands him a pen.

Seconds later, McGraw says, "Now, after I read each right to you, you'll initial beside each statement indicating you understand that specific right. Do you understand?"

He's slow to answer. "Yes."

McGraw begins reading the first right from his copy. He waits each time after reading the statements for Dennis to write his initials next to each one.

When done, McGraw says, "You have agreed to answer all of these questions without us making any promises of leniency or any other promises to you, and you agree we have only asked you to answer truthfully, is that correct?"

"Yes."

McGraw reaches for the forms and begins his questioning. "Do you know Kendal Wilson?"

Dennis becomes fidgety and looks down at the floor.

"Have you heard that name before," Roark says. "Emily made several calls to her."

"She's a friend of Emily's. Kendal was in nursing school with us. But the girls didn't associate much."

"Then why would she call her?" McGraw asks.

Dennis rubs his mouth and shakes his head. "I don't know."

"Is something bothering you?" Roark asks.

"No…no ma'am."

"Tell us what you know about Kendal?" McGraw says.

He doesn't look at the detectives. "Don't know much."

McGraw looks at Roark. *He's lying.*

"Emily wrote in her diary that she wanted to get some of the money like you did, and if she didn't get it, she was going to the authorities," McGraw says. "What money did you get and from whom?"

The surprise look on Dennis' face when he heard she had a diary, reveals that he knows more than he's telling them.

"I guess it's going to come out sooner or later," he says, looking at the floor and crossing his arms in front of him.

"What is?" Roark asks.

Dennis is slow to answer. "Kendal called Emily about testing a drug on her patients. Kendal had finished testing it on five of her patients, but the doc needed more patients in his study. Emily brought me into it because she was afraid of her super. We met with Kendal and the doc and I agreed to do the research, that's all."

"What kind of research?" McGraw asks.

"I tested his drug on twelve of my patients for three weeks. It's a drug to make people forever young. And it works."

McGraw glances at Roark. *Donna Harvey*, McGraw thinks.

"So, you were paid to do the testing?" Roark asks.

"Yes," he says, still looking at the floor.

"Who is this doctor?" McGraw asks.

He looks up. "Oh, do I have to give his name? He's such a good person, trying to help people."

"His name!" McGraw demands.

Dennis doesn't answer.

"Dennis! Give us his name!" Roark says with emphasis.

"Mordecai!" he shouts, still looking down.

Roark almost rises out of her chair.

"You mean, Dr. Michael Mordecai the researcher at Biogen Labs?" McGraw asks.

"Yes."

"How much did he pay you?" Roark asks.

"A thousand dollars."

McGraw knew the answer from Emily's diary.

"Why did Emily threaten Dr. Mordecai for money? Was it to keep her quiet?" Roark continues.

Dennis looks up. "Yes."

"Let me get this straight," McGraw says. "You got paid for testing Mordecai's drug on your patients, and Emily, being desperate for money, wanted to be paid hush money because what the doc was doing was illegal, and Biogen knew nothing about it. So, if he didn't pay up, she was going to the police? Does that cover it?"

Dennis nods, again. "Yes. Am I in trouble?"

"Testing drugs on patients without their knowledge or consent and not being an approved FDA clinical trial, I'd say you will be facing some serious charges." He pushes a yellow legal pad in front of Dennis and tells him to write down everything he just told them, and stands.

"Detective Gomez will come for you."

Roark waits until Dennis finishes writing down his comments and leaves when Gomez comes in.

Roark meets up with McGraw in the bullpen and says, "I really feel sorry for him."

"I know. Unfortunately, money has a way of leading people down the wrong path. Did you interpret his body language?"

"Yes. When you looked at me, I knew what you were thinking. His body language told you he was lying. I can see what you mean that body language can be better than a lie detector, if interrogation is done properly."

McGraw asks Roark, "When we discussed the hush money with Dennis, who flashed into your mind that could have hurt Emily?"

"I immediately thought—Mordecai. He surely didn't want her to go to the police."

"And you're probably right."

He calls out to Kramer, who is at his computer. "Kramer, we'll need to hold Dennis Murray. Gomez is with him."

"Yeah, boss."

McGraw turns to Roark. "I need to make a phone call. Give me a few minutes and let's all meet at the table."

Roark and Kramer go to the center table to wait.

Minutes later, The boss and Gomez return. McGraw stands at the head of the table while Roark and Kramer sit, but Gomez chooses to sit at his desk, next to them.

McGraw begins. "Sergeant Roark and I interviewed Dennis Murray, the boyfriend of the missing girl, Emily Joyce. What we've learned are the following:

A lady named Kendal Wilson recruits Dennis Murray and his girlfriend, Emily Joyce, both of whom are nurses, to participate in a clinical trial, testing an anti-aging drug on their patients without FDA approval."

Gomez raises a hand.

"I know what you're thinking, but let me finish," the boss says.

He continues. "Emily backs out of the testing part because she has a snoopy, tough supervisor and is afraid she'd find out about her testing a drug on the patients. Dennis, however, joins in and treats his twelve patients with the drug. All patients do well. He is paid a thousand bucks by a doctor who oversees the tests. Emily has money problems and is in dire need of cash.

She calls Kendal Wilson and threatens to go to the police if she isn't paid hush money. Soon after she disappears. I know you're wondering who the doctor is, so let's discuss him. Who thinks they might know?"

Gomez says, "You mentioned the doc was testing his anti-aging drug. That made me think of Donna Harvey. You remember Benny said the homeless guys at her house were given something by a man to make them feel younger."

"So, Donna Harvey's involved," Kramer says

"And whose home did we see her go into?" Gomez asks.

Kramer answers. "Dr. Mordecai."

"He's our doc," Gomez says.

"Before we started this meeting, I called my lawyer friend, Gary Apoian, and asked him what are the consequences of anyone testing a drug on his patients in a trial not approved by the FDA, and without the patient's knowledge or consent, but no one died?" McGraw pulls out a sheet of paper from his pocket and begins reading from it.

"Gary said, 'An intentional violation of FDA rules is a felony, irrelevant that nobody suffered harm. Punishment is in the range of $500,000 and up to three years in federal prison.' He also stated the Citation: 'Criminal fine and Enforcement act of 1994, PL (public law) 98-596.'"

"So," Roark says, "everyone involved is a felon."

"Yes," the boss says, "And they are: Kendal Wilson, Dennis Murray, Donna Harvey, and Dr. Mordecai. We have Dennis in custody and we'll need warrants to bring in the others. But I want to hold up on Dr. Mordecai for a bit."

"Why is that, boss?" Gomez asks.

"I sense there's more to him than meets the eye."

Kramer gestures with his head to alert the boss that the chief is coming. Captain Dipple, the big guy, comes up behind McGraw.

McGraw turns around. "Capt. Whatta we have?"

"Another body in East Lake, cowboy. This time it's a woman. Here's a file on what I have so far. She's all yours."

The chief looks over at the team. "I see you're busy having a meeting."

"Yes. Just closing out. About to come to your office to give you an update."

The chief is slow to answer, staring at the group.

What's his problem, McGraw thinks. *Probably wondering if we're plotting against him.*

"I look forward to our meeting, cowboy," the chief says. "I'm sure you all are on top of things as always." He turns and heads back to his office.

McGraw says, "Okay, guys. From what we've discussed, who do we have in East Lake?"

Everyone said the name: Emily Joyce.

"I agree," he says. "Kramer and Gomez, get out to East Lake and do your thing. Sergeant Roark and I will follow."

Chapter 48

When Kramer and Gomez arrive at the lake that afternoon, patrol officers have secured the area with yellow tape tied around trees and are standing around waiting for the detectives to arrive. Larry, the assistant M.E., is removing a black plastic bag covering the victim's body lying on a tarp by the shore's edge.

"Oh, here come Mutt and Jeff. Guess the case will be solved now," Larry says.

"You know it," Gomez says. "You guys cut and slice and throw the dice, while we use our brains to figure things out."

"That'd be the day," Larry says, as he completely removes all the duct tape and the black bag covering the body.

"Okay, guys, cut the crap," Kramer says. "We got serious work to do before the boss and the sarge arrive."

Larry frowns. "Wait a minute. Are you calling the Lieutenant, 'the boss?'"

"Yeah, why?"

"Man, that's Lieutenant McGraw. Probably one of the best detectives in the country, and you guys call him boss? That's a no, no in my opinion."

"He's a great guy," Gomez says. "He likes it. And who cares about your opinion?"

Larry shakes his head. "I just don't get it. I would never do that."

"How about getting back to the vic?" Kramer asks, "and letting us do our thing?"

Larry brushes the hair from the female victim's face. "A redhead and she was probably kinda pretty," Larry says.

"Who found the body?" Kramer asks.

He points to the gentleman siting under a tree in his portable fishing chair about twenty yards away, looking a little perplexed. "He hooked the bag around her body and she came up, and he froze, and said he just held on to it and called 911."

"Got a name for the fisherman?" Gomez asks.

"Charles Penn."

Kramer says. "Here comes the boss (he emphasizes 'boss') and the sarge, so we'll go interview Mr. Penn."

Larry looks up at Kramer and shakes his head.

"Howdy, Larry," McGraw says.

"How you doin,' Lieutenant McGraw and Sergeant Roark?"

"Another vic with a nasty gash, I see. What can you tell us?" McGraw asks.

"At this point, we have a redhead female, probably in her late twenties, throat gashed badly just like the guy we pulled out weeks ago. Also cuts on hands and arms, and stabbed several times in the abdomen. Still had her clothes on, so I don't believe she was molested."

"We know who this one is. She's Emily Joyce. Any idea how long she's been in there?"

Larry shrugs looking puzzled. "You know her, how?"

"Long story, McGraw says. "How long in the lake?"

"I'd guess forty-eight to seventy-two hours, but we'll have more on her later."

McGraw and Roark slip on gloves and squat to look over the body.

"You're right. Those gashes look like the ones on the vic you pulled out weeks ago," McGraw says.

"Could be the same killer," Roark says. "The gashes may be his signature."

"Can we see her hands?" McGraw asks.

"Some cuts and scratches," Larry says as he lifts her arms. "The poor thing tried to fight her assailant off. There's some discoloration of skin, some bloating of the tissue and even decay starting. Some gas build up in her body made it easier for the fisherman to pull her up. He's over there with Gomez and Kramer sitting in the lawn chair. The bags the vic was in were held together with duct tape. We may be able to get latent prints from the tape, but he probably wore gloves."

"I think that's enough for us. You can take her."

"Thanks, Lieutenant McGraw."

"Tell Dr. Philip, I'll be in touch."

"Yes, sir."

Gomez and Kramer are with Mr. Penn when McGraw and Roark walk over to them. Gomez walks up to the boss. "Fisherman's name is Charles Penn. Lives in north Atlanta and has been fishing here for a couple of days. Was out in his boat when he snagged the vic's body. Said he hasn't seen anyone around."

McGraw moves over to the fisherman. "Mr. Penn. I'm Lieutenant McGraw with Homicide APD and this is my partner, Sergeant Roark."

"Please to know you," the white-haired man probably in his seventies says, doesn't rise from his lawn chair. "Call me Charlie."

"Okay, Charlie. Nice meeting you."

"Did you see anyone suspicious around here before you snagged the body?"

"As I told the other detectives, I've been out here for two days and never saw one human. Very peaceful out here."

Charlie is wearing coveralls with lures pinned to the front and to his cap. Reaches into the red cooler chest next to his chair for a Coors light and yanks on the ring to open it, and takes a drink. "Been thirsty."

"How's the fishing here?" Roark asks.

"Pretty good." He bends over and removes the lid from a bucket and lifts a string of blue gill, each the size of his big hand.

"How long will you stay out here?" Roark asks.

"Only a couple more days. Getting tired of sleeping on the ground. Miss my bed."

"We'll let you enjoy your times outdoors," McGraw says. "We may want to talk to you again."

"I ain't going nowhere. Your detectives have all my information."

"Thank you," Roark says.

The detectives walk over to Kramer and Gomez.

"You got all the info on Penn, the times he was fishing, and the kind of fishing line, and hook he used that brought the vic up?"

"Yeah, boss," Kramer says. "This ain't our first rodeo."

The boss smiles, and says, "Just a reminder. We may want to talk to him again."

Kramer nods looking at Gomez who is making a face at him.

McGraw turns to Roark. "Let's see if we spot anything unusual around here."

They walk around the area where the assistant M.E. laid Emily Joyce and then move up to the road's east entrance. There were tire tracks that followed up to the small parking area.

"Looks like our killer drove a vehicle down close to the lake," McGraw says.

"Oh, look. Here comes Will Deaver walking, Buddy. Hi, Mr. Deaver." Buddy jumps on Roark. "He is so playful," she says.

"He likes people," Deaver says.

McGraw asks, "Will, I know you walk Buddy a couple times a day. Did you notice anything unusual around here during your walks the last three evenings?"

"Not much going on." He frowns. "Wait a minute. A couple evenings ago when Buddy and I were on our evening walk, I saw this man fly out of here like a bat out of hell in an old Chevvy. I couldn't tell what year it was."

"Did you get a good look at him?"

"The street lights helped. My eyesight isn't as good as it used to be, but I saw he had on the same kind of mask that the other guy did. And what looked like blood on him. Not sure, but it looked like it. Again, I was afraid Buddy was going to get hit as he zoomed out of here."

"So, you're sure it was the same mask?"

"How can anyone not remember the Frankenstein Monster?"

"Thanks," McGraw says," You've been very helpful."

"Hope you catch him. Come on Buddy, we gotta get out of here," he says, pulling on the leash again.

"Our masked man," Roark says.

"Yep, you can bet the driver was Michael Mordecai."

"What's the next step?" Roark asks.

"We're done here. As soon as we get back, I want to have another team meeting."

Arriving back at headquarters, McGraw grabs a cup of java, goes to his desk, places a call to Dr. Philips, the M.E., and learns that she did find a Y-chromosome in the blood taken from Emily Joyce's apartment, which verifies that the killer is a male. She also reports she found a hair with its root in the hand wound of Emily Joyce. She can get DNA from it to see if it matches the Y-chromosome DNA and the other DNA on file. The blood sample forensics turned in to her should identify Emily Joyce's DNA with that in the apartment.

An hour later, McGraw meets with his team at the center table. When everyone is settled in, he says, "I've asked Sergeant Roark to record this session for our report. You'll recall we have wondered about the motivations of our killer."

"You mean the Frankenstein monster," Gomez says, followed by a laugh.

Kramer gives him the eye for interrupting the boss.

"As I was about to say, from the diary of Emily Joyce and from interrogating Dennis Murray, we can for the moment infer that Dr. Michael Mordecai is our killer because he was going to meet with Ms. Joyce to discuss money and she let him into her apartment. We'll be able to confirm it once we get the DNA results from the M.E. For now, I'll call him "M." So, if M's our killer, what could be his motives for killing Dr. Corey Keller, Alan Borowitz, and Emily Joyce? Let's review what we know about the vics one at a time.

"For Dr. Keller, M's thought was, his boss, Keller, was deliberately dragging his feet in getting FDA approval for the clinical testing of M's anti-aging drug, which first must go through an in-house committee for approval.

According to Dr. Jessica York, M and Keller had many verbal fights over the lab testing of M's drug, and over the usual committee's slowness in acting on applications for FDA approval. He at times would fly off the handle and rush out in the middle of a meeting."

"Even so," Kramer says, "killing Keller doesn't help M. The Biogen committee and the FDA still must approve his drug for testing even with Keller out of the way."

"Good point, Kramer. The type of personality of M should shed light on his action in killing Keller. At this point, we can ask, is M a psychopath or sociopath? Well, today, docs relate psychopathy and sociopathy to what they call antisocial personality disorder (ASPD). However, psychopathy should be regarded as a particularly severe subtype. Sociopaths lack empathy for others, have poorly regulated emotions, impulsive behavior, and outbursts of anger. They are immensely impatient, easily provoked, attempt to control others with threats of aggression, lie for personal gain, show a tendency to physical violence, and have superficial relationships.

"However, it is reported that sociopaths and psychopaths do share in similar traits. They have a poor inner sense of right and wrong. They can't seem to share or understand another person's feelings. Psychopaths are cold hearted. Sociopaths are hot headed."

Silence.

Gomez looks over at Kramer and then at Roark.

"I see a puzzling look on your faces. You must be wondering if M is a psychopath or a sociopath," the boss says.

"No, boss. I'm wondering how you know all this stuff," Gomez says.

"Research, Gomez. Research. After reviewing what I just presented about ASPD, what type would you say M is?"

"A sociopath," Kramer says.

"A psychopath," Gomez says.

"Keep all this in mind. There's more. We'll come back to this."

"What about Alan Borowitz, boss?" Gomez asks.

"Borowitz is a different story. He refused to take part in the drug trial. With the limited knowledge he had in the medical field, Borowitz knew what M was giving to the homeless men was illegal and he could rat on him. M learned Borowitz was addicted to cocaine, and M, being a charmer, felt no compassion for Borowitz's addiction problem. Instead, he used it to his advantage, tempting Borowitz with the drug to keep him quiet. But M knew Borowitz couldn't be trusted, so to keep him from going to the authorities he enticed Borowitz to rendezvous at East Lake where M gives him enough cocaine to kill a horse. Borowitz shoots up and dies. Then M slashes him and dumps his body in the lake."

"Doesn't that demonstrate that he's cold hearted?" Roark says.

"Yes, it does," the boss says.

"But I don't understand, why the Frankenstein mask?" Roark asks. "How does that fit in?"

"M doesn't use it to frighten his subjects. He use it only as a disguise to get a thrill. He chose the bizarre mask to tell us, 'I'm in control. Come and get me, if you can.'"

"And now, Emily Joyce," Kramer says.

"Yes. Emily Joyce. She threatened him. She was going to the authorities if M didn't pay her hush money. All this is clearly written in her diary, even though she didn't write M's name in it. Dennis told us the whole scenario. Emily threatening M like Borowitz did, which would have thrown him into a fit of rage. Consequently, he probably arranged for them to meet at her apartment to discuss how much money she'd accept to keep quiet. It's obvious from the crime scene, M went there to kill her. He enters and probably sweet talks her and when she was relaxed, he grabs her, she fights back, evident from the bruises and cuts on her arms. He, being stronger, subdues her, slashes her throat with his dagger, but in the process, he cuts himself and she scratches him. His DNA could be under her nails. When she's down, he kneels next to her body, and like a mad man, he stabs her several times—"

"—Don't mean to interrupt, boss. But that sounds like a psychopath, Kramer says.

"I agree," Roark says.

Gomez nods.

McGraw continues, "Finally, M rolls Emily's body up in large lawn bags. Her apartment being in the back of the complex and close to the stairs is somewhat hidden. It's reasonable to assume that he didn't wear his mask at that time because he didn't want her screaming and attracting attention. He knew he could throw her body in the trunk of the stolen car, and then take off for East Lake. After dumping her, he'd put on the mask and races out of the area."

"Any questions?"

"When are we gonna bring in Donna Harvey and Kendal Wilson?" Gomez asks.

"After we get warrants."

"What about M?" Gomez asks, then frowns. "Why are you smiling, boss?"

"The Y-Chromosome found in the blood at Emily's tells us the killer is a male, but it doesn't identify the killer. But we've gotten another break. Nora found a hair in Emily's hand wound, being wrapped in a lawn bag kept the water out. The hair has a root, which means she can test it for DNA. You guys got M's wine glass from the restaurant, and if it matches the Y-chromosome DNA and the hair root, we have our man—Michael Mordecai.

We have Dennis's DNA, and we can be certain he's not our man. We could get an affidavit for probable cause against M since we have Dennis Murray's testimony and Emily Joyce's diary, but I think we'd better hold off on M until we hear from Dr. Philips."

He pauses, then says, "If M gets wind that Dennis Murray, Donna Harvey, and Kendal Wilson are in custody, all hell is going to break loose."

"The way he butchers his vics, and the way his mind works, he could turn into a ferocious animal when backed into a corner," Gomez says.

"He'll kill anyone in his way," Kramer says.

"So, is he a sociopath or a psychopath?" the boss asks.

"Psychopath," they say in unison."

"I agree."

"What about shadowing him, boss," Gomez says. "We know where he lives."

"We know from his record; M usually gets to work around seven-thirty or eight and leaves around six. It varies at times, but that's normally his routine," McGraw says.

"What about it, boss? We can do it."

"Hold up." McGraw looks at Roark but doesn't say anything.

"What? What's on your mind?"

"Wondering if Jessica York would tell us if M has been showing up to work."

"Only way to find out is to call her," he says.

"I'll give it a try." He pulls out his notebook from his desk drawer and calls the number for Biogen. "Operator, this is Lieutenant McGraw, APD homicide, I'd like to talk to Dr Jessica York. Thank you, I'll hold." McGraw looks at Roark and shrugs. "Yes, I see, okay. Could you connect me with Dr. Mordecai? Thank you." Seconds later, he listens and says, "Okay, thanks."

"What, what?" Roark asks.

"Jessica has left, and M is on leave." He turns to Kramer and Gomez. "Go to M's house and ask to talk to Dr. Mordecai. Call in what you find."

"Will do," Kramer says.

Gomez is behind the wheel of the black Dodge and eases it up in front of Michael Mordecai's' home.

"There's her van in the driveway," Kramer says. "I see a woman's head through the kitchen window. Most likely Donna Harvey. We can kill two birds with one stone here."

"Let's hop out and do our duty," Gomez says.

They amble up the sidewalk that runs between a well-manicured lawn with lots of bushes and trees. Kramer arrives first and lifts the golden knocker a couple of times. The door opens and a lady fitting the description of Donna Harvey smiles and asks what she could do for them.

"We'd like to talk with Dr. Mordecai. Is he in?" Gomez asks.

"Dr. Mordecai left about an hour ago for a short vacation. Fishing, I believe."

"Are you Donna Harvey?" Kramer asks.

"Yes, I am. Do I know you?"

"Sorry. We're with the Atlanta PD. I'm detective Kramer and this is Detective Gomez."

"Who is it?" a voice calls out from the kitchen. Seconds later, a lady in a wheelchair appears at the door next to Donna Harvey."

"Hello. I'm Michael's mother. How can we help you?"

"They want to talk to Dr. Mordecai, Gail," Donna Harvey says. "They are with the police."

"Oh. He left this morning for a fishing trip."

"Do you know in what area he might be?" Kramer asks.

"No, I don't. Michael doesn't include me in any of his plans. Sorry."

"Thank you for your help, Mrs. Mordecai. I wonder if we can talk to Ms. Harvey outside?"

Donna steps out and Gail watches.

"Ms. Harvey, we need to take you in for questioning." Gomez says. "Please get your things and come with us."

"Is this about Dr. Mordecai's drug testing?"

Kramer nods.

"Just give me a few minutes to gather my things and call Gail's neighbor Judy to stay with her."

Standing in the doorway, they notice the expression on Gail Mordecai's face. Donna Harvey apparently told her she had to go with them.

Gail wheels over to them. "Is my boy in big trouble, officers?"

"Not able to discuss it, ma'am," Kramer says. "Sorry."

“Why are you taking Donna? What has she done?”

“Ma’am, I’m really sorry, but we can’t discuss anything with you,” Kramer says.

They wait until they get Donna to the car and cuff her. Gomez gently guides her into the back seat.

“We’ll get your van later,” Gomez says, as he slips in behind the wheel.

On the way to the station, Kramer calls in and reports that Dr. Mordecai has left to go on a fishing trip and that they are bringing in Donna Harvey.

Chapter 49

Kramer and Gomez usher Donna Harvey into the homicide division and introduce her to Lieutenant McGraw and Sergeant Roark. The boss informs her she is an accomplice in Dr. Mordecai's testing scheme and they need hold her for questioning.

She says nothing.

"Put Ms. Harvey in One," McGraw says.

When they return the boss tells his junior detectives to get the address of Kendal Wilson from Roark and bring her in. Roark has tracked Kendal's address, which she hands to Kramer.

McGraw and Roark enter Interview Room One and the female officer standing watch, leaves the room. Roark had a recorder and notepad while McGraw is carrying a folder. Roark explains to Donna Harvey that the questioning session will be recorded. Donna nods but says nothing. Roark flips on the recorder and enters the day and time.

"Please give your full name and occupation, Ms. Harvey," Roark says as she flips on the recorder.

"Donna Harvey Vanderbilt, I'm a nurse who works with homeless men through my church."

With the recorder running, McGraw rises and removes two forms from the folder and slides one in front of her, and holds the other one in his hand. By law I must inform you of your legal rights, in accordance with Miranda ruling. I'm going to read each of these rights to you as required by law. You'll see on the form you have, that there's a place for your name, date, and time. Please fill that in now."

Roark hands her a pen. After she finishes, McGraw says, "Now, after I read each right to you, you'll initial beside each statement indicating you understand that specific right. Do you understand?"

"Yes."

When done reading all the statements, McGraw picks up her sheet and says, "You have agreed to answer all of these questions without us making any promises of leniency or any other promises to you, and you agree we have only asked you to answer truthfully, is that correct?"

"Yes."

"What do you do for the homeless?" McGraw asks, continuing the questioning.

"Bring them to my home. I have rooms in the basement. Usually 12 men. We feed them and help them get on their feet and maybe get some work."

"It's our understanding that you assisted Dr. Mordecai in the testing of his drug on 12 of your homeless men for about three weeks," McGraw says, "Is that right?"

"Only eleven. Had one chicken out."

"Who was it?"

"Alan Borowitz?"

"Why didn't he participate?" Roark asks.

"Said he didn't like being a guinea pig."

"Did you realize that testing a drug without the FDA approval is a felony?"

"Not really. All I cared about was making my men better. That's my only mission in life."

"That's a noble one, but in this case, testing a drug on them wasn't the wisest thing to do," McGraw says.

She shrugs as if it didn't matter.

Roark looks at her notes. "You work for Dr. Mordecai, taking care of his mother, right?"

"Yes. She's a lovely person."

"How did you get involved in the testing of Dr. Mordecai's drug?" McGraw asks.

"Dr. Mordecai told me my guys would feel stronger and younger. It did just that."

"You're fortunate no one died," Roark says.

"He said that wouldn't happen."

"When did you see Dr. Mordecai last?" Roark asks.

"This morning."

"Did he say anything to you?"

"I was in the kitchen with Mrs. Mordecai making her tea when he went to the door with a cloth suitcase. His mother asked him where he was going. He said, away for a while. She became very upset because she had doctors' appointments and he never mentioned going away. It was no problem. I took her. I like Dr. Mordecai, but not the way he treats his mother. She's a jewel, and…and, well, he's not so nice at times."

Roark looks at McGraw. *He's in the wind.*

"Do you know if he owns a cabin somewhere?" McGraw asks.

She shrugs. I don't."

"Did his mother say where she thought he might have gone?"

"No, ma'am."

"Would you tell us if you knew?" McGraw asks.

"It'd be hard, but, yes, I think I would."

"Donna, does Gail know what her son has done?" Roark asks.

"No. He tells her nothing about anything. They don't speak much." She pauses. "Dr. Mordecai spends all his time in his office. Rarely comes out even when I'm not there, his mother told me."

"What does he do in there? Any idea?" McGraw says.

"He keeps the door closed. But the few times he's asked me for something I'd take it and only stand in the doorway. I can see he likes his scotch and is always working on something at his desk. He has this big picture on the wall." She shudders. "It's scary. There are times when the door is closed, I hear mumbling coming from his office."

"What about that picture that makes you shake all over?" McGraw asks.

"Seeing the man with a dagger in his throat. Blood all over his shirt."

McGraw glances at Roark. *Dagger in the throat.*

Roark pushes the notepad and pen across the table. "You need to write all that you told us."

"Everything?"

"Yes."

Donna Harvey reaches for the pen and begins writing.

McGraw walks out and stops at his desk when he sees Kramer and Gomez ushering a narrow-faced pretty woman in her thirties, with long shiny auburn hair, sparkling eyes, and red lips, into the pit.

Kramer told the boss that Kendal didn't seem surprised when they appeared at her condo, cuffed her, and brought her in. She said on the way to the station that she suspected someone would be coming for her because of her involvement in the testing of Dr. Mordecai's drug in her patients. When asked why she thought that, her answer was a surprise. Mordecai told her to be ready for it before he left town. She didn't know where he went.

"Put her into I R Two, and get Esther to stand guard inside the door.

"Will do," Kramer says.

"We'll be there shortly." He turns to Gomez. "Begin processing Donna Harvey Vanderbilt in one."

"Vanderbilt?" Gomez says. "Finally, a last name."

McGraw reaches for his Braves cup and walks over to the coffee stand. Minutes later, Roark enters and grabs her cup, and meets the boss at his desk. After a few sips, she says, "Noah, I feel sorry for Donna. Her mission in life is helping people. She seems to have a good heart."

He takes several more swallows of his coffee while in deep thought. "In our line of work, we aren't supposed to allow our emotions to come into play, but we're human, too. The DA may go a little easy on her."

Roark finishes her coffee. "What about that painting she described in M's office. He likes daggers."

"Looks that way," Noah says. "Let's go see what Kendal has to say."

McGraw and Roark enter Interview Room Two and Esther leaves. Roark has a notepad and recorder. She explains to Kendal Wilson that the questioning would be recorded, and Roark flips on the recorder and gives the date and time.

"Please give your full name and occupation," Roark says.

"Kendal Wilson. I work as a nurse at the Jefferson Assisted Living facility."

McGraw stands and pushes a sheet of paper in front of Kendal and tells her by law he must Mirandize her. He explains the process as he did with Dennis and Donna Harvey.

"I understand perfectly and I have nothing to hide," she says.

When completed, McGraw continues with his questioning. "How long have you been working at Jefferson?"

"Nearly five years."

"What is your role there?"

"Role?"

"What do you do there?"

"I have patients that I'm responsible for."

"Did you test Dr. Mordecai's drug, RapTOR on any of your patients?"

She nods looking at the floor.

"I need a verbal reply. How many patients?"

"Five."

"And how long and what were the results?"

"My patients became stronger, better skin and more agile after three weeks."

"Did anyone die from the drug?"

"No."

"Did you know that testing a drug without FDA approval is a felony?"

"No, I didn't. Thought I was doing something good for my patients."

Roark asks, "Why did you only treat five patients. Doesn't seem like very many."

"They were the only ones that fit the requirements Dr. Mordecai had established."

"You and Dr. Mordecai are very close. Is that correct?" Roark asks.

"Yes. We're engaged to be married."

McGraw asks, "We need to talk to Dr. Mordecai but haven't been able to reach him. Do you know where he might be?"

She shakes her head. "I don't. Neither his mother nor I have been able to reach him. We both have tried."

"Does he own a cabin or some property somewhere away from the city?" Roark asks. "We were told he's gone fishing."

She smiles briefly. "Fishing? Michael wouldn't know the first thing about fishing."

"If he doesn't own a cabin, do you have any idea then where he might go?" McGraw asks.

She shakes her head. "No."

"Would he leave the state?" Roark asks.

"Detectives, Michael lives in his own little world. It's hard to tell what he might do. Your guess is as good as mine."

"Did Dr. Mordecai ever mention East Lake to you?" Roark asks.

McGraw, looking at Roark, feels himself frowning.

"East Lake? That sounds familiar," she says.

"Does it ring a bell?" McGraw asks. "Think hard. It could help us locate him."

Kendal appears to be in deep thought. McGraw and Roark look at each other. Roark shrugs.

"Detectives. I don't know…" She stops in mid-sentence. "This may be nothing, but Michael mentioned once in passing that someday he might buy a piece of land on the far side of the Lake that he had his eye on. That was all and I don't even remember why he even mentioned it."

"Was that a few years ago?" Roark asks.

"Yes. I didn't think any more about it at the time. Michael dreams a lot."

"Thank you. I think we're done here," McGraw says.

"What's going to happen to me?" Kendal asks.

"You'll be processed and it will be up to the DA," McGraw says.

He rises. "Sergeant Roark will stay with you until Detective Kramer comes to process you. In the meantime, you will be required to summarize all you've told us."

Roark passes the legal pad across the table to Kendal.

Back in the squad area, McGraw tells Kramer to process Kendal Wilson once Roark is done with her.

Fifteen minutes later, Roark comes into the pit after Kramer relieves her.

"What made you think of East Lake?" McGraw asks.

"It just hit me. M threw his two vics in East Lake. He even met Borowitz there to kill him, and then dump his body in there, and, after he took Emily from her apartment, he threw her in there, too. Why there? I thought maybe he had some attachment to the place."

"Brilliant thinking," McGraw says. "We'll go out there and look around once we search his home and office. For now, I'm going to meet with the chief. McGraw's about to leave his desk when his cell vibrates. He picks up and answers it. Dr. Philips, the M.E., is on the line. "What do you have for us, Nora?" He listens intently. "Great news. You've made my day. Thanks."

"What?" Roark asks. "Don't make me wait."

"Dr. Philips got a match from the hair root DNA, the Y-Chromosome and the DNA on the glass."

"Mordecai!" she shouts."

He nods. "Yes."

"Thank goodness," she says.

McGraw heads to the Chief's office.

Chapter 50

McGraw knocks on the door jamb of Chief Dipple's open door. He waves McGraw in.

"Come in, Cowboy."

McGraw selects one of the chairs facing Dipple and sits.

"Got Dennis Murray, Donna Harvey Vanderbilt, and Kendal Wilson in custody. Our killer, Dr. Michael Mordecai, is in the wind."

"So, you think he's your man?"

"Definitely. The Y-chromosome from the blood collected from the vic's apartment, and a hair in her hand wound that had a root, and Mordecai's DNA on the wine glass were worked by Dr. Philips. She just called me. The DNA on them belong to Mordecai. He's, our man."

"What's your plan?"

"I'm getting a search and arrest warrant for Mordecai."

"Go for it."

"He's hiding out somewhere, but we're going to go to his home and search his office for anything that might tell us where he went."

"Any idea where he might be hiding out?"

"That's the 128-dollar question."

The Chief frowns. "I've heard of the sixty-four-dollar question, but never a 128-dollar question."

McGraw smiles. He loves to pull the Chief's chain. "Well, this one is tougher, so it's going to take twice the effort to find this guy."

The chief forces a laugh. "If anyone can, you can, Cowboy."

"Thanks for the confidence, Chief," he says as he rises and leaves.

Back at his desk, McGraw fills out an affidavit to get an arrest warrant for Dr. Mordecai.

"What are you working on?" Roark asks.

"An affidavit to get an arrest warrant for Mordecai. That's the only thing left."

"Maybe he called his mother," Roark says. "Probably wishful thinking on my part."

"He's not going to take a chance calling anyone. He knows we can ping his calls. Anyway, his mother would be the last person."

Roark says, "Maybe we'll find a clue in his office. We know he spent all his time in there."

"I was thinking that, too. Hopefully, he screwed up and left us a clue in there."

Chapter 51

The next morning around nine, McGraw and his team arrive at Mordecai's home where they meet up with Chris and his forensic team. As they clamber out of their vehicles, McGraw, with a search warrant in hand, tells them, "We must be careful in how we approach Mrs. Mordecai. She's in a wheelchair and we don't know her overall health."

"Sure thing, boss," Gomez says. The others nod their approval.

At the door, McGraw lifts the golden knocker a few times, Seconds later the door is opened by a middle-aged, attractive, well-dressed woman with a nice hairdo, and a pleasant smile.

"I'm Lieutenant McGraw and this is Sergeant Roark and two of our team members along with our forensic team. We are from the Atlanta PD. Are you Mrs. Mordecai's daughter?"

"Oh, no. I'm her neighbor, Judy Marks. I've been helping Gail call around to get home services for her. She's wheelchair bound and needs help."

"May we come in? We'd like to talk to Mrs. Mordecai."

"Yes, please." She moves aside and then closes the door. "I'll have to get Gail for you."

"Thank you," McGraw says as they all enter the foyer and wait. In a few minutes, Judy Marks is wheeling a slender, brunette woman with streaks of gray, into the foyer. "Hello. I'm Gail Mordecai. I understand you are looking for my son…oh, I know those two," she says pointing to Kramer and Gomez.

The two detectives just nod.

"Yes, ma'am. I'm Detective McGraw, this is Detective Roark," he says, pointing, "and those two that you know are Detectives Kramer and Gomez, and this is Chris with his forensic team. How are you, ma'am?"

"I'm ok." She frowns. "Quite a large group of you."

"Yes, ma'am."

"I know he's done something, but no one ever tells me anything, certainly, not Michael. May I ask what he's done?"

McGraw hesitates as he wonders how he's going to break the news to her. "Yes, ma'am. He's been involved in testing his drug in patients without FDA approval, which is against the law."

"I see." She looks up at the lady behind her. "Judy, would you wheel me into the living room? Detective McGraw, would you all please come with me?"

"Yes, ma'am," McGraw says."

They move into the spacious room with wall-to-wall carpet, expensive furniture, lots of plants, and filled with lots of sunshine.

"I'd like to know what else Michael has done. You see, I know my son."

"Ma'am, he's believed also to have harmed people as well as testing his drug on innocent subjects," he says.

"You mean he's killed people?"

"Yes, ma'am."

Silence.

No visible tears in the mother of a son who is a bad seed. But sadness fills her face.

"Are you okay, ma'am. Do you need a doctor or family member?"

"You're very kind, detective. I'm fine. Are you going to search his office?"

He pulls out a folded sheet of paper from his jacket pocket. "I have a warrant to search his office and home. Chris and his forensic team will record what they find."

"Go ahead. Judy, would you show them to Michael's room and office?"

"Certainly. This way," she says as she leads them to a large room off to the right. "This is where he works and lives," she says, pointing to the room with the door closed.

"I don't believe it's locked," Judy says, as she turns the doorknob and pushes against the door. It swings open. She moves out of the way. "I'll show the others to his bedroom."

"Thank you." McGraw and Roark move into the large room with a shiny mahogany executive desk in the middle of the room, on which are stacked books and scientific journals, followed by Chris and his team, who are prepared to record any evidence. A high-back leather chair has been pushed away from the desk indicating that Michael might have been in a hurry. The wall to their left is covered with bookshelves filled with the classics, and in the corner near the door is a white apartment fridge on top of which are a bottle of Scotch and several whiskey glasses. Behind M's desk are two large windows with wood shutters and two large green plants on each side.

"Look at this," Roark says as she moves to the wall to their right on which hangs Mordecai's college degrees and awards. In the middle is a large painting. "Here's what makes Donna Harvey shudder," Roark says as she stands a foot from it.

In the painting, only the head and shoulders of a man in a white shirt are shown in a plush room background, with his head titled backwards, mouth widely opened, eyes closed, expressing extreme pain. Blood is spattered on the front of his shirt from a dagger handle sticking out of his neck. Forensics documents the painting.

"I'd say, this is what motivates Michael," McGraw says. "We need to look around to see if we can find the Frankenstein Mask."

Roark moves to the desk. "Looksee here. We got him," she says.

McGraw walks away from the painting to her. "Whatta, you have?"

"A scotch glass. His DNA." Forensic records the glass and bags it.

"While we already have confirmation, it wouldn't hurt to have it," he says, handing it to forensics. McGraw pulls out all the desk drawers. No mask. Roark rummages through the materials on top of the desk and opens all the books.

She frowns. "All this scientific stuff. How does anyone digest all this information."

"The same way you digest investigative techniques and forensics."

"Boss, we've gone through his room," Kramer says. "Forensics has bagged his hairbrush even though we have his DNA, but nothing else."

"We're done here," McGraw says.

"Man, look at that painting," Gomez says. "M's definitely our killer."

Chris removes the painting.

"We have enough evidence. Now we must find him," McGraw says.

They walk over to Gail Mordecai, who is visiting with Judy in the living room. Chris and his team are first to depart.

"Mrs. Mordecai, we're done here. We thank you for your cooperation," McGraw says.

"I hope you find him," she says. "He needs to face up to what he's done. Will you let me know what happens?"

"Yes, ma'am. I'm sorry to disturb you."

She only smiles and nods.

Outside, Roark says. "Here I go again. That poor woman, all alone. She knows, but he's her son. That's tough."

"Did I ever tell you, you have a kind heart?"

"Not enough."

He smiles. "God looks at the heart."

Roark is in tears.

Before entering the Silverado, McGraw tells Roark, "I think it's time to follow your hunch and go out to East Lake and look around. Give me a minute, I'll be right back." He walks over to Kramer and Gomez and tells them to follow him out to East Lake.

"Sergeant Roark has a hunch he's hiding out there."

"That's as good as any," Gomez says.

Chapter 52

Michael has been driving around town this afternoon thinking about what he'll say to Jess before leaving for the lake. He must get her to agree to push the bigshots at Biogen to attach his name to the discovery of RapTOR.

There's no one else who would see that I'd get credit for my discovery. She's been a good friend.

He pulls the red Corvette into her driveway leading up to her home.

She may have hurt feelings and may not want anything to do with me since I took leave and haven't talked with her in a couple of weeks. She knows nothing about what I have been doing.

Michael opens the car door, slides out with an arm full of notebooks, and walks up to her door and knocks.

He notices an eye looking through the peep hole in the door.

"It's me, Michael."

The door opens and Jess is in her sweats.

"Are you going for a run?"

"Just got back. Where have you been?" she asks with hands on her hips.

"Didn't they tell you I took a couple weeks' vacation?"

"No, and there is scuttlebutt going on around the company."

"What kind of scuttlebutt?"

"That you are involved in Corey's death and the police are looking for you. M&M, is that true?"

He pauses. "He tried to stop the testing of my drug."

"You're wrong. He was working on your behalf. It was the committee."

"I didn't know."

"What have you done, M & M? It's like I don't know you."

"I guess I should tell you."

"Tell me what?"

"A few nurses, working in nursing homes, have been testing my RapTOR on their patients."

"You what?"

"Jess, hear me out! RapTOR really works. The patients do become younger, more agile and develop younger looking skin just as we thought."

She looks puzzled. "How in the world did you accomplish that?"

"I worked late at night in the lab filling capsules with my drug. I went over the protocol with each of them before they administered the drug. We've tested RapTOR on twenty-eight patients total and not one died. I'm excited about the results. Here is all the data," he says, setting the notebooks on her coffee table.

"Michael, you know what you've done. Testing a drug without FDA approval can send you to prison for a long time."

"Jess. Listen. I was willing to take that chance to see if RapTOR works in humans. You should see how young the patients look."

"Michael, you need to turn yourself in to the police."

"What? I can't do that. I thought you'd be happy that all our hard work paid off."

She turns away.

"You're not thinking about turning me in, are you?" he says, squeezing his fists into balls.

"No. But you must leave now. I could be charged as an accomplice."

"Jess, you aren't listening. My drug will make people forever young. I could win the Nobel Prize."

"Michael, listen to yourself. You're not acting rational. You've broken the law. You must go. Now!"

"Okay but promise me one thing. That you'll make sure I get credit for RapTOR at Biogen." He points. "There are all my notebooks that cover such exciting data. Will you make certain that I get credit for my drug?"

"Yes, yes. But you must go!" she says pushing him to the door and opens it.

"You promise, Jess, that you'll definitely make sure I get full credit for my drug?"

"I will do my best. I promise. Please go!"

"Good. Thanks."

As he leaves, he feels vibration from the door being slammed shut behind him.

I thought we were best of friends. Never would have ever thought Jess would turn on me.

Chapter 53

McGraw maneuvers the Silverado a couple of times on the two roads leading in and out of East Lake on the east side with Gomez and Kramer following in an unmarked black vehicle.

"God knows where Mordecai is," Roark says. "There's a lot of land on the far side of the lake that would make a good buy and a good hiding place."

McGraw stops by the edge of the lake, reaches for his binoculars, and steps out. He scans the area on the other side of the lake. After several minutes, he returns to the Silverado and slides in.

"You're right. There's a park and a waterfall at the far end of the lake. Several tents are close to the park."

"Is there a way in and out?" Roark asks.

"Yes. The problem is: if he is in one of the tents close to the road, and he spots us, he's a goner."

"Is the road close to the waterfall?"

"Yes."

"Could we enter on one side of the waterfall without being seen?"

"I believe so. Why?"

"What if, and I mean, what if, we were to enter the road by the waterfall where those in the tent couldn't see us, and we get out and walk around the waterfall?"

"If he spots us, he could get out before we get back into the monster," McGraw says.

"If we're careful and move with caution, we might be able to get him."

He pulls the vehicle over to the side of the road. "I have an idea. I'm going to have Kramer and Gomez enter through the other road that is close to the tents and park before entering the park area. If they walk in, hopefully they can sneak up on him as he comes out of the tent."

"That is, if he's there."

"He's there."

"How can you be so sure?" she asks.

"Because you said so. Remember, you said Mordecai had an affinity for this lake is why he dropped two bodies into it."

"I remember. But I'm not as right as you always are, boss."

He smiles. "You can't butter me up. You're right on this one."

McGraw slips out, goes to the unmarked black car behind him, and tells his detectives the plan. Back in with Roark, McGraw tells her all is set, and drives off around the lake to the other side. He moves slowly into the park area and keeps the Silverado hidden by the falls and parks. He reaches for his cell.

"Kramer?"

"Yes, boss."

"Your position?"

"We just got out and we're walking at the edge of the road where there is a lot of brush and trees."

"Do you see anyone?"

"No. Either the campers have gone hiking or they're inside asleep."

"That might be good," McGraw says. "Do you see M's white caddy?"

"No, boss. There are three cars over by the race track that runs around the center of the park area. Just a minute, boss."

"Do you see something?"

"Yeah. Gomez spotted a guy in his binoculars, running the track, but it's not M."

"Maybe I'm wrong thinking he'd come here," Roark says.

"Give it a rest. Stop beating up on yourself. M is no dummy. He's here. I feel it."

"Oh, I forgot. That feeling again."

"You know I'm psychic."

They laugh.

"Kramer?"

"Yes, boss."

"Give me the description of the cars. Can you see the plates through your binocular?"

"There's a black Nissan Sentra, a silver Toyota Corolla, and a red Corvette."

"Corvette? Roark says. You don't think M bought a Corvette?"

"Or rented one. It must have a V-8 engine that could shoot out of here like a missile."

"But why would he mimic Corey Keller in this way? I don't understand his mind," she says.

"Copycat, He's copying Keller's behavior, authority, and lifestyle. M had respect for Keller even though he hated his guts. He's now stupid with power. He's feeling invincible and I'm expecting him to do something crazy."

McGraw asks Kramer if the Corvette is a convertible.

"No boss. But it sure is pretty."

"Give me the plate number."

"It has a dealer's license plate on it."

"Give me the number and dealer. I'd bet my last dollar M stole the D-tag after renting the Corvette" McGraw says. He turns to Roark and hands her the dealer and number he wrote down. "Call the dealer and ask if Mordecai rented a Corvette. They may not know he's the one that stole the D-tag."

Minutes later, Roark says, "Michael Mordecai bought the Corvette. That's why the D-tag is still on the car."

"Boss? A guy just came out of the tent with his back to us," Gomez says. "I'm looking through my binoculars waiting for him to turn around. He can't see us. Boss, it's him. He's going over to the Corvette."

"We have this exit covered," McGraw says.

"He's opening the driver side door and is reaching in for something, It's weird. He's just standing behind the door looking around," Kramer says. "It's like he senses something."

"He may just be overly cautious," Roark says. "He knows we're after him."

"Stand down," the boss says. "If he spots you, he'll hop in and ram you as he races out, and we'll lose him. Get back to your car and let me know when you're there."

Seconds later, after racing to the car, Gomez says, "We're back."

"What is M doing?"

"He's sitting behind the wheel with the driver's door still open."

"On three, let's move in on him. Ready. One… Two… Three. McGraw puts the pedal to the metal and the wheels squeal as he shoots in. Mordecai slams his door shut and shoots out of his spot with Kramer rushing at him. Kramer tries to do a 180 in front of Mordecai, but he skillfully maneuvers around Kramer and barrels out with McGraw racing after him.

"He's heading for I 20," McGraw says.

"Man, he's really barreling it," Roark says.

After two minutes, without hesitation, M is on I 20 doing 90. McGraw flips on the strobe lights and siren and is keeping up with him in the left lane. Up ahead of M, a truck pulls out into the left lane to pass a car doing about 40. Mordecai weaves to his right to avoid slamming into the truck and crashes into the slow-moving vehicle, knocking it off the road and down the embankment. McGraw brakes and moves into the right lane. M loses control and careens off the road, landing twenty yards away from the road, overturning several times, fenders flying off.

McGraw pulls the Silverado far off to the side. Kramer and Gomez pull up behind him.

They hop out and rush to the Corvette. The detectives are quiet as they look at the lifeless body sandwiched in the crushed carbon fiber body. M's head is crushed and blood is everywhere.

"It's gonna take the Jaws of Life to get him out of there," McGraw says.

"The firemen and EMTs should be here shortly. But doesn't look like they can do much for him," Gomez says, as McGraw is squatting down looking in over part of the exposed body.

McGraw says. "He's gone."

"I hate to say it, but live by the sword, and die by the sword," Roark says.

"It's Karma," Kramer says. "Mimicking Keller caused him to end up like him."

"I was wondering what he was thinking when he went off the road," Gomez says.

The End

A Note to Readers

It's a great feeling when authors finish their novels. The gratification doesn't stop there. Readers interested in their genre must be reached. We are told that people don't read much these days because of all the electronic gadgets, but we believe there are still many readers looking for an interesting story, whether in print or in ebook format. We hope you've found it in *Forever Young*—interesting and enjoyable, as much as we did in writing it.

Thanks for reading *Forever Young.*

We encourage reviews and greatly appreciate them. If you'd write one where you purchased the book, we would be very thankful. Reviews help readers find new stories. You can find more of Magarian's titles in paperback and ebook on Amazon or at your favorite online retailer.

Every quarter, I have a drawing for a free autographed copy of my latest novel. Please go to my website and sign up. How to directions are given.

I am happy to report that the Magarian website has been completely revised as an inaugural venture to coincide with the publication of *Forever Young*. Those of my readers that are signed up on the old website will be active in the new site. Please go there and check it out.

Detectives Noah McGraw and Holly Roark have become enduring fictional characters to many of our readers. It is pleasing to hear how they enjoy our detective thrillers, and how they feel close to the two detectives.

Website: www.robertmagarian.com
Email: author@robertmagarian.com

Acknowledgments

Writing is a lonely task, but one I fully enjoy. Having a team that helps bring life to the novel is exciting. I wish to thank all those who have contributed in so many ways.

Many thanks to my *co-author, Detective Mike Isaac* (ret.), for his expertise and contribution to this novel, and who wishes to dedicate his efforts to his mom and dad, Jeanne, and Mike, who taught him at an early age to have a love for reading.

Colonel Scott Waldrup, Police Chief, Mascoutah, IL PD, my co-author of our novel, *The Tongue Collector*, for his insight and expertise in police matters and suggestions. Your continued support is greatly appreciated.

Editing: Nancy Hancock, the consummate language scholar and eagle-eyed corrector and best advisor a writer can have. Thank you for making this novel the best it can be.

Robert Ferrier, my first writing teacher, who was a tough instructor that put me to the test. I appreciate all he did for me, and so appreciate his encouragement.

Carolyn Wall, author/teacher, my second teacher, who taught me the love of writing and how to build a story with conflict. She is so appreciated for supporting me and encouraging me. Thanks for keeping my spirits up.

Cover Design: Peter O'Connor in the UK. He can be reached at www.bespokebookcovers.com.

Print Formatting: Amy Atwell, Author E.M.S.

My family: Thanks for your support. Love you all.

ROBERT MAGARIAN, B.A., BSPh, Ph.D., is professor emeritus of medicinal chemistry and pharmaceutics. He has been writing fiction since his retirement and has created several fictional characters in medical and detective thrillers. The two most popular characters are Detectives Cowboy Noah McGraw and Holly Roark of the Atlanta PD. Magarian is introducing Detective Mike Isaac (retired) as his investigative collaborator in *Forever Young*.

Magarian is the author of five thriller novels, *The Watchman, Seventy-Two Hours, You'll Never See Me Again, A Crime to Remember, The Tongue Collector,* and now, *Forever Young*. In addition to his fiction, Magarian is the author of two essays: *Follow Your Dream*, and *A Journey into Faith*. He lives with his family in Norman, Oklahoma.

MIKE ISAAC, B.S., MPA, RN, began his Law Enforcement career in 1984. He was assigned to the Paramedic, Patrol, and Criminal Investigations Divisions. He served on the Critical Incident Stress Management response team at the Oklahoma City bombing and supervised the crisis and hostage negotiations at his department. He instructed academy officers in CISM, police response to mental health calls, and numerous investigative topics. He retired as Lieutenant in 2020.

Made in the USA
Monee, IL
25 September 2023

43406959R00142